THE TIES THAT BIND THE SOUL

Old Souls Book 2

C.G. GARCIA

ISBN-10: 0615975747
ISBN-13: 978-0615975740 (Paperback)

Dedicated to all my readers. You're the best!

CHAPTER ONE

"This is probably far enough," Hahri whispered as he pulled his head back behind the bale of hay Issai and he were crouched behind.

The covered wagon they had snuck onto had been one of the largest on the southern road to Kairash, its twin columns of hay bales so packed together that it had been difficult to squeeze in among them and out of sight. They had managed to push enough of them more closely together that they had just enough room to crouch or sit sideways between the first two rows of bales.

Although hot and uncomfortable, Issai was infinitely grateful for the chance to sit down. By the time they had walked the relatively short distance to the road, he had been winded and ready to collapse. He never would have made it the entire distance and was relieved that he didn't have to confess his weakness to his companion.

He was already feeling loads better even though they had only been riding for about a half-hour. He suspected that it was because their shoulders had been touching for most of the ride and that Hahri had purposely sat as close as possible to him for that very reason.

The wagon was currently stopped somewhere in the city. Hahri had taken the opportunity to sneak a peak.

"Where are we?" Issai whispered back.

"Looks like somewhere in the Merchant District. I never made it this far into the city last time, so I hope you know the way to the bathhouse."

Issai pushed on the smaller boy's back, urging him out from between the bales into the almost nonexistent aisle. "The Merchant District is east of the road we need to take. We'll have to double back a few blocks, then go north."

Hahri groaned. "We're a lot farther away than I'd hoped. Someone's bound to recognize me before we get there. I wish we knew this city well enough to risk taking a more roundabout route. We still have several hours to kill before we can even enter the bathhouse for Purification purposes."

Issai silently cursed Hahri's lack of a cloak. While he had left his with his pack, Hahri's had been taken before the slavers had stuffed him into the cage. The only other garment besides the spare shirts he'd had in his pack had been a monk's robe, and they both had agreed that it would attract too much attention. Issai had never seen a novice monk walking around without at least one mentor, and Hahri hardly looked old enough to pass as a full-fledged monk.

Staring at the back of the other's head as they squeezed themselves towards the wagon's opening, inspiration suddenly struck. He reached over and yanked the tie from Hahri's hair.

"Ow! What are you doing?" Hahri hissed in a stage whisper, a hand darting up to rub the back of his head as he turned around to glare.

Issai held up the tie. "The *Shi* that know about you will be looking for a boy with his hair in a tail, not that bird's nest." He smirked as the other frowned indignantly. "It could buy us more time."

"Or we could just use those knives you're so proud of and shave your head while *I* wear the cloak," Hahri grumped as Issai stowed the tie in his money pouch.

"I'll pass. Head itches too much when the hair's growing back."

Giving him an incredulous look, Hahri turned around with a snort. He carefully peered around the side of the wagon and jumped out, Issai on his heels. Their unsuspecting patron was currently inspecting one of the hooves of his two horses, his back to them. There were quite a few people traveling the road on foot or with carts, but no one even glanced at them as they hurried to join the flow of foot traffic heading west.

Issai still felt a little tired, but nothing that would prevent him from gutting a few *Shi* if it came down to that. Hahri walked directly in front of him, a position that allowed them to better assist the other no matter the direction of attack.

By the time they could see the first houses of the Residential District in the distance and not so much as a wayward child jostled them in the rapidly thickening crowds, Issai was so tight with tension that he was one unexpected cough away from flicking a knife into his hand. His paranoia also seemed to be feeding into his companion. Hahri's back visibly became stiffer and stiffer the closer they got to their destination. It also didn't help that the buildings were starting to look shabbier, the roads not so well cleaned of the common waste of both man and animal, and it became apparent that they would have to pass through the seedier parts of the Merchant District.

Eyes hidden beneath his hood, Issai assiduously scanned the crowds for the slightest signs of danger. He also made a point of looking for the blond kid that had tipped him off about Hahri's capture. He still wasn't sure he believed that bastard slaver lord when he had claimed ignorance of the boy. He wanted to tie up that loose end if at all possible before they left the city.

He was so keen on watching the faces off to his left that Issai would have missed seeing Hahri step out of the crowd towards a tailor's shop had that abrupt movement in the corner of his eye not caught his attention. Hahri paused at the large, dusty window beside the shop's entrance just as Issai caught up to him.

The ancient boy leaned closer to the glass as if studying the various garments barely visible beyond the grime and murmured, "I think we've got a tail. The man's been five people ahead of us since about a quarter-hour ago. He keeps looking back. It could be nothing, but..."

"Agreed." Issai's eyes darted briefly towards the alley to the left of the shop, then back to the other boy.

Hahri smiled minutely.

They both turned and walked off as if to go to the next shop over. Issai glanced surreptitiously down the alley and noted that it was particularly long, branching off twice to connecting alleyways running horizontally between a cluster of buildings. Though he didn't like it, it was a risk he could accept.

"Now," he breathed, darting down to the second connecting alleyway at a neck-breaking speed, Hahri a half-step behind him.

He turned to the left into the alley so sharply that he briefly skidded into the back wall of a shop before bouncing off to resume his run. Hahri had shot past him during his stumble and was already turning north down what was seemingly turning out to be a maze of alleyways connecting the backs of dozens of shops.

As he turned the corner, Issai spared a glance behind him and was relieved to see the alley was empty behind him. If that man had indeed been following them, it appeared that they had lost him.

Up ahead, the alleyway ended with the back wall of a shop, and yet another connecting alleyway ran parallel to it from west to east. Hahri had just started to turn left at the corner when he inexplicably stopped dead in his tracks and whirled around to face the opposite direction.

Two more strides and Issai was just reaching out to grab the other boy's arm when the shouts finally reached his ears. He whipped his head around towards the sound even as he slid to a halt next to Hahri.

Two men wearing the uniform of the City Guard stood side-by-side about a hundred strides down the alley, shouting encouragement to another couple of guardsmen who were currently grappling with someone farther back where the alley dead-ended against another shop. The person was desperately trying to push a smaller figure back behind them while at the same time trying not to be taken down by the guardsmen.

"Somebody help us!" a tenor voice cried desperately among the jeers and laughs.

That voice was like a slap to Issai's face. He *knew* it. In fact, it was a voice he had last heard yesterday.

However, before he could speak, Hahri grabbed his arm roughly and hissed, "It's her! It's Korin's little girl!"

Huh? Issai stared at Hahri in disbelief before peering down the alley at the small body the other was trying to protect. He could just make out short, dark hair and what looked like a long, dark walking stick clutched in the child's hands, held out horizontally like a flimsy barrier. Come to think of it, Korin had mentioned that the girl carried a sword...

Then the figure struggling with the guardsmen briefly lifted a familiar blond head, and Issai was once again reminded of his earlier shock. Now was not the time to puzzle out whether they were right or wrong.

"You're not going to believe this, but I think I recognize the boy the guardsmen are attacking. He looks and sounds like the kid that told me you had been attacked." Issai slid his knives into his hands. "Even if that isn't the right girl, I definitely want to talk to that boy."

Hahri nodded. "Let's go."

The other boy shot ahead and bashed the first two guardsmen in the back of their necks before Issai could even run past. He doubted that they had even heard Hahri coming; they crumbled to the ground without uttering a sound.

The last two guardsmen had finally managed to force the blond boy to the ground, one of them currently sitting on his back while the teen thrashed frantically, trying futilely to buck him off. The other was advancing on the child, a long-staff raised menacingly in his hand as the small figure backed into the shop wall, the stick or sword or whatever it was still being held out as a barrier between them. Issai's blood ran cold. The City Guard usually carried only short-staffs and swords. Could these men be *Shi*?

Hearing his approach, the guardsman sitting on the boy turned his head towards Issai just as he slashed a knife across the man's neck as he ran past, the momentum driving the blade so deep that it scraped across the bones in his neck. He kicked the gurgling and bleeding body off the boy before it could fall on him and turned in enough time to see Hahri dodge the swing of the remaining man's staff.

Hahri grabbed the guardsman's head between his hands before he could straighten and gave it a vicious twist. The sound of the man's body as it hit the ground seemed louder than a clap of thunder in the now preternaturally silent alley.

Issai flicked the blood off his knife and bent to hastily wipe the remainder off on the dead man's uniform. He slipped them both back beneath his sleeves, his eyes riveted to the teen frozen facedown on the cobblestones. He was surprised that the boy hadn't tried to flee.

He reached down and grabbed the back of the blond's shirt, hoisting him up onto his feet. He then roughly tugged him over to the nearest wall and flung him against it, locking him in place with a hand still bloody from his latest kill pressed firmly against the teen's chest.

He trusted that Hahri would deal with the girl.

"So," Issai said calmly, taking in the blond's pale face and the utter terror radiating from dark brown eyes. Yes, he was definitely the same boy. "Mind telling me what you're doing here with that child?"

His mouth opened and closed a couple of times before he stuttered, "I was—I was just—"

Just as before, the boy couldn't seem to talk around the knot of terror that had lodged in his throat. His whole body was shaking so hard that the hand Issai had pressed against his chest was probably the only thing that kept him upright.

"You're Senn and Kye."

That unknown voice froze any forthcoming words on his tongue.

Issai slowly turned towards its source, only to find the

child looking directly at him with the most piercing, un-childlike expression he had ever seen on someone that young. Although the kid had lowered the stick/sword to the side, the stance was still defensive. Issai was still too far away to verify the eye color, but this person definitely looked like the same "boy" he had seen stealing in the Rihottan marketplace.

He gave a curt nod.

"So you've met Korin recently..." Hahri presumed, immediately drawing her eyes to him.

Hahri was still standing next to the last man he had killed, his hands open and arms hanging in a loose, nonthreatening manner at his sides. It seemed he had made no attempt to move closer to her.

Her hand tightened on what Issai now believed was her sheathed sword, but her hard expression remained unchanged. "Yes."

"Where is he now?" Hahri asked. He toed the body at his feet. "Did these men or someone like them take him?"

Her eyes narrowed. "Don't get the wrong idea," she all but growled. "Yeah, I saw him at the temple, but I left on my own and was on my way out of the city when those bastards ambushed me on the main road. I managed to run away. I was about to turn down a dead-end street here in the Merchant District, but that boy," she gestured at the blond with her chin without taking her eyes off Hahri, "came running out of nowhere and grab-bed my arm, pulling me in the opposite direction. A lot of good that did me as I ended up trapped by those guards-men, anyway."

"They weren't guardsmen," the blond teen suddenly spoke up, cringing when Issai looked back at him sharply. He still looked scared enough to wet himself.

"More slavers?" Issai said skeptically. "You sure seem well-informed on the matter. Over the course of two days, you've appeared at two places where these so-called slavers have attacked people. Why would you go out of your way to first, track me, a stranger, down to tell me about slavers attacking my friend, then today coincidentally stumble upon someone that knows us who also just happens to be running from these slavers-in-disguise? The only thing that makes sense is that you're the one setting us up for ambush in the first place!"

The teen was shaking his head frantically. "But— but—I had no *idea* you even knew each other!" he cried, his eyes darting over Issai's shoulder to Hahri as if pleading with the auburn-haired boy to save him. "All I saw was a little boy running from a bunch of men, two of whom I've seen chasing after kids a lot of other times. Some of those kids I knew, and they always, *always* turned up missing afterwards! Everyone in this city has at least heard of the Mahze. What else was I suppose to think?"

Issai scowled. "That still doesn't explain why—"

"Hey! What are you doing down there?"

Issai stiffened and turned towards yet another unexpected voice, cursing when he saw four city guardsmen running towards them. Several more were just emerging from around the corner of the same connecting alley Hahri and he had passed through. Dammit! There were too many of them to be *Shi* or slavers-in-disguise. One of the shop owners must have witnessed some of the commotion here and sent for the real Guard.

"Captain! These men are dead!" a guardsmen squatting beside the first two fallen men called out.

Killing one or two guardsmen was one thing, but killing an entire squad would likely bring the wrath of the crown down on them. Issai grabbed the boy by his wrist—having every intention of beating the truth out of him later—and turned to Hahri.

"Already on it," Hahri said, moving towards the girl.

Issai pulled his captive down the alley, intent on bowling over any guardsmen that dared stand in his way. He felt someone quickly come up directly behind them, but instead of going around, they slowed down to match his pace. Then Hahri shot past him to his left, and Issai realized that it was the girl, probably using him as her shield.

He gritted his teeth and sent two guardsmen flying to the opposite walls as he barreled through them with more force than he had initially intended. Issai knew that he shouldn't feel irritated, that it was a very logical thing for someone as small as her to do, but he did. He already had his hands full with Hahri; he didn't want to have to babysit another, Old Soul or not.

Speaking of babysitting, the blond teen was currently trying to pull his wrist out of the vise-like grip Issai had on him, his eyes wide and rolling like a terrified horse's, but Issai just tightened his hold. There was no way he was letting the boy get away a second time!

Issai caught up to Hahri at the corner where the remaining guardsmen had taken up a defensive line, the ancient boy pausing only long enough to down the three unfortunates directly blocking his path, before all four continued straight down the alley, leaving a dozen or so to give chase. Hahri's strikes had looked particularly brutal. Issai only hoped that Hahri hadn't accidentally killed them. They really didn't need a repeat of what had happened back in Nisei.

Up ahead, he could see a mass of moving bodies walking past the end of the alley. Finally! Either that was the main road they had been aiming for, or a smaller thoroughfare running north and south through the district. At this point, Issai didn't care which it was as long as they would no longer have to run around blindly in this gods-forsaken maze of alleyways!

Then without warning, the passing crowd seemed to disappear from view around the mouth of the alley, and Issai got a brief glimpse of the empty street before a sudden rush of bodies began to crowd into the alley.

"*Dammit!*" Hahri cursed angrily just as Issai realized those were guardsmen coming at them from the front, too.

What did that witness tell the guard station—that they were murdering the whole damn block? It was inexplicable that they had sent more than one squad for a brawl in an alley.

"Don't stop! Just barrel through!" Issai said as he matched his pace to Hahri's, still dragging the blond teen behind them even as the other pleaded for him to let go. "It's the only chance we've got without killing everyone." He spared a glance behind him at the girl. "That goes for you, too."

If she replied, it was lost in the cacophony of shouts as Hahri and Issai slammed into the human avalanche bearing down on them like twin battering rams. Issai managed to make it halfway through the writhing mass before he was knocked to the ground, losing his grip on his captive's wrist as he frantically tried not to get trampled or stabbed in the confusion as legs swayed and tripped over fallen bodies and each other.

Cursing, Issai elbowed two men trying to grab his arms hard in the stomach and scrambled on his hands and knees around their legs as they crumbled, retching, to the ground. Then Hahri was somehow behind him, dragging him by the arm even as the auburn-haired boy kicked a guardsman coming at them with a sword from behind hard in the crotch.

Issai had enough time to see a blond head running away back south towards the heart of the Merchant District before he was yanked back onto his feet and tugged in the opposite direction.

"That brat just left us here and ran away!" Hahri growled as he shot off to the north, presumably giving chase.

After a breath's hesitation, Issai followed before any guardsmen still standing could get within reach to tackle him. He was *pissed*. That damned brat had escaped him yet again! It was as though the gods were determined to keep any and all answers from him by throwing these ridiculously brutal roadblocks in front of them. As if that weren't bad enough, now one of those roadblocks included another brat who had decided to thumb her nose at all of them!

I should just kill them all!

CHAPTER TWO

Had the girl's aim not been for the congestion of the main road, then catching up to her would have been a simple thing. However, watching the way she just seemed to slip into and glide between the almost non-existent spaces among the currents of people, animals, and carts moving in both directions without touching anyone, Issai could finally understand why Korin had failed to keep her within his grasp. Her agility was nothing short of astounding. He wondered if she had even needed their help back in the alley.

They had been chasing her for a good quarter-hour now, and neither he nor Hahri had managed to erase any of the distance between them. No other cities lay to the immediate north of Kairash, only a few farms and after that, the mountain range that separated Sarim from the kingdom of Vayllus. The map he had studied a few days earlier had shown no northern roads that allowed travel directly through the mountains into Vayllus, so he couldn't imagine that was her goal.

Despite that, although she had moved to the edges of the crowd several times, she had made no attempt to leave the main road. It was as if she realized that she had no chance of eluding them without the cover of the crowds.

That made Issai wonder exactly how much Korin had told her about them, or for that matter, how much she knew about Old Souls. For all he knew, they weren't the first Old Souls that had crossed her path. Before meeting Hahri, he had always figured that there were at least one or two more Old Souls other than him because of the different stories circulating around about them. Some, like the Violet-eyed Old Soul legend, had to do with him, and others didn't relate to him at all. The thought that there may be a great deal more beings like them than he had ever anticipated didn't sit well at all with him.

They were nearing the Residential District, which in a way was ideal since the bathhouse they were to meet Korin at was located somewhere within. The crowds were also thinning, and apparently, Hahri decided it was the most opportune time to just start shoving everyone out of his way rather than trying to harmlessly squeeze by them. He really hadn't wanted to attract any more attention, but...

Issai was a couple of strides away from Hahri and quickly caught up to him as the crowd before them became aware of the impending danger through all the squawks and curses of Hahri's victims and parted willingly to let them pass. When only four people separated them from the girl, she suddenly darted off to the right down a narrow street of boarding houses, running as if her soul depended on it.

Issai immediately pushed himself out of the flow of people and gave chase. By now they had probably attracted the attention of a few patrolling guardsmen, not to mention the ones from earlier that were no doubt still in pursuit. If they were to have any hope of making it to the bathhouse later, then they had to catch her *now* and go into hiding.

A sharp wind blew by him and Hahri materialized next to the girl as she abruptly jerked to a halt with a cry of surprise, her left arm gripped tightly in the auburn-haired boy's hand. As Issai slowed and approached them, Hahri hastily jerked to the side as the girl delivered a vicious kick straight towards his crotch. He quickly grabbed her other wrist when her hand started to reach for the sword hanging from her belt, and she winced when she attempted to rip her wrist from his grip.

Issai caught a glimpse of what looked like a white bandage peeking out from beneath Hahri's hand, reminding him of the other boy's arrow wound. He hoped it hadn't been reopened in the struggle.

He stood close, ready to grab her if she managed to break free, but to his astonishment, Hahri abruptly released both the girl's arms. As she squawked and teetered backwards, he smacked her soundly on the side of her head like an exasperated parent disciplining an especially precocious child.

"Jeez," Hahri huffed, a hint of annoyance in his voice, as he looked down his nose at her, "we just saved your ass back there, so the least you could do is stop for a moment and hear us out." He jerked his chin in Issai's direction and grinned. "You're as bad as *he* was!"

Issai tensed, completely expecting her to bolt again, but she just lowered her hands from where she had instinctually grabbed her head and stared at Hahri with a confused frown as if he were an animal she wasn't quite sure she had ever seen before.

He knew the feeling.

Hahri glanced around them. A small crowd of gawkers had begun to gather on the porch of the boarding house directly in front of them. Issai could feel the eyes of several more boring into his back like a physical touch.

"Come on. We need to get out of sight before the wrath of the City Guard catches up to us."

When she stiffened and looked ready to flee again, Hahri looked at her pointedly. "I don't think I need to remind you that slavers *and* those who hunt our kind are out in droves right now. Even if you'd rather not come with us, we're the best chance you have of getting out of this city alive and free."

With a *whoosh*, her sword was suddenly free of its scabbard and pointed directly at Hahri's heart. To his credit, the other boy didn't even flinch, just met her eyes calmly with the inhuman gaze Issai had come to hate. She stepped back a little shakily and glared at him for a long, tense moment before turning her glare warningly at Issai.

"If either of you touches me again, I'll slice you open—got it?" she snarled, but she reluctantly sheathed the sword.

"Yeah, we've heard," Hahri said with a shrug. "We're supposed to meet Korin at one of the bathhouses tonight under the guise of having our 'souls purified.' We should be able to find a cellar or something to hide in until then."

Issai glanced around at the now conspicuously empty area. "Save the explanations. We're probably only moments away from being found. Let's go."

Several hours later, using the cover of darkness and a

couple of hooded cloaks stolen from various clotheslines for Hahri and the girl, they walked straight into the bathhouse as if they had every right to be there. Hahri led them over to the first monk they saw and told him that Korin was expecting them for tonight's Purification. Just as Korin had promised, they were immediately shown to a small room without question. It contained only a small table in the center with a couple of benches, a pitcher of water with three small cups, and another door at the back.

"Brother Korin should be here within the hour," the monk assured them as he left the room.

"Stay there," Issai said and immediately made a bee-line for the other door, a knife clutched in his hand.

Light from the room beyond was visible beneath the door. He paused for a moment, but with all the people in the bathhouse, he couldn't really tell if anyone was in the room or not through his other sense. Everyone but Hahri and the girl felt equally distant from him. He slowly open-ed it a crack and carefully peered inside. He could just make out the long edge of a sunken bath and a couple of stone benches against the right wall.

He pushed the door completely open, but did not enter, his eyes immediately doing a quick sweep of the room and the bath, but found no one. The room was just a little bit wider and longer than the first room. In the bathhouses Issai had visited previously in this kingdom, he had either bathed in the large communal bath or when he could afford it, in the smaller, single baths.

However, the singles had been in rooms barely large enough to walk around the metal tubs they housed. He had heard that some of the larger bathhouses offered bet-ter accommodations to wealthy travelers, though he had never seen them. Maybe this was one of them.

He nodded towards Hahri, who was still standing by

the exit, and made his way over to claim one of the benches at the table. Although Hahri quickly joined him on it, the girl made no move to follow.

Hahri glanced at him with what looked like amusement before turning his attention to their newest addition. "So," he began, his tone casual, "are you gonna talk to us now, Kid?"

She had been watching them both suspiciously from the moment they had entered the bathhouse, but now the look she directed at Hahri was of silent fury. From the moment she had followed them into the thick of the Residential District, she had not uttered one word—out loud at least. Her eyes had spoken volumes, especially when Hahri kept asking her name at random intervals as they snuck around through various properties searching for a suitable place to lay low.

Her silence only seemed to feed his desire to pick at her relentlessly. Having been on the receiving end of such attention, Issai could only be glad it wasn't him this time. Throttling Hahri in front of her was probably not the best way to win her trust.

Along the way, the auburn-haired boy had taken to calling her "Kid" in the most condescending way possible. Frankly, Issai was surprised she hadn't left them both lying in the road in small pieces and fled the kingdom. The way she had glared at him when she wasn't busy slicing Hahri to shreds with her eyes said that she blamed him as well for the other boy's behavior.

When they had finally found a root cellar that looked as if it hadn't been entered in ages, she had stomped over to the farthest corner from them and completely refused to have anything more to do with either of them, be it an offer of food or another bout of questions, until it was time to leave for the bathhouse.

"Stop. Calling. Me. That."

Although her words were said softly, they were so sharp that they could have drawn blood from the very air.

Hahri shrugged, seemingly unconcerned that he was a breath away from having his nuts cut off. "I have to call you *something*. I work with what I'm given."

Issai sighed. He'd better intervene before any blood was shed. He was way too drained for any more life-or-death healings today.

He gave his companion the evil eye before turning his attention to the fuming girl. "Did the monk tell you why he was so determined to talk to you?" he asked carefully.

The suspicion was back in her eyes. "Shouldn't you be asking *him* that?"

Her hand gripped the hilt of her sword tightly, but she thankfully made no move to draw.

Issai shook his head. "That's not what I mean. Did he tell you about us? About Old Souls?"

"He said I was one," she replied tersely. "What of it?"

Issai resisted the urge to curse. Not even he had been this tight-lipped in the beginning. She was harder to talk to than even regular people.

"Exactly," Hahri cut in, probably sensing his distress. "Good to see we're on the same page."

She was so perplexed by Hahri's words that she forgot to glare at him as she said, "What the hell are you going on about, asshole?"

Her tone and words sounded all kinds of wrong coming out of what was in essence a ten-year-old girl. Issai suddenly realized that it was because she wasn't even trying to hide what she was anymore. He would never again question the unnerved looks his various parents and siblings had given him over the centuries even when he thought he was acting normal for the age he appeared.

He had always wondered what it was that always gave him away. The answer was obvious; he had just refused to see it until now after it had been so blatantly thrown in his face by this pseudo-child. Creatures such as themselves had never been mortal, so why did he ever think he could act like one? Might as well ask a lion to be a mouse. People, after all, had an uncanny ability to always sniff out what didn't belong. It was no wonder the *Shi* always had no trouble picking him out of a crowd even when they had no idea what he looked like.

Hahri's sudden bark of laughter thankfully pulled Issai from his unsettling thoughts. The girl once again looked ready to spit nails.

Perhaps lucky for them—Hahri especially—the door abruptly swung open before any of them could speak again, nearly smacking the red-eyed girl square in the back had she not demonstrated that breathtaking agility once again to instantly pivot out of the way. Her sword was out and pointing straight at the intruder before either boy could even rise.

The look of utter shock on that pale, familiar face had Issai instantly choking down a laugh. No matter how stupid Korin the Watcher's face looked with his eyes bugged out and his jaw seemingly hanging halfway to his knees, Issai didn't think it was appropriate.

Of course, with Hahri in the room, he should have known it would be a wasted effort. The ancient boy laughed so hard, for a moment it seemed he would fall off the bench. Issai was tempted to push him off anyway.

"Get in here, monk, and shut the door before this idiot blows our cover," Issai commanded.

Korin stared at him in confusion for half a breath before hastily complying. The girl stepped away from the monk and sheathed her sword, flashing a widely-grinning

Hahri a look of disgust. The look Korin turned to the pseudo-child after he shut the door was so openly relieved and ecstatic that Issai feared the man would burst into tears. That was something he *did not* want to see. Ever.

"You said two days," she said shortly to Korin.

She made her way over to the empty bench and sat on the edge directly across from Issai, eying them all warily as if she expected them to pounce on her at any moment. Her hand was gripping the hilt of her sword so tightly her knuckles were white.

Korin nodded, his face suddenly serious. He reached into an inner pocket in his robes and pulled something white out that Issai couldn't immediately identify. He then walked over to the girl, his eyes suddenly just as wary as hers, and slowly placed what was in his hand on the table before her. It was a piece of folded cloth small enough to be a handkerchief, its edges embroidered with a simple, straight line of blue thread.

"Thank you," he said quietly and gingerly sat down on the same bench as far from her as he could manage without the threat of falling off.

After glancing at the cloth briefly, she neither touched it nor denied its ownership, though her expression seemed even more guarded as she watched the blond.

Issai wondered what that was all about even as he studied the monk with a critical eye. His movements had been very stiff and deliberate, as though he was trying not to aggravate an injury. Issai half-wished Hahri would open his big mouth and question him about it, but his com-panion was suddenly being uncharacteristically quiet, cerulean eyes watching the monk and girl keenly.

"Well," Korin said into the heavy silence, clearing his throat nervously, "I thought the trembling within me had lessened a bit, but…I really did not expect to find you three here waiting for me."

"So I gathered," Hahri said dryly. "Honestly, I don't quite know how we managed it, either. Senn and me at least. That we ran into the kid as we were coming here was pure coincidence."

Placing his folded hands on the table, Korin leaned a bit closer towards them. "Was it *Shi* or slavers that took you?"

"Both," Hahri replied with a scowl. "Damn bastard hit me from behind. Some idiot lord of the Mahze clan decided to become a *Shi* after running into Senn as a child a few years back. Long story short, they used me as bait for Senn. We ended up spending the night in a couple of cages where they usually keep the kids they snatch. It was deep in a cave directly beneath a building in their compound in Yuzu. Crazy bastard wanted to eat *both* our guts."

"*What!* Why?" Korin exclaimed, his eyes widening with horror. Even the girl's eyes widened for just a moment. "Wouldn't just one of you—"

Hahri nodded. "Yeah. We wanted to know why too, so once Senn managed to send everyone running and screaming for their lives, first by gutting one of them, then spraying my blood all over their lord, we asked the bastard."

"Wait! What do you mean 'sprayed your blood all over their lord'?" Dark eyes immediately began searching up and down Hahri's body, looking for injuries.

Hahri visibly shuddered. "Trust me, you don't want to know, and I don't want to think about it too closely. It worked; that's all that matters. We had the bastard begging to spill what he knew before the end. He said some bastard named Soujin told him he could become something like a god if he consumed a thousand Old Souls, that Soujin, himself, had done this and could now create immortals at will with his gained power. He claimed to have witnessed a girl becoming an immortal."

Korin frowned. "I have never heard of such a thing," he said. "Nor have I heard of the name 'Soujin.' It's not one I have heard used in this kingdom since its founding."

"You've been in this kingdom *that* long?" Hahri remarked in something like disbelief. "That's even more surprising than when you said you had never heard of an Old Soul until you met us!"

Issai rolled his eyes. "You get excited about the strangest things. I'm more concerned about what he said about the name, Soujin." He turned to the girl. "Have *you* ever heard the name mentioned anywhere?"

She shook her head. "I've only been in this kingdom for a couple of seasons, so…"

The look Korin shot the girl was indecipherable, turning away sheepishly only when the scowl returned to her lips.

"Hmm—makes me think the bastard lied to us now," Hahri said. "Either that or Soujin isn't his real name."

It was Issai's turn to scowl. "Or he's a foreigner. Now I trust what that slaver lord said about that boy I keep running into even less."

"What boy?" Korin asked.

"Maybe you know him," Issai replied hopefully. "He's got the same coloring as you—blond hair, dark eyes, between fourteen and sixteen, about Kye's height. He told me he was a native of this city, which could be true enough given its ethnic history. He was the one I mentioned to you before I left to chase after Kye, the one who told me he had been taken. I thought I had lost him

23

for good, but then after running from a potential tail along some back alleys in the Merchant District, who do we stumble upon but that same boy. Only this time, he had her," he nodded towards the girl, "with him, and they were surrounded by four possibly fake guardsmen."

Something changed in the monk's expression. He suddenly looked afraid. "Four guardsmen?" he repeated, his eyes shifting worriedly to the girl.

Issai eyed him strangely. "Yeah," he replied slowly. "One of them was after her with a long-staff. City guardsmen never carry those, but *Shi* always do."

If anything, Korin looked even more troubled. "I think I might have met them as well early this morning. They were waiting for me in my room. No one even knew they had entered the temple, though they claimed otherwise." He turned to the girl. "They were asking a lot of questions about you. They said the Guard had been trying to arrest you for some time now."

They stared at each other for a long while. Issai exchanged a puzzled look with Hahri, but neither one said a word.

"Yes, I know," the red-eyed girl finally said a few, tense moments later, a bit reluctantly.

Korin nodded. "I see," was all he said.

See what? Issai almost growled with frustration. He was definitely missing something here, probably a lot of somethings. Problem was he had no idea how to ask about something that potentially could be a sensitive subject with them. He had already screwed up once with Hahri; the gods knew he didn't want to deal with that kind of repercussion again.

"*Shi* or whoever, they're all dead now, so you don't have to worry about those four anymore," Hahri told Korin.

"Except that maybe that blond kid had ties to them," Issai reminded him. "You of all people should know how loose ends can come back to bite you."

Hahri made a face. "Point taken. So Korin, do you know the kid?"

"Without a name, you could be talking about hundreds of boys in the city. Besides, I left Kairash five years ago. Even if he is someone I knew, I would have only known him as a child and might not recognize him today."

"We'll just have to search for him tomorrow, then," Hahri said, unperturbed. "Senn's right. The whole thing definitely reeks. The way things have been going the last couple of tendays, we don't have the luxury of ignoring anything even remotely suspicious anymore. Is it still safe to stay here all night?"

"Given that the temple was unknowingly breached, it's probably much safer here for the time being. At the very least, we should not be roaming the streets at night for any reason, not even to seek shelter within the temple walls. In the morning, we can leave with a group of my Brothers and follow them on their morning rounds. Their presence alone should provide us with protection as we search. I am not so sure that even those *Shi* would dare attack a group of monks in public."

"Well, if they do, you can always knock them flat with that weird voice of yours and legitimately claim that you did it to protect your Brothers," Hahri quipped, though the grin he wore was decidedly more malicious than amused.

"Let us hope that it does not come to that," Korin said, eyeing them all a little guiltily before settling his gaze on the girl. "Which reminds me, I never did ask you if my Gods' Voice caused any lasting damage?"

Wary red eyes narrowed sharply. "I *knew* it was your fault!" she hissed angrily.

Korin drew back with wide eyes under the heat of that sudden fury. "What—"

"Don't pretend that you don't know!" she spat, jumping to her feet.

Issai stiffened when she drew her sword and pointed it straight at the monk's neck, but a hand squeezing his arm warningly kept him from rising as well.

Wait, Hahri mouthed when Issai frowned questioningly.

The girl was so angry that she couldn't hold the sword steady. "That damned buzzing! It started right after you hit me with that infernal power! You said yourself that those two suffer from it, too, and I saw you *attack* them just as you attacked me! *You* did this to us! You had better be able to fix it, or I'll slice your throat right where you sit and thumb my nose at the gods you so love as I watch you die!"

"Unfortunately, Kid, we were having problems way before the monk sent us flying," Hahri interjected, more nonchalantly than a person who had just had his own throat cut just that morning had any right to be able to do. "It's a nice theory, but ultimately it's wrong. If all you're feeling is a little buzzing, then be thankful you're not like us. What we feel is pain."

For a beat, Issai was absolutely positive that she was about to turn her blade on the blunt boy. In that brief moment, it wasn't anger or even blind fury that he saw swirling in her eyes; it was a touch of madness. Then she viciously stabbed the point of the sword into the hardwood between her feet and let out a wordless sound of pure rage.

"Hey—I get it, okay," Hahri said softly, his eyes

unexpectedly a little sad as he watched her tantrum. "We all get it. You want answers—maybe not the same ones we seek—but that's why we met up here, to hopefully find some of them. That's all we can really ask of each other no matter how much we may wish otherwise."

Issai couldn't quite believe that the auburn-haired boy was still daring to talk to, to *reason* with, someone who was obviously infinitely more unbalanced than any of them—they who were arguably pretty unbalanced themselves. However, whatever kind of crazy the ancient boy was currently exhibiting, it was apparently exactly the kind needed to counter the girl's unfathomable rage. The fire seemed to drain out of her with every word out of his mouth until only a suspicious scowl remained.

She yanked her sword from the wood and sheathed it before plopping down onto the bench again, looking for all the world like a sulky child. "All right, then," she snapped. "Why do *you* think this is happening to us now?"

Hahri shrugged, the strange sadness thankfully gone from his eyes. Issai found that look almost as disconcerting as when the Old Soul persona showed through.

"The 'why' may be as simple as Senn and I meeting and you and Korin meeting. The 'how' and the reasoning behind it is a different story, one we were hoping to learn by talking to you two."

"If you don't mind my asking," Korin spoke up tentatively, "how did the affliction first come about for you two?"

His face was still pale and moist with the shock of facing such an inhuman wrath so unexpectedly, but to the monk's credit, the hands resting on the table did not tremble.

Hahri glanced at Issai, clearly questioning. Issai

frowned. How much did he want to reveal to these two virtual, and in the girl's case volatile, strangers? It seemed that the other boy was leaving that decision up to him once again, and the fact of the matter was they badly needed all the information they could get. He would just have to tread carefully.

"It was after our initial contact," Issai replied, skirting on the details. "I looked into his eyes and just like that, a connection was born between us, one that is aggravated by distance. As far as I know, neither one of us did anything in particular to make it happen."

He turned towards the girl and was a bit disconcerted to find her staring at him intently. "What?" he felt compelled to ask, a bit more sharply than he had intended.

"Was it worse?" she asked, her voice just as cutting. "After you were hit by *his* Voice?"

"If you mean the pain of our connection, then no." Issai supposed he could understand why she still clung to her initial theory even when told it was flat-out wrong. The buzzing within her would make perfect sense if it were indeed a consequence of Korin's attack. "After I completely healed the damage it caused, there were no lasting effects."

Her eyes flitted towards Korin then back to him. "You really can heal wounds with only your mind?"

He nodded, and her expression shifted into something unnamable. He had wondered if Korin had told her about that. Apparently, she had talked more with the monk than she had initially let on.

"If that's true, then why haven't you used it to rid yourself of that damned affliction?" she demanded.

Issai stilled instantly. Why hadn't he done it? That was answered easily enough. It was because, until now, it had never once occurred to him to try. Words could not describe how unbelievably stupid he felt at the moment, even given the fact that he had only dealt with physical wounds that he could see. That he had never even thought to try was what was inexcusable.

However, he would rather gut himself on a *Shi*'s sacrificial altar than admit any of that to the brat or the monk. "Because I don't even know what exactly is hurting and why," he said. "My ability to heal deals with absolutes, not speculation."

His answer seemed to blacken her mood threefold, quite a feat considering the tedious line she was already walking between fury and plain irritation. "So does that mean you can't heal the damned buzzing in me either?" she pressed.

Suddenly her reaction made perfect sense. "I can't heal anyone but myself," he confirmed, "and now, only because of this inexplicable connection that formed between us, Kye as well."

Korin nodded thoughtfully. "Perhaps there is nothing in need of healing at all. For me, it's as if my soul is trembling, like the gods wanted us to find each other and made this our beacon."

Issai half-expected Hahri to make some snide remark, but it was the girl who snorted in disdain instead. "Yeah, a beacon to torment us," she sneered. "What other reason is there for any of this other than for a new way for us puny mortals to struggle along for their amusement?"

"That's not the way the gods work..." Korin protested with dismay, looking over at both Issai and Hahri for affirmation. "Just look at Senn and Kye. They never would have found us if they had not been sent visions to guide them to the right path."

Issai winced internally at the monk's sudden enthusiasm. They really didn't know why Hahri had felt compelled to seek out these two particular people. That was the whole point of coming here to meet them. He didn't like how the monk just chalked it all up to the will of the gods as if that was the only detail that mattered. It reeked too much of the game he feared it was for his own comfort. The girl may be more right than she realized.

"Don't make it sound so cut and dry," Hahri warned, echoing his thoughts. "If the gods truly wanted us here, then they damned sure have a poor way of going about it. Senn and I have been chased by more *Shi* in the last couple of tendays than we have in the last few centuries. We couldn't even stay in a place long enough to enjoy a bath without being ambushed. Hell, just this morning, I was manacled to a slaver lord's idiotic idea of a sacrificial altar beats away from being *eaten alive* while a circle of more idiots stood around and jeered like it was the grandest party they had ever attended. Forgive me if I'm still a little dubious about that explanation."

"But you made it out alive..." Korin protested.

"Yeah we did, but that was *all* Senn."

"That's happened to me, too."

The silence was instantaneous as all eyes turned to the girl. She had spoken so quietly that her voice had almost been unrecognizable.

"You've been captured by *Shi* before?" Hahri asked.

"If you mean a bunch of men in dark robes who stripped me naked and tied me to a slab of stone before cutting out my guts and eating them while I was still alive, then yes," she replied tersely. "It's happened more times than I can count."

Korin's face twisted into the most blatant look of horror and disgust Issai had ever seen on another's face. Hearing it from the mouth of a little girl must have finally made all the atrocities they'd suffered at the hands of the *Shi* real.

She looked directly at Korin. "They called me an Old Soul just as you did."

Issai didn't think the monk's expression could have looked any worse, but now, not only was he horrified, but Korin also looked as though he was about to be violently sick. Once again, the girl's tone had been layered with so much subtext that it undoubtedly alluded to an earlier encounter between the blond and her. He wondered what the monk had done to inspire such obvious animosity against him, though he doubted that it was half as bad as Korin's expression suggested.

"That settles it then," Hahri cut through the following silence. "The four guardsmen that attacked the kid were definitely *Shi*. It's getting way too dangerous to remain here. I say we hightail it out of the city as soon as we find that blond boy and get whatever information he may have out of him."

Issai nodded. "We should also try to find more information about Soujin at the same time."

Hahri turned to the other pair. "We set out to find you, not because a vision told us to, but out of a desire to find out what it means exactly to be an Old Soul and why we exist at all. Knowing that, then it might be possible to find an end to this urge to *do something* that Senn and I have felt ever since our first lives as well as an end to this newest affliction we all are suffering. Our reasons for being here in this room right now may be different, but perhaps our ultimate goal is the same. Will you stick it out with us, at least for a little longer?"

"Of course," Korin replied without hesitation. "Whether you believe so or not, I believe that the gods set me on this path, and I have every intention of following it to its end, whatever end that may be. Perhaps it will lead to a way to quiet the pain in all of us." He turned to the girl and continued hesitantly, "I will make it my priority if that is your wish. Will you stay with us and let me help you?"

Rather than reassure her, Korin's words only seemed to add to her agitation. The same wary scowl she had worn in the beginning was back on her face.

"We'll be here all night," Issai pointed out as he rose and slung his pack over his shoulder. "Talk it over some more with the monk if you like, but I want a bath, then sleep. We should take it in shifts in case someone does decide to attack us here, monks or no monks. The way our luck's been going lately, it's almost guaranteed to happen, and Kye and I haven't slept in over a day. I'd rather have a couple of hours under my belt, at the very least, if it does happen."

Korin looked questionably at the girl, who hesitated a moment longer before nodding curtly. Maybe the blond would be more successful in learning her name than Hahri. Issai really didn't want to have to call her kid or girl, too.

"Give us at least five hours, then we'll switch," Hahri said, as he followed Issai into the second room.

"A gold coin says there'll be blood in there by midnight," Hahri offered as Issai dropped his pack onto one of the stone benches against the wall.

The sad thing was that his companion was probably right, and for the first time, he was immensely grateful that the one he had been saddled with was Hahri. True, the auburn-haired Old Soul was confusing as hell at times, but given his other choices, Issai would've either ended up dead or a murderer.

He smirked. "You say that like you even have a coin

to your name."

Hahri grinned and pulled a small, leather pouch from his belt for the other's inspection. Issai knew damn well that it had not been there before they had entered the city.

He waved it away. "All I can say is I hope the bastard deserved it."

Hahri's grin widened maliciously. "Oh, definitely."

He threw his cloak untidily beside Issai's pack and dropped the pouch on top. "So," he said as Issai turned to do the same, "are you gonna try it?"

Something in the overtly casual tone Hahri used instantly had him on edge.

"Try what?" Issai asked warily as he looked sideways at the smaller boy.

All traces of humor had disappeared from those cerulean eyes.

"To break the Bond."

CHAPTER THREE

"I'm sorry," Korin said as soon as Kye and Senn left the room. "Had I known what those blasphemers had done to you…"

The girl sneered and turned away. "I don't need it."

He nodded, knowing this would be her reaction, but he had needed to say it anyway. He noted that she had yet to touch the handkerchief on the table and wondered if she planned to leave it there. He had given it to her in the small hope that it would make her a little bit more receptive to him, but...

At least she had agreed to remain with them for the time being. That had to count for something.

Korin fidgeted on his side of the bench, wondering if he should go sit opposite her. He hated not being able to see a person's face when he was talking to them, but he wasn't altogether sure she wouldn't immediately stab him in the gut if he tried to move any closer to her—or move at all for that matter.

"If I ask you a question," she spoke suddenly, her eyes

fixed to the opposite wall, "will you answer me honestly this time?"

His heart sped up excitedly. That she had initiated the conversation was definitely a step in the right direction.

"Yes. Ask whatever you wish."

She looked at him briefly before returning her gaze to the wall, a small frown pulling at her lips. "Do you really believe all that crap you told me yesterday about our souls being connected, or were you just spewing some Temple bullshit?"

His mouth instinctively hardened into a thin line of disapproval. Why was everyone so hostile towards the Temple? She was worse than even Kye, her biting words now and before alluding to a personal vendetta against the gods rather than just animosity towards the Sons of the Temple. He wanted to ask her, but he knew relations between them would have to thaw considerably before he dared try.

Korin had given a lot of thought to how he would handle their next meeting, what questions he would ask, while he had sat in this very room last night waiting in vain for Senn and Kye. Her question rendered all of his preparations irrelevant, and now he was once again at a loss of how to proceed. He knew without her telling him that this was his last chance to convince her to stay.

"I assure you, I would not have said any of it if I did not believe it to be true," he said quietly. "I truly believe that it was by the will of the gods that we met when we did and that by Their power, our souls were connected."

"Ignoring the fact that we can't even touch each other without pain," she said sardonically, "let's say you're right. They purposely bound our souls together, and now we can't even go two paces from each other without feeling like we have a swarm of pissed off bees battling it out inside our bodies. What could the gods possibly hope to accomplish by doing such a thing?"

Thankfully, it was a question he had considered at length. "At first, I thought it was because my earthly life was finally coming to an end," he replied. "You were the first person I had met in all my many lives that had any kind of similarity to me. I thought the gods had sent you to me to become the Watcher in my stead, that it would be my final duty to show you the path you would walk.

"However, after meeting Senn and Kye and learning a little about Old Souls, it's possible I was mistaken. The reason we were brought together here may be as simple as the gods wanting us to complete a task, one that only beings such as ourselves have the power to accomplish."

Korin watched her tensely, but she said nothing, her eyes remaining fixed to the wall. He had expected her to rage at him again. After all, if she really did have nothing but disdain for the Temple, then the thought of doing the gods' work should have had her immediately fleeing out that door. Yet, she just sat there stiffly and silently glared at the wall as if trying to knock it down by sheer will.

"You know," she said after a long moment, finally turning to look at him with a curiously blank expression, "I don't even know how many years have passed since I died the first time. Thousands surely, but I've long since lost count. Now, by your reasoning, we were created with this twisted kind of immortality to do Their dirty work here in the mortal realm. So tell me, monk, why have They waited so damned long to get things going? Why now? Or better yet, why keep us in the dark about it? I don't know about you, but *I* have never heard Them say *one damn word* to me. It just doesn't make sense to let us sit and rot for so long."

Korin was stunned. That was the most he had ever

heard her speak. Her words made something inside of him shift uncomfortably, leaving him feeling a little off-balance. From early on, he had always felt his sole purpose was to serve the will of the gods. It had never been in his character to question that will, even though he frequently wondered why he was the one chosen to serve in such an extraordinary way.

Of course, he had never had any of the gods speak to him directly either, but he had never expected them to, no matter how many times he had desperately wished it. Instead, it was the duty of all monks to read the signs given them and act accordingly.

However, explaining all of that to her would do him no good here. She was not a monk and could not be expected to understand, much less accept, that kind of reasoning.

"I cannot answer any of that at this time," he admitted. "I would be lying if I said I could. Sometimes, things only become clear in the end. I have always faced every obstacle in my life with that in mind."

The look she gave him was incredulous. "That's a really stupid way to go about things," she said bluntly. "You're like a blind man knowingly walking straight towards the edge of a cliff, so sure that there will be steps going down when you get there. Even though I've sliced you up twice now, you still approach me like you're positive I won't do it again. It's like you have no regard for yourself at all. Are you that much a slave to the gods?"

He smiled gently. "The gods do not force anyone to do anything. They might point us in any number of directions for Their own reasons, but it's ultimately up to us whether or not we choose to listen. I could have chosen to stay in Aideya after you ran from the temple, but I wanted to see where this path led. Because of that choice, I was able to rescue some unfortunate children from the clutches of slavers. Had I not decided to pursue you, I never would have even known about them, and now, because of Senn and Kye, we have the chance to find out more about Old Souls together. We have a chance to calm the trembling in our souls. I do not think those two have told us even a fraction of what they know about all of this."

"Of course they haven't," she scoffed. "*They* aren't stupid, and that's saying a lot considering I'd like nothing more than to cut out the brown-haired one's tongue. Only *you* expect everyone to willingly blab all their secrets to a total stranger. Being a monk doesn't give you the right to be a nosy asshole."

"Yes, I hear that often," he said with a laugh. "I do not mean to come across as so overbearing, and I apologize for it."

"Stop apologizing so much," she said crossly. "I said I don't need it."

He smiled sheepishly. "Is there anything else you would like to ask me?"

She regarded him silently for a long moment, her expression still unreadable. There was something infinitely unnerving in the way those red eyes just stared at him without blinking once, but he forced himself not to fidget and calmly returned her gaze.

Finally, she sighed heavily as if frustrated and carefully laid her sword onto the table. She then shifted on the bench, straddling it in order to face him directly. Her legs were barely long enough to allow her feet to dangle over the sides.

"How did you know I was a girl?" she demanded. "When I'm this age, most don't find out until they're getting me ready to slice open."

Korin frowned. "I don't know how you can talk about having something so horrible done to you so non-chalantly."

"Don't change the subject," she said sharply. "How did you know?"

He held his hands up, placating. "I had a vision, that time in the temple after that strange force slammed me into the door. I saw a young, redheaded girl of about sixteen, and somehow I just *knew* she was you, knew it with all my being. It was because of the implications of that vision that I thought perhaps you were one whose existence was similar to mine."

The fear was back in her eyes, except this time she didn't turn away or try to hide it with anger. It was the most honest expression the ancient monk had ever seen her wear.

"That was Saiya," she said softly.

Korin was instantly confused. "Saiya?" he repeated. "You mean—I was wrong about the vision? The girl wasn't you?"

She frowned and shook her head. "For a monk that's lived as long as you, you're pretty slow on the uptake," she snapped.

He stared perplexedly at her for a couple more breaths then inhaled sharply. "Your name...!"

She smiled thinly. "Yes, and that was what I looked like the first time I died."

Break the Bond...

Issai should've seen it coming; a tenday ago he would have, but after everything they had been through in the last two days, their strange bond was one of the few things he had come to terms with. It had even been useful. Without it, he probably would never have found Hahri in time to save him. Apparently, his change of heart had not been as obvious to Hahri as he had thought.

He paused in the process of removing his belt and slowly turned to face the other boy, fearing what he would see—or not see—in those cerulean eyes. He was infinitely relieved when the gaze he met was swimming with emotion and not inhuman and cold.

Did he want to break the Bond—if Hahri would've asked that as the Old Soul, Issai would not have known how to handle it. He probably would have gotten angry. Things would have likely gotten tense and distant between them again, and that was something neither one of them could afford at the moment. Yet, not only was there clear sentiment, for the first time, there was also something vulnerable in the smaller boy's expression. Although it made him uncomfortable, it was something he could answer.

Issai shook his head. "No, I want to *understand* it," he said firmly. "As much as it can be a pain in the ass, it does have its uses. Besides, didn't I already say I'd stick it out with you?"

"You did," Hahri replied slowly, "but…"

"But what?" Issai demanded, scowling. "Do *you* want to break it?"

Hahri sighed heavily and raked a hand through his hair in clear agitation. "That's not what I meant at all. I'm not doubting your words. I just wanted you to know that it was an option you could take, that *we* could take if any unsettling issues come up in the future."

Issai's frown deepened. "Even if I wanted to break it, what I said to the girl earlier was true. Without knowing how or why the Bond exists, you might as well ask me to heal a tear in the air. I don't think it's something we should be mucking about with so recklessly. Look what happened to me the last time I healed us…"

"We really should get to the bottom of that, you know," Hahri said. He rubbed his injured arm thoughtfully. "Maybe when you try to heal my arm, we can experiment a bit."

"Trying to heal your arm *is* the experiment," Issai pointed out. "As I said earlier, I'd rather not do anything until we both have gotten some sleep. I can't trust my control otherwise."

Hahri shrugged. "That's fine. We should take advantage of our current accommodations as much as possible. Hate to say it, but the kid wasn't just being nasty earlier when she called me a horseshit-smelling bastard. Even after being drenched and changing shirts, I can *still* smell a bit of that damn dungeon we spent last night in on both of us. Honestly, I'm surprised the monks didn't turn us away at the door."

Issai grimaced. He had smelled it too, of course, but the smell had so thoroughly permeated his nose last night that he hadn't been altogether sure if that lingering stench wasn't just in his mind. Now that he knew for sure, a bath was the most sensible thing the other had suggested all day.

A few moments later found them both soaking up to their necks in water that was pleasantly hot. From everything he knew about the Temple and their teachings, Issai had expected the water to be bone-chillingly cold, especially in a city this close to the mountains. However, having never undergone a Purification himself, he had no way of knowing if a heated bath was normal or a luxury only offered to the Temple's more wealthier worshippers.

Maybe he would ask Korin about it later.

Speaking of things he wanted to ask about...

"There's something that's been really bothering me," Issai ventured as he handed his companion one of the soap squares he had found in a small alcove along the edge of the bath.

"About Korin or the girl?" Hahri asked absently as he began to run the soap through his hair.

"No, about you."

Hahri froze. The soap plopped into the water, instantly forgotten, as the auburn-haired boy lowered his arms and slowly turned to face him.

"I really don't like the vibe I'm getting from you now," he said, his words edged slightly with tension. "It feels a lot like fear, and I'm not sure I want to know what could scare you."

Issai scowled. Fear? He didn't think he was *that* worried about the other's answer.

"I said it was *bothering* me," he replied coolly.

Hahri matched him stare for stare. "Nevertheless, it's something you feel strongly enough about that I'm able to feel it, too. Is it something I did?"

"More like something you said. Remember back in Rihott when those *Shi* first started chasing us in the marketplace? You let out a curse, one in the Vornan language."

Hahri's shoulders relaxed a bit. "What, '*saat*'? Wow, I can't believe you actually know that language. It's one that died out thousands of years ago."

"I know," he said quietly.

Hahri tilted his head curiously. "Why does me saying that word bother you?"

"I once knew a boy who used that particular curse," Issai said. "He's the only one I've ever heard use it, especially in that particular language. The word had long fallen out of use by the Vorn during the time I lived among them, but he always said that he liked the way it flowed from his tongue."

And just like that, all the emotion disappeared from Hahri's face and Issai found himself unexpectedly facing the Old Soul.

"Was his name 'Alik'?" the ancient boy asked.

Issai inhaled sharply. That name was like a punch in the gut.

"How did you...?"

"*Because Alik was me*," Hahri said in Vornan.

It was Issai's turn to go completely still. "Wha-what?" he choked out in disbelief.

"You were Jov."

Although said as a statement, Issai could practically taste the implied question, as though the other wanted him to contradict him. Issai very much wanted to oblige him.

"I was."

This time not only could he see the shock animate the other boy's previously emotionless eyes, Issai could also feel Hahri's jumble of emotions bleed into his own shock.

"But..." Hahri began, but then shook his head, unable to complete the thought.

He didn't need to because Issai was almost absolutely sure that they were both thinking the same thing. How could they have known each other in a previous life and not known the other was an Old Soul? Or more importantly, why had the Bond not manifested then?

As it was, Issai could barely even remember Alik, just bits and pieces of places they had gone together, a conversation or two. He couldn't even remember what he, himself, had looked like during that life, never mind what

Alik had looked like. Really, if it hadn't been for that odd curse word, he probably wouldn't have remembered Alik at all.

"What do you remember of Jov?" Issai asked carefully.

"He was a kid," Hahri said after a long moment of thought. "Maybe twelve or thirteen. Odd thing is I can't remember him as any older or younger. I think I was a couple of years younger than him. We used to climb the mountains behind our village. Whether for fun or a specific purpose, I couldn't tell you. Other than that, nothing."

Hahri suddenly frowned. "Come to think of it, I can't even remember how or when I died during that life."

Issai felt his chest tighten in dismay. "Yeah, I can remember those mountains," he said slowly, "especially one in particular. Do you know what happened to the Vornan civilization?"

Hahri's frown deepened. "Not really. I think I once heard a story that they had incurred the wrath of the gods and were wiped out as punishment, but I think that as likely as the gods coming to the earth to dance on Kairash's city wall."

Issai grimaced. "Oh, they were wiped out all right, but whether or not the gods were responsible is up for debate. The largest peak erupted, so violently that I heard only pieces of the island remained above the water. The rest was blown to bits and scattered across the ocean."

Hahri's eyes widened. "When did that happen?"

"You said you don't remember how you died?" Issai continued as if the other hadn't spoken. "Well, neither did I until the life after Jov when I heard talk of the calamity that had befallen the Vorn's island."

"After Jov—wait—we *died* during that eruption!"

Hahri exclaimed. "Is that what you're saying?"

Issai nodded. "It was the only reason I could think of to explain why I couldn't really remember the life I had led as Jov when I could remember all the others so clearly. Just think about it. An eruption that violent would've destroyed our bodies completely in the blink of an eye. Who's to say that it didn't also damage our souls somehow?"

Hahri gripped his hair on both sides of his head and tugged in agitation. "I lived as Alik relatively close to when this all began; he was like my fifth or sixth in-carnation. All this time, the *centuries* I spent looking for you, and you're telling me we forgot we knew each other because *some damn mountain decided to blow its top!*"

"You have to admit, it makes the most sense. Didn't you even wonder why you couldn't remember how you died?"

Hahri laughed humorlessly. "I don't even remember which life came after that, so I must've not been too bothered by it if it didn't leave enough of an impression on me to remember now."

"After hearing about the eruption, I wasn't too bothered about my sudden amnesia either," Issai admitted, "and I never ended up in that part of the world again, so I never saw the decimated island. Maybe if I had, something might've poked at my memory." *Maybe I would've found you sooner...*

"I still can't believe that we forgot something so important," Hahri insisted.

"Maybe we didn't. Maybe neither one of us admitted that we were an Old Soul," Issai pointed out.

Hahri shook his head. "When I remembered about us climbing the mountains, I got the impression that it was something we had done many times. I can't believe

45

neither one of us showed our abilities while doing something so dangerous, especially when we were still little more than children." His eyes abruptly lit up in excitement. "Hey—do you think Korin and the girl might've been there, too?"

The thought gave Issai an unpleasant jolt. "If that turns out to be the case, then what you said about the gods being responsible for the island's destruction becomes a little more plausible. Either that or it would have to be the biggest coincidence in the history of humanity."

"We'd better ask them first thing in the morning. This could be more important than any of us realize."

"If the girl's still here, you mean."

Hahri grinned. "No, she'll definitely still be here. For all her threats and violence, beneath all that noise, she's just as curious about us as we are of her. Otherwise, she would've never agreed to follow people as questionable as us. Maybe after trading a few stories, we'll be able to make more sense of everything. After all, if I hadn't cursed back in that marketplace, then we might've never known that we had crossed paths before. It's not like either one of us would've remembered that life at all if I hadn't inadvertently thrown you that clue. There's no telling what other things we might uncover."

"Hopefully something more useful than and not as infuriating as shared amnesia," Issai griped as he shoved Hahri's dropped soap along a small wave of water back at the other boy.

"It's too early to feel so disappointed," Hahri said as he snatched the soap up and resumed washing. "Now that I know something important may have happened way back when, you can bet your ass I'm gonna poke and prod that memory until I bleed all the secrets out, even if it takes me the rest of this life to do it."

"Don't hold your breath," Issai muttered.

He glared down at the soap square in his hand. Who would have thought that what he had believed was the simplest of his piles of questions would have opened such an unexpectedly complicated door. He should have known better than to ask it when he was so physically and mentally exhausted.

Now, with the knowledge that a large piece of the Old Soul puzzle may still exist somewhere in his memories, he would never get to sleep, and that was something he really couldn't afford.

"*Saat*!" he spat.

CHAPTER FOUR

Issai shot to his feet at the sound of the door squeaking open, both knives fisted in his hands before he had even opened his eyes. His heart pounded as though he had been running for hours.

"Put those away; you're gonna give him heart failure," came the sleep-muddled voice at his side.

He immediately looked down at Hahri who was stretched out on one of the stone benches wrapped in his cloak, gazing up at him blearily. Had he been asleep? The last thing Issai remembered doing was trying to recall more about his time with Alik. His eyes flickered over to the opened doorway where Korin stood, his expression still a bit startled. If the monk was here to wake them, then apparently he had.

"Sorry," he told the blond, slipping his knives back into their sheaths. He rubbed a hand down his face. "Is our shift up?"

"Yes," Korin replied as he hesitantly stepped farther into the room, "but maybe I should have let you both sleep a bit more."

"It's fine," Issai said as he felt Hahri stand up beside him.

He glanced behind the monk's shoulder and was relieved to see the girl still sitting at the table in the other room, even if she was glaring at the opposite wall. Despite what Hahri had said, he really hadn't expected Korin to convince her to stay. Especially when everything the ancient monk did and said seemed to rub her the wrong way.

"We have something we want to discuss with both of you before you go to sleep, anyway," Hahri said.

"Oh?" Korin remarked, looking interested. He glanced behind him. "Saiya?"

The girl whipped her head towards them so fast that Issai was surprised he didn't hear it crack. The glare she directed at Korin was sharp enough to draw blood. For a moment, she looked ready to jump up and skewer them all with the sword on the table, but then she let out a heavy sigh and abruptly turned away.

"Do want you want," she said in a voice that sounded disinterested.

Hahri rolled his eyes and strode into the room, plopping himself down right across from her. Issai quickly followed, wanting to be in elbowing distance before his companion could open his mouth.

"So, 'Saiya' is it?" Hahri said once they were all seated. His smile was friendly. It made Issai instantly suspicious. "Much better than 'Kid'—*ow!*"

Issai couldn't help it. The laugh spilled from his lips before he could cover his mouth at the look of startled indignation on Hahri's face as the auburn-haired boy rubbed his knee where the girl had apparently kicked him.

"You deserved it," Issai said, not able to keep the

amusement out of his voice completely.

"Hmph! Traitor…" Hahri sniffed, the face-splitting grin ruining the effect.

Issai heard a delicate cough, and he turned his attention to their so-far quiet, fourth member. The monk was looking at Hahri and him as if they were some unknown life-form.

"What?" Issai demanded tersely.

Korin shook his head. "No, it's just—after so many centuries of life, seeing you in this moment and various others before, I cannot fathom how you can act so convincingly like the teenaged boys you appear to be. Especially when it appears it's not an act at all."

"And you're just an old fart in a young body, so what's your point?" Hahri shot back.

Issai could've sworn he saw Saiya almost smile.

"You just proved it," Korin countered, looking more perplexed than offended at the insult. "At times, it's like you really did not mature past your teen years. It makes me wonder what you have been doing all this time."

"Oh, you mean besides suffering through infancy, looking for an idiot like you, and running for my life from a bunch of psychos who are trying to have my guts for breakfast, not a whole damn lot, I guess."

"I think that about covers it for the both of us," Issai couldn't help adding, completely deadpanned.

"Oh, well, yes of course…" Korin replied, suddenly discomfited. "I truly did not mean to offend…"

Saiya snorted. "I told you you're too nosy," she said.

"He's a monk," Hahri said with a shrug as if that explained everything.

For him, it probably did. Issai personally thought the ancient monk was just awkward when having to deal with anything unrelated to the Temple. The gods knew he, himself, had trouble dealing with people, period. If Hahri had not had the personality he did, their little group probably would have imploded from the start.

Damned if he would tell Hahri that, though.

"And on that note..." Issai interjected, looking at Hahri meaningfully.

The ancient boy nodded. "Yes, we had something to ask you two before we got sidetracked. Did either of you ever live among the Vorn?"

"The Vorn?" Korin echoed thoughtfully. "No, I have not. In fact, I do not believe I have ever heard of them. Were they a civilization on this continent?"

"No."

The answer surprisingly came from Saiya. Issai's heart sped up in both anticipation and dread. Could it be?

Saiya was looking at Korin with something like disbelief. "Are you really that sheltered?" she asked incredulously. "Even people from the slums all around the world have heard *that* story. The gods practically wiped out their entire island from existence as punishment for some great sin or other. I'm shocked that you monks don't use it as a warning to us perpetual sinners in your sermons."

"The island was about a hundred spans east of the Salali continent," Hahri told him. "About as far away from here as you can get. I suppose if you've never lived in any continent other than this one..."

"I have not," Korin replied. "Except for my first life, I have always been born in these lands, and even then, I was born on a boat that was little more than a hollowed out log as my people were fleeing their homeland to this continent."

"Hmm—I wonder why," Hahri mused. "I've been born practically everywhere."

"Same here," Issai said.

Both of them turned to look at Saiya nearly in tandem.

"Same," she said curtly. Then a bit more hesitantly, "Though never on that island."

Hahri sighed, his expression disappointed. "Well, so much for that."

"Why is that island so important?" Korin asked. "Did the gods really destroy it?"

"Well, if They *were* responsible, then They did it when we were on it," Hahri replied. "Senn says he found out in his next life that one of the mountains blew, but the problem is that neither one of us remembers much of anything of those lives, never mind how we died. Until last night, we thought the first time we had met was a few tendays ago. Turns out we knew each other on the island, and neither one of us remembers the other as an Old Soul. That's why we wondered if you two had lived there during that time, too."

"I always just thought it was nothing more than a story," Saiya said. She fixed Hahri with a hard stare. "You think it has something to do with Old Souls, don't you."

Hahri shrugged. "It might, or as Senn suggested, being erased so completely might've damaged our souls somehow, and that's why we can't remember much of anything of that life. We thought it odd enough to ask you about it just in case, but..." He shrugged again.

"You were right to ask us," Korin said. "I probably know the least amount about Old Souls of all of us here, but despite that, I will help with as much as I can."

"Even if that help requires you to use your Gods' Voice on our behalf?" Issai asked shrewdly.

Korin looked at him sharply. Issai met the blond's gaze just as strongly, challengingly.

The monk slowly nodded. "If I must."

"Trust us, you will," Hahri said. "Just in the last tenday, we had what amounted to a small army try to corner us just outside of Subu. I don't know who commanded them, but they were *Shi*, every one of them. Who knows where they are now. We also can't be sure if the slavers that took me won't try for us again, seeing as how we killed their lord and a good many more of the bastards while escaping their compound. That's why we probably shouldn't stay in this city longer than another day or two.

"You can ask around about Soujin. The locals know you, but more importantly, they *trust* you. You're more likely to hear the truth than any of us. We'll concentrate on keeping an eye out for that blond kid."

"Don't just assume that I'm going to follow you on whatever harebrained chase you all have concocted," Saiya cut in, scowling at all of them in turn. "The only thing I care about right now is to stop this maddening humming inside, and I haven't heard one word said yet about how you're planning on doing it. If the only thing *you* care about is chasing after phantoms, then I'm outta here."

Hahri sighed. "So impatient. Of course we've thought about the Bond. In fact, Senn and I plan on experimenting a bit with it while you two take your turn sleeping."

"Good, then you can just keep the monk here with you while *I* go take a bath," she retorted as she slid off the bench, sword in hand. She pointed the scabbard at them. "If any of you even *think* of going in there before I'm finished, then it'll be me instead of *Shi* who guts you this time."

She fixed Korin with a particularly nasty glare. "Let's see you make good on your promise to help me. I won't wait forever."

Then she turned on her heels and marched into the next room with the air of a martyr walking to her death, slamming the door behind her with more force than necessary.

Hahri snickered. "And you accuse *us* of acting like children," he said, smiling at Korin widely. "You're gonna have your hands full for quite a while. Do you think we should tell her that the door locks from the other side?"

"There's no way in hell I'm going anywhere near that door," Issai said wryly even as he winced internally when he realized he had not thought to lock the door himself. "She probably means it, and I've had enough holes punched in me in the last few hours to last me several lifetimes."

"Speaking of holes," Hahri said as he lifted the sleeve of his left arm to reveal the bloody bandage. "Care to try now?"

He nodded. Yes, he had made the other boy wait long enough.

Korin gasped. "What happened?"

"Arrow," the ancient boy replied absently as he was unwinding the bandage. "The slavers really didn't want us to leave their compound alive. It's not as bad as it looks; it entered pretty cleanly without damaging the bone or veins. Hurts like hell, though."

The blond turned to Issai. "Should I move away?" he asked worriedly.

"That would be best," Issai agreed. "I'm not all that sure I can do it, so the less distractions I have the better."

"But—I saw you heal him back in Rihott…"

"That wasn't his wound," Issai said. "It was mine."

"What do you mean?"

Issai hesitated. He caught Hahri's eye briefly, and the other nodded minutely.

"Distance pain isn't the only thing we share through the Bond," he admitted, watching the monk's reaction closely. "We suffer each other's wounds, though Kye is the only one who has them manifest physically. I only feel the pain of his injuries."

Korin stared mutely at him for a long moment with an unreadable expression. "That is nothing like the bond I have with Saiya," he finally said. He pulled open his robes a bit and revealed the bandages beneath, confirming Issai's earlier suspicions of injury. "She cut me pretty badly with her blade before she was stopped. There was never any indication that she felt any of it, and believe me, that kind of pain would have brought anyone to their knees."

Hahri whistled. "She did that to you, and you still chased after her? You've got a lotta nerve, monk. I'll give you that."

"You two are the only other Old Souls either of us have ever met," Issai said, ignoring the other boy's teasing. "Who's to say what's typical for our kind and what's not? There may not even be any more Old Souls other than us four or there may be hundreds more. My point is, what may be true for us may not necessarily hold true for you. You should keep that in mind before attempting to copy anything we may do in regards to the Bond."

"Of course," the monk was quick to agree, even as he regarded Issai with that strange expression again.

Issai thought it best not to call him on it for the moment. One problem at a time. Besides, he was certain that Korin would bring up whatever was bothering him all on his own.

"Should we grasp hands like the last time?" Hahri asked as he straddled the bench to face him.

Issai emulated the other. "It might help, although..."
He caught himself and glanced over at Korin who had
moved over to the far corner of the room. "No. Never
mind. It should be fine."

Although his companion's eyes narrowed a bit, he
otherwise gave no reaction to Issai's words. What had
happened to him last time was not something he was
ready to discuss with anyone other than Hahri. At least
his near slipup had reminded the other boy of it, and
hopefully, it would make him more cautious of any
actions henceforth.

He clasped Hahri's hands tightly, took a deep breath
to try to calm the sudden anxiety that knotted his throat,
and closed his eyes. Issai figured the best way to go about
it was to treat Hahri's wound as though it was on his own
arm instead. He imagined the torn flesh on the surface,
then the layers beneath straight through to the exit
wound. Once he had that image firmly implanted into his
mind's eye, he released his command to heal.

For a couple of beats, he felt the center of his left
forearm begin to heat up, and elation and relief coursed
through his entire being. Then the heat abruptly vanished,
and startled, Issai opened his eyes.

Hahri blinked at him in confusion before looking
down at his arm with a frown. Issai followed his gaze and
instantly cursed. The wound still looked completely the
same, down to the bits of scabbing and the red, inflamed
skin surrounding the hole.

"On to the next plan, I take it?" Hahri said lightly.

Issai glared down at the offending wound as if his
failure was somehow its fault. "Yeah," was all he said as
he stared down at it for a long while before closing his
eyes again.

Because of the heat he had felt briefly in his own arm,

he obviously had activated his healing ability successfully, but apparently, it had turned off when it had found nothing to heal. If healing himself did nothing for the other boy, then the only thing left to do was to try to somehow send his healing energies to Hahri directly through the Bond.

The problem was, he had no idea how to even approach such a feat, much less how to accomplish it, when he had no idea what it was that bound them together and why. There was no telling what kind of calamities he might cause them by blindly messing around with what could very well be their souls.

His thoughts drifted to the time when he had shared the vision of the white blossom fields with Hahri, and then inevitably to the unsettling incident when it had seemed he had *become* Hahri for that brief, terrifying moment. Issai hadn't thought about it at the time, but maybe something similar had happened in both instances. After all, he wouldn't have even known something was amiss the second time if he hadn't felt Hahri blink.

There was no way around it. If he wanted to have any chance in healing Hahri's wound, he would just have to man up and try to invoke that state on purpose.

"Try to concentrate on giving me some of your strength," Issai said softly, opening his eyes to look at Hahri seriously. "Just thinking about doing it may even be enough."

Cerulean eyes widened. "You're gonna...!"

He nodded. "I think it might be the only way."

Hahri pursed his lips worriedly. "Are you sure? Is healing such a small wound worth that kind of risk?"

Issai caught and held his eyes. "The next time it might not be 'such a small wound.'"

The ancient boy swallowed thickly and slowly nodded.

Satisfied, Issai closed his eyes once again, and focused his entire attention on feeling the closeness of the other boy with his other sense. Once it reached the point where he felt as if he was practically wearing Hahri's essence, he tried to determine if any of the jumble of emotions he was currently feeling were in fact Hahri's. He thought the anxiety he was feeling was a bit too much, so Issai zeroed in on that sole emotion and allowed himself to almost drown in it.

That's when he felt himself suddenly squeeze his own hands tightly. Had he succeeded? Unlike before, Issai saw nothing but darkness, but he hoped that was because this time Hahri had his eyes closed as well. He dared not try to open his own to test it. Maybe next time there would be time enough for more experimentation, but he definitely didn't want to push his luck any more than he already had.

Issai turned his attention to his left forearm. Yes, he could feel the fever in the skin, feel a pain that seemed to throb in time with his heartbeat. He immediately set about tracing the wound in his mind's eye exactly as he had done before, and before he could lose his nerve, he released the mental command to heal.

His arm instantly exploded with heat, worse than he had ever felt during a healing, and Issai very nearly pulled away in surprise before catching himself and forcing himself to stay as still as possible as what felt like the flames of a forge continued to eat into his arm. He only prayed that he wasn't making a huge mistake by not ending it.

Then the heat slowly began to subside until he could only feel a slight tingle on the surface of his skin. Deciding to take a gamble, Issai slowly opened his eyes, hoping he was prepared for whatever he might see. It was still a terrible jolt to his psyche when he found himself staring into his own face again. He forced himself to look down at Hahri's wounded arm instead of screaming and was infinitely relieved when he saw nothing but smooth, unmarked skin.

Maybe it was because he had crossed beyond the threshold of sanity long ago, but he decided to test one more thing. Once the idea had popped into his head, he just could not leave it alone. Issai raised his right arm, wondering all the while which one of the two, if not both, would obey his will. When Hahri's arm, and only Hahri's arm, lifted, still tightly clasping his own hand, Issai immediately let it drop, so creeped out by the whole thing that he once again lost himself within his sudden panic and jerked away from the other boy with his entire being.

His whole world seemed to tilt violently, and then his back and head slammed into something hard, knocking every bit of breath from his lungs.

"*Saat!*" Hahri hissed somewhere above him as Issai's eyes teared, and he gasped for a breath that just wasn't there. Hahri also seemed to be breathing heavily.

A few more desperate gasps triggered a violent coughing fit, and as Issai's whole body seemed to spasm, he felt a hand lightly touch his shoulder.

"No! Stay back for now!" Hahri warned from somewhere above him, sounding a bit hysterical. "I don't know what—just stay right there for now, okay!"

Issai still couldn't see through the tears in his eyes even as he rolled onto his side gasping like a fish out of water. It was official now. He had to be the most idiotic asshole that ever lived, and when he could breathe properly again, he would be sure to tell Hahri this. His whole body stung as though he had been dragged facedown by a horse from here to Daisha.

He heard a door swing open with a *bang*, and he

hoped to the gods that it was Saiya and not one of the other monks. The last thing they needed was to cause a ruckus.

"What in the three hells happened to them?" demanded a childish voice.

"I do not know," Korin answered, his voice tight and frantic. "Senn was trying to heal Kye's wound on his arm. Then something strange happened to the air, almost like it thickened until you could practically taste it—like my mouth was full of copper coins. Soon after, Senn roughly pulled away and fell backwards off the bench."

"Don't glare at me," Hahri rasped, still sounding slightly out of breath. "I don't know what happened either, only that he did manage to heal my arm."

"If you...give...me a...damned...moment...I'll tell...you!" Issai tried to snap, but it sounded feeble even to his own ringing ears.

"Can you get up?" Hahri asked worriedly.

Issai took in a few more deep breaths before he replied, "Yeah. Just...give me a...hand."

He saw Hahri kneel down beside him before grasping his shoulders and pulling him up into a sitting position.

"I did something really stupid again," he muttered ruefully as the auburn-haired boy pulled him up onto his feet long enough for him to stumble back onto the bench.

"You can tell me about it later if you want," Hahri whispered into his ear before straightening up to sit back down onto the bench beside him.

Issai nodded and let his head slowly fall until it was resting on the table's surface. He coughed a couple more times, still not quite able to breathe normally.

"Is the wound *completely* healed?" he asked against the wood.

He knew it was but decided to feign ignorance. He wasn't quite ready to tell Korin or Saiya about what he had done just yet.

"Yeah, just like all the others," Hahri confirmed.

"So what did you do?" Saiya demanded.

Issai raised his head just enough to see both Saiya and Korin standing near the opened door to the bath. Although she was dressed in the same clothes, her feet were bare and her hair was dripping water and darkened to almost black.

The best thing to do was to tell a very diluted version of the truth. Flat out lying would probably bring him more trouble than it was worth down the line. "I couldn't heal him the same way I heal myself, so I tried to do it through the Bond. I focused my mind on that connection and managed to send my healing energies down it, but then I started to become lost within that connection. I started to panic a bit and managed to tear myself free. The result was what you walked into." He laughed self-deprecatingly. "I played with fire, and this time the consequence was I got burned."

"What was it that you touched?" she asked, looking more interested than he had ever seen her. "Did you see anything?"

"Maybe Kye's soul," he answered honestly. "Maybe something else. There's just no way to know for sure at this point. It's not like I was physically using my eyes and hands."

He could almost see the wheels turning in her head. "Do you think it's something I can try with him?" she asked, jabbing her thumb in Korin's general direction.

"Probably," Issai said warily. He took a deep breath and was pleased when his lungs didn't ache all that much anymore. "Whether or not it's wise to do so will be up to you two. As I told the monk earlier, your connection is a bit different than ours. What worked for us may not work for you. You also probably shouldn't try anything when either of you are tired. That's why we waited until after we had gotten some sleep to make the attempt. In hindsight, this was probably not the best place to muck about with what could be our very souls."

Her eyes narrowed. "Then we'll just have to go somewhere more suitable." She turned to the monk. "As much as I'm loathed to say this, I watched your temple quite a bit, and the monks didn't seem all that bad here."

She glanced speculatively between all three of them for a long moment before settling her gaze on Issai. "Tell you what—I'll help you look for the blond kid until you find him, even if it takes all year. In exchange, you two teach me everything you've discovered about this damned Old Soul bond, and *you*," she jabbed her index finger into Korin's stomach as if it was her sword, making him wince, "get us another room in your temple that's a bit more secure than the last one because after all of you are done hunting down all of your answers, we're going to stay there until we figure out how to break the connection permanently. I don't care how many slavers or *Shi* may be circling the place. That's the deal. Take it or leave it."

Wondering how they had all so thoroughly lost control of the situation to someone who looked as though she had barely learned to lace her boots, Issai raised an eye-brow to Hahri as if to say "can you believe this?"

But then he caught a glimpse of Korin who looked a breath away from bursting into tears, and all he could do was snort in amusement and nod his consent along with everyone else.

CHAPTER FIVE

"I can't believe the brat actually allowed the monk to go back there with her to sleep," Hahri said as he dug the tip of one of the warped slaver daggers he had picked up back in Yuzu along the edges of the large emerald embedded in the hilt of a second, trying to pry it out.

Issai watched him silently even as he listened for voices beyond either door. It had been a while since he had heard any beyond the door to the bath. He was dying to talk to Hahri about all the craziness he had just experienced, but was loathe to do it when there was a chance the other two, especially Saiya, could be listening.

"At this point, she probably sees him as less of a threat than us," Issai replied. "Even though he has his Gods' Voice, I seriously doubt he has ever killed anyone with it, whereas we've killed a fair amount without batting an eye in the short time she has known us."

"There is that," Hahri agreed, "but I think it was more because she wanted to, despite your warning, secretly poke at their bond while the monk's asleep. That man is so ridiculously trusting that I doubt the possibility even occurred to him."

Issai frowned at the door. "If she does, then she's even stupider than I thought." He turned and regarded his companion seriously. "What I just did was beyond idiocy, Hahri. I don't know what you experienced on your end, but for me, it was a little frightening. I'm starting to regret not telling them the details because I wonder if either one of them realizes how dangerous all of this really is."

Hahri set the daggers down onto the table and turned his full attention on him. "It was pretty frightening for me as well," he admitted. "I didn't want to say anything earlier, but my whole body still stings pretty badly." He crossed his arms and rubbed them a couple of times. "I can do this, but it brings no relief; it doesn't seem to affect the irritation at all. But that's not the part that scares me."

He dropped his arms onto the table and leaned in a bit closer to Issai. It took every ounce of control Issai had within him not to flinch away. "Almost from the time that you did whatever you did the second time you tried to heal me, I couldn't move at all. I could still feel my body, feel myself breathing, feel my heartbeat, but no matter how hard I tried to move, to open my eyes, my body simply wouldn't obey. Then literally from one breath to the next, all I could feel was *you*. Your emotions, I mean. They were so strong, just so—*there*—that it felt like I had completely lost myself."

"You felt like you were *me*," Issai interjected softly, his words tight with tension.

"Yeah. I didn't understand what you meant when you told me the same before, but now I get why you had such

THE TIES THAT BIND THE SOUL

a hard time trying to explain what you experienced to me. Yet, even though it was pretty overwhelming, I still couldn't say it was *scary*." Those cerulean eyes suddenly seemed to pierce right through him. "What scared me was that my head looked down and my arm lifted, and it wasn't me that did either of those things."

Issai hung his head. "Go ahead, say it. I'm an asshole."

One beat of dead silence, two, and then his head shot up in surprise when instead of the well deserved affirmation of his idiocy, the other boy promptly started laughing in his face. Hahri was laughing so hard that his balance on the bench became seriously threatened.

"You are something else, you know that right," Hahri wheezed out between chuckles, tears of mirth shimmering in his eyes. "And here I was wondering what you would say when I told you, but never in a million lifetimes would I have ever thought those three words would ever leave your mouth!"

Issai scowled. "I don't know why I even bother anymore. Apologies are simply wasted on you."

"Oh no," Hahri said. "That was the best apology anyone has ever given me. Truly it was. If it had been *me* inside your head, I probably would've done worse and felt half as guilty afterwards."

Issai felt the edges of his lips lift despite himself. "True."

"Just promise me that you'll start thinking a little more instead of just reacting when things get a little weird, and we'll call it even. I have a feeling that things are gonna be nothing but weird and unsettling from here on out, and sorry, but the pain of us being wrenched apart is annoying as hell!"

Issai made a face. "Don't worry. If I have to heal you

again, I'll never let things progress that far again."

"An Old Soul should never say 'never,'" Hahri quipped with a grin.

Issai just shook his head. Really, he didn't know why he had been so worried about the ancient boy's reaction when time and time again, Hahri insisted on treating everything like one big joke. Granted, he did feel much better about the whole thing because of his companion's flippant attitude, but sometimes Issai just wished that Hahri would take his concerns as seriously as he did. He didn't like feeling so foolish afterwards for worrying so much.

Hahri picked up the two daggers and began trying to dig out the emerald again. "You know, I was gonna suggest I try to divine the blond kid's location like I did Korin and Saiya's while we have the time and the privacy, but…" He looked over at Issai and smiled wryly.

Issai shifted uncomfortably. "You say that even though you're still hurting from the last time we supposedly touched souls. Wouldn't that be like throwing salt on a wound?"

Hahri shrugged. "We don't have to do it right this moment. We still have several hours before the monks Korin wants us to follow around will be done with the Purifications for the night. I'm sure the pain'll have faded by then. It always has before. I'm game if you are."

Issai sighed. "Well, I *am* tired of chasing after brats, and it might free up more time to ask around about Soujin. After all, the boy could still turn out to be a dead end."

"Or a goldmine," Hahri replied absently, a frown of concentration stretching his lips as he picked at the jewel in earnest.

"I wouldn't go that far." Issai reached for the pack at

his feet and began rummaging around for his whetstone. Might as well sharpen his knives while he had the chance.

"So, have you remembered anything else about Alik and Jov?" Hahri asked after a moment of working in companionable silence.

Issai was squinting at the edge of one of his blades, looking for chips. "No, but it did get me thinking about something else that's been really bothering me."

Hahri looked up from his work. "Something to do with me again?"

"Well—more to do with me than you, really," Issai replied. "Thinking of Alik made me reconsider the question of why I seemed to know things I shouldn't about your personality from day one. That maybe initially touching souls as we did back in the forest didn't necessarily transfer the knowledge as I first thought so much as awaken memories I already held within my soul."

Hahri's eyes were thoughtful. "I see what you're getting at. If that proves to be true, then it's quite possible that more of those memories can be discovered with the right prodding."

Issai sighed. "Why does everything seem to require us to screw around with our souls? Is it too much to ask for a straightforward answer?"

"You wouldn't want things to become boring would you?" Hahri teased.

Issai snorted. "After all the 'fun' we've had in the last couple of tendays, boring actually sounds fantastic."

"Put in that context, I suppose a dull day or two wouldn't be so bad, though I wouldn't count on it just yet. I'm just glad that we were able to get a little sleep here without someone trying to break down the door."

"Speak for yourself. I don't think I got more than a couple of hours. My damn brain wouldn't shut up. Didn't you think about your time as Alik at all?"

"Course I did," Hahri scoffed. "I just don't obsess over things like you do. Maybe that's why you couldn't remember anything else despite trying so hard. These kinds of things have a tendency of popping up in your thoughts when you least expect them."

"You say that, and yet you haven't said one word about remembering anything else, either."

"That's just because I haven't gotten around to telling you yet."

Issai nearly dropped his knife. "*What!*"

Hahri smiled sheepishly. "I would've told you earlier, but I wanted to see if you had remembered anything first. I'm not all that sure of its accuracy, and I had hoped you would confirm it. You see, I was thinking about the one clear memory I have of hiking up one of the mountains with Jov, and seemingly out of nowhere, an almost over-whelming feeling of excitement and anticipation washed over me. It wasn't just the normal excitement at the thought of an adventure, either. There was purpose be-hind it, like there was something at the summit that I was dying to see. Also, I'm pretty sure that the mountain we were climbing that day was the one you said erupted."

"That's even worse than not remembering anything at all," Issai complained. "Why would we risk such an ob-viously dangerous climb while our bodies were still so young?"

Hahri shrugged. "Maybe because it was that important, or maybe because we knew we'd just be re-born again if we died. Who knows? I'll just have to sleep on it again and hope something else will come to me. You should think on it as well, even if that hike is something you don't remember at all."

"I *have* thought about it," he grumbled. "Over and

over and over again and not even a vague feeling of recognition to show for it. You might as well be talking about somebody else for all I can remember."

The emerald Hahri had been working on suddenly shot out of the dagger's hilt, nearly hitting Issai square in the eye if he hadn't jerked his head to the side at the last moment. Hahri didn't bother even trying to hold in his laughter.

Issai glared at him half-heartedly. "I swear, sometimes I think the gods really did send you to me for the sole purpose of irritating me for their amusement."

"Would you have preferred they sent *Shi*?"

"Exactly what part of the last few days makes you think they didn't?" Issai said dryly. "Although—speaking of *Shi*, there's something else I realized last night, something about the life I lived after Jov. It was the first time I was caught and sacrificed by a *Shi*."

Hahri stared at him for a long moment with an undeterminable expression. "Makes me think that old adage of tragedies coming in pairs is true," he said finally as he rose to retrieve the jewel that had nearly poked Issai's eye out. "...and why some things were forgotten in the first place."

Violet eyes widened as Issai swiveled around to face the auburn-haired boy, who was squatting with his back turned to him. "Don't tell me...!"

Hahri clenched the green stone in his hand more tightly before turning to look at him. The mirthless smile that stretched his lips was all the answer Issai needed.

"Are you sure you do not want to wear one too?" Korin asked Saiya for what seemed like the hundredth time, holding out a white set of monk's robes he had borrowed from one of the novices that were to accompany their group.

Issai and Hahri stood behind him at the door, already wearing a clean set of monk's robes over their clothes, hoods drawn and ready to go.

"I'd rather go naked," Saiya said flatly, eyeing the garment like Korin had just plucked it from a manure pile.

Issai expected to see the same disapproval flash across the ancient monk's face as he had when Hahri had been intentionally goading him about the Temple, but Korin's expression was more anguished than anything. Did it really mean that much to him what Saiya thought about his association with the Temple?

He was beginning to regret not asking the monk more questions while Saiya had been in the bath. The blond was, after all, still practically a stranger. While not exactly forthcoming, Saiya at least had made her expectations of them clear. What did the monk expect to gain out of all of this?

"But—what if the men Senn and Kye defeated yesterday were not the same four who confronted me?" Korin fretted. "You could be recognized—"

"They were the same ones," Saiya cut him off.

"How do you know that for certain?" Korin pressed.

"How do you think, monk? I saw that little show you put on for them in your room. You sure are a convincing liar for a monk. Even I would've believed your stupid face had I not already known better." She snorted disgustedly. "I had hoped you'd died of heart failure when I saw you keel over so suddenly. That way, I would've known for sure if this damn buzzing would've disappeared along with you."

"You were in the room when I talked to them?"

Korin asked incredulously. "But where…I thought you had found me much later!"

"No one ever thinks to look up," she said with a shrug. "Besides, you monks keep your rooms so dark and gloomy that I could've hidden an entire army up in the rafters, no problem." She pulled the hood of her cloak down over her head until it covered her face down to her nose. "This'll be enough cover, especially with a couple of novices around my age tagging along."

Her sword was safely belted at her side and hidden beneath the folds of her cloak.

"Or you can hold her hand as we go along, pretend she's one of those street kids you're so fond of," Hahri suggested with a completely straight face, though Issai wasn't fooled in the least.

To make matters worse, the monk immediately looked down at Saiya speculatively as if he were seriously considering it even though the stiffness of Saiya's stance coupled with the near snarl on her lips suggested that the blond would lose a hand if he so much as tried it.

"We'll just keep her and the novices in the center of our group," Issai said quickly before Korin could open his mouth, shooting Hahri a dirty look. "Now, let's go before your Brothers decide to leave us behind."

"Where should we look first?" Korin asked as they walked down the narrow hall to the main communal bath chamber where the other monks were hopefully still waiting.

Issai and Hahri exchanged a glance. An hour before they had awoken the others, they had tried to divine the blond boy's whereabouts using the same method that had succeeded in leading them to Saiya. It had been a colossal failure. Neither one had gotten so much as a vague feeling of direction. They had tried for almost the full hour before admitting defeat.

Hopefully Korin wouldn't remember it was something they could do. The last thing Issai wanted was for him to question them about such a touchy subject in front of Saiya.

"Well, the last time I saw him, he was running back towards the heart of the Merchant's District," Issai replied. "That's as good a place as any to start. If we don't find him there, then we can go on to the marketplace and so on."

"So, what's this about 'keeling over'?" Hahri asked.

"It was just exhaustion," Korin replied with an embarrassed smile. "It seems running with you two along with going a day without sleep was more than my body could handle. It's nothing to worry about now."

Five monks and three novices awaited them in the main chamber next to the atrium. Although it was still pretty early, a dozen or so men were already enjoying the bath. Issai glanced at them from the corner of his eye as they crossed the room, but no one was even looking in their direction.

The monks warmly greeted all three of them each in turn, but surprisingly asked them no questions. Not even the youngest among them, a boy aged somewhere between Saiya and him, gave them so much as a sideways look. Issai wondered what exactly the ancient monk had told them to explain their presence that they were accepted so readily without comment.

Some of his misgivings must have shown on his face because Korin touched his arm and said, "Do not worry. They know we are looking for somebody just as they knew I was looking for Saiya. They will be discreet."

He then turned to the group of monks before Issai could reply and said, "Let us go to the Merchant District first. Feel free to conduct whatever business you may have there today as you see fit. We shall follow your lead as we conduct ours."

There were more people on the main road than Issai would have liked, but it was not so crowded that they had to worry about being jostled or inadvertently separated. Hahri and he walked side-by-side at the rear with Saiya and the three novices sandwiched between Korin and the older monks.

Now that he was really paying attention to the faces all around him, Issai realized how dumb it was to ask Korin if he recognized the boy based on only a description of blond hair and dark eyes. So many teenaged boys fit that general description on this road alone that had he wanted to talk to each of them, it probably would've taken all day.

Seeing a cluster of guardsmen upon entering the Merchant District reminded Issai that he, Hahri, and Saiya were still fugitives. Even if the men they had killed yesterday were discovered to be imposters, the fact remained that men had been killed. The Guard would not forget the matter so easily.

Issai resisted the urge to pull his hood farther down over his face as their group walked past. None of the guardsmen were currently looking at them, and he didn't want to needlessly draw anyone's attention to them.

The monks' first stop was at a potter's shop. Issai settled himself against the wall outside along with one of the older novices while half the monks entered the shop and the other half went with Korin and Saiya to another shop across the street. Hahri grabbed another novice and all but dragged him to a shop a couple of buildings over.

After only a moment of silence, the novice at his side cleared his throat and said hesitantly, "Can I help you with your search?"

"You *are* helping," Issai replied absently as he scanned the flow of people walking past.

He felt the boy fidgeting beside him like an erratic breeze blowing across his skin. "But…" the boy began, then thankfully fell silent.

When the teen had opted to stay outside with him, Issai had been half-afraid that the boy would pelt him with questions the moment his mentors were out of ear-shot. As Hahri could attest, nothing set him on edge more than being cornered with questions he had no intention of answering. It was a distraction he could ill afford at the moment. However, a desire to be useful was something else altogether.

Issai spared the novice a glance. The boy was frowning down at his boots, the pale skin of his face tinted pink with either embarrassment or frustration. In that moment, it really was uncanny how much the young monk looked like Korin. His eyes and hair were the exact shade of the ancient monk's, though the boy's hair was cropped much shorter than Korin's. Issai wondered if perhaps they were related.

"Your presence alone is enough," Issai assured him. "A monk is almost as invisible as a child, and right now, that's what we need the most."

He spotted Hahri and the other novice leaving the building up ahead. His eyes followed them as they crossed the street to enter another. He suddenly wished that Hahri had asked one of the adult monks to go with him rather than a novice that was probably no older than twelve.

"You know," Issai said, turning to look at the novice again, "there *is* something else you can do. If you see anyone staring at us or hanging around any of the shops the others are in for too long, give my sleeve a tug."

Issai was mildly surprised when the boy merely nodded solemnly and turned dark eyes to stare out at the passing crowd. He had expected at the very least a question or two. Maybe working with monks wouldn't be as tiresome as he had assumed.

Both groups emerged laden with purchases about a half-hour later without incident, and they continued on their way, stopping only long enough for Issai to enter one of the shops to collect Hahri and the novice.

"Any luck?" Issai asked once they had fallen back to the tail end of the group.

"Nothing on either one," Hahri replied with a frown. "None of the shopkeepers I talked to know or have heard of someone named Soujin. I did see a lot of apprentices coming and going from the back door of a couple of shops, so it's possible I could've missed the blond kid if he was a worker, but..." He shrugged. "If he really is one of the Mahze, then I seriously doubt that he had a legitimate reason for being in this district when he and Saiya crossed paths. He could already be long gone from the city, and this'll turn out to be a huge waste of time just like you said."

"Whether we run across him here or in another city, for a chance to punch him in the face for making me look for him more than once, I'd say that alone makes it worth it, even if he turns out to be useless."

Issai turned his eyes back to scanning the crowd before him, and just like that, there he was as if summoned by their conversation, standing as conspicuously as a tree in the center of a river against the flow of foot traffic that was forced to step around him. Their eyes met across that human sea, and only the blatant relief in the boy's entire demeanor made Issai

75

reign in his initial impulse to charge the blond and make good on his threat and simply keep walking towards him at the same sedate pace.

Issai had expected a flash of fear, maybe panic in those eyes—but relief? Did the boy actually *want* to be found? The thought immediately set off all kinds of warnings in his head. Had the blond been standing there all along waiting for any of them to appear?

He felt Hahri move a bit closer to his side as Issai continued to stare down the boy, watching for any sign that their target intended to flee. His eyes flickered over to Hahri as the other boy deliberately brushed his hand briefly against Issai's own as he moved up to whisper something into Korin's ear. The ancient monk glanced back at Hahri momentarily but otherwise did nothing.

Then Hahri made his way over to Saiya, who visibly stiffened at his approach, and did the same. A few moments later, she nodded slightly without looking at him. Only then did he turn to Issai and give a curt nod.

Once again, it seemed that Hahri was leaving their next move up to him.

Their small group continued to walk past the blond teen with no apparent recognition until Issai was finally within earshot.

"Follow us," Issai muttered without looking at the boy as he walked past, hoping that he hadn't misread the situation. At this point, they really couldn't afford any more mistakes.

Two beats later, the skin on his back began to crawl, signaling the encroachment of his personal space from behind. He dared not turn around to confirm it was the boy. Who knew how many hidden eyes were turned on them? Instead, he turned his head slightly towards Hahri as the auburn-haired boy fell back into step with him.

"Korin says the monks want to stop by the weavers for some linen before sending half of us back to the temple to deliver the goods they've accumulated so far," Hahri said quietly, his eyes darting meaningfully over his shoulder.

Issai nodded. The temple provided them with a neutral, relatively safe place to talk.

The only question now was whether or not "talk" was what the enigma behind them wanted as well.

CHAPTER SIX

The walk back to the temple seemed to last a lifetime as Issai struggled to not keep peeking over his shoulder to make sure that the blond teen was still following them. He was so wound up with tension by the time they were only a few blocks away from the temple that he nearly dropped the bundle of linen he was carrying for the monks when he suddenly felt a sharp tug on his right sleeve. Expecting a pickpocket, Issai was surprised to meet the worried eyes of the blond novice that had helped him before, instead.

"Someone is following us, I think," he said softly.

Issai frowned as the boy stared at him expectantly. The young monk was *still* watching everyone for him?

"A blond boy around my age?" he asked just to be sure.

Black eyes widened in surprise as the novice nodded.

Well, at least Issai knew that the teen was still following them, though he wondered just how conspicuous his overeager spy had been while keeping tabs on him.

"Don't look at him," Issai warned. "All is as it should be."

Looking a bit confused, the novice nodded without comment and hurried back to join the other two novices ahead.

"What was that all about?" Hahri asked quietly, eying the retreating novice curiously.

"I'll tell you later," Issai replied without looking at him. He didn't want to do or say anything that may spook the blond teen behind them.

Once at the temple, they were immediately met by a group of monks clustered around the entrance to the main atrium as if they had been waiting there specifically for their group. Issai instantly stiffened in suspicion, hanging back a bit to cast a sharp eye over everyone as the monks of their group began talking to the others.

It was still early enough that most of the worshippers wanting to attend the midday sermon had not begun to arrive. Various monks, novices, and citizens passed through the moderately sized room all around them, but not so many that Issai had to worry about anyone coming too near. He was grateful that Korin still had his hood up and his back to the entrance or else they might have been mobbed.

Hahri automatically stayed at his side, glancing at him briefly before turning his eyes on the group of monks as well. Issai caught a brief surge of confused tension from the Bond as if Hahri was wondering why Issai was suddenly on edge.

Korin handed the pottery he had been carrying to the two monks he was talking to while Saiya stood, a silent shadow, beside him. After a few more friendly words, all but two monks retreated to one of the doors on the far side of the atrium, along with the three novices. The blond novice cheerfully waved to Issai as they left. He relaxed a bit.

The ancient monk beckoned Issai and Hahri forward.

"The Prior has arranged a couple of rooms for us for as long as we have need of them," Korin said as the remaining monks took the linens from Hahri and Issai and retreated as well with a final nod to their Brother. "We can go there now if you like."

Issai discreetly glanced over his shoulder to see what had become of their target. He was relieved to see the blond teen standing within the atrium a few paces to the right of the main entrance, arms crossed and fidgeting nervously as he looked beyond the opened doors, giving the impression that he was waiting for someone to appear. From that angle, the blond would have a clear view of the wide path that intersected the temple grounds directly from the main road.

For his sake, Issai hoped he wasn't.

Issai turned to Korin. "I think it would be better if you issued the invitation on our behalf," he said, eyes turning questionably to Hahri, who nodded his approval. "He may not know that you are the Watcher, or that you are connected to us at this point, and it might make him feel more secure if a monk were to mediate between us."

Korin looked at Issai sharply. "You are not planning on hurting him are you?" he demanded.

Hahri rolled his eyes. "Just go do it, monk. This is a matter between Senn and that boy. Only that boy holds the key to his fate now."

Korin opened his mouth as if to object, then slowly closed it until his lips were stretched into a thin line of open disapproval. He glanced back and forth from Hahri and Issai's unmovable, hard expressions to the almost disinterested look on Saiya's face, and his frown deepened.

"Fine."

The blond teen was still facing the doors when Korin tapped him on the shoulder. Hahri snickered when the boy nearly jumped out of his boots at the apparently unexpected contact. Korin drew back in just as much surprise, holding his hands up in a placating manner, before leaning back in to speak.

After a while of back and forth conversation too low for Issai to hear, the boy turned to look at the group of Old Souls briefly, before turning back to Korin and nodding. Issai's heart sped up in excited anticipation when the two blonds began walking towards them.

"A gold coin says the monk promised him his safety anyway," Hahri offered.

Issai snorted. "With terms like that, you might as well rob me and be done with it."

Out of the corner of his eye, Issai observed Saiya looking at them both with a strange twist to her mouth that he couldn't immediately attribute to a specific emotion. He didn't think it was anything hostile, but it made him uncomfortable nonetheless.

The boy stopped about five paces away as Korin continued over to them. "He says he only wants to talk," Korin informed them, "...to Senn especially."

Issai raised his eyebrows. "Really? Hard to believe when he couldn't get out of my sight fast enough yesterday."

Korin shrugged uneasily. "He was quite adamant that it had to be you." The ancient monk sounded almost baffled.

Issai exchanged a meaningful look with Hahri before he turned to the fidgeting boy and beckoned him with a crook of his hand.

"Lead the way," he said to Korin.

They silently followed Korin deeper into the temple to a fairly nondescript wing of granite walls and very little light that housed the monks' living quarters. The Rihottan temple they had stayed in previously had not been quite as austere.

After passing dozens of virtually identical doors, they filed through the one Korin had indicated. Along the way, Issai had slowly allowed himself to fall back until only the boy was behind him. Only when the blond stranger had closed the door behind him and was turning to face them did Issai dart forward and shove the teen hard against the door, one of his knives pressed threateningly against his throat.

"Can you tell me one reason why I shouldn't just run this across your throat?" Issai growled.

"Senn!"

A sound of bodies colliding followed, and a muttered "wait" from Hahri assured Issai that he would not be interrupted.

"B-because—I want you to help me," the teen pleaded, his eyes wide and earnest even as he trembled in fear.

Issai's eyes narrowed. "And why would I do that?"

"Because we're the s-same."

"The same?"

"Old Souls."

Suddenly it felt as though all the warmth had been sucked out of the room, causing something within Issai's mind to stutter and freeze. Hahri's exclamation of "What!" behind him sounded as faint and muddled as if he had shouted it from the bottom of an ocean.

"I don't believe you," Issai heard himself say quietly,

the chaos that currently was his mind so removed from the rest of him that it was as if he was someone else watching the scene unfold from the back of the room.

"It's not like I expected you to," the boy insisted, swallowing nervously. "All I ask is for you to hear me out, and in exchange, I have information you might find useful."

"What makes you think that I would believe anything coming from the mouth of a Mahze?" Issai spat.

"*Mahze?*" the teen repeated, the confusion so evident in that single word that it gave Issai pause. Then the blond's eyes widened. "You think I'm... No!"

He grabbed Issai's arm, the blade at his throat seemingly forgotten in his sudden panic.

"I would *never*...those *scum*..." the blond squawked, his face screwed up in blatant disgust.

Issai irritably tried to shake off the boy's grip without inadvertently digging his knife's blade into the blond's neck, but that only seemed to make the boy's fingers tighten more determinately around his forearm.

"If you aren't Mahze," Issai scoffed, "then explain to me how you even know I'm an Old Soul."

"Because I'm being held prisoner within this city by another Old Soul!" he anguished. "Fettered by chains inside a prison of his making, neither of which anyone can even see—not even *me*! He told me that I was an Old Soul, too, that I was one of many that he's been trying to find. He said some of the others were two boys around my age, one with violet eyes, and possibly a red-eyed boy around nine or ten."

"This Old Soul, do you know his name?" Issai asked, still skeptical.

"He said his name was Soujin."

It seemed everyone but Saiya instantly sucked in a

startled breath. Of all the names the boy could have dropped, he never expected it to be *that* one. Could it be that the Soujin who had trained the slaver lord Rahzan to be a *Shi* was an Old Soul himself? The very idea was just outrageous enough that Issai could not completely dismiss it.

Seeing the same astonishment mirrored in Hahri's expression, Issai made up his mind. He pulled the knife from the teen's throat, grabbed a fistful of his shirt, and dragged him past Saiya to the cot against the far wall.

"Explain," Issai commanded as he deposited him onto a folded blanket, stepping back with his arms crossed to give the apprehensive boy a little room. He did not put his knife away.

Both Hahri and Korin stepped up to stand on either side of him. Issai was a little surprised that, after his initial protest, the ancient monk had yet to say or do anything. For the moment, he hoped it stayed that way.

The blond teen visibly cringed under their wall of scrutiny and fisted his hands tightly on his legs as if to steady himself before he began, "My name is Keison. Up until two tendays ago, I was just an apprentice to a potter in the central part of the Merchant District. I'd just finished my nightly duties and was about to leave when a man dressed in the silks of a lord came into the shop. The master had already gone home, so I used that as an excuse to tell him to come back in the morning.

"He didn't say a word; he just stared at me for a few beats, like he was trying to figure out if he knew me or not. Then his hand shot forward towards my chest, and I suddenly felt like my insides were being pulled apart! All I could think was that he'd punched a hole in me with his bare hand and was ripping my heart out because the pain was so awful. I didn't think it was possible for a person to hurt so badly. But when I looked down, there was no blood, no heart, nothing but his outstretched hand curled like he was holding something more than air. I'm not even sure if he touched me at all. I mean, my shirt wasn't even torn! But my chest was still screaming with an unbearable pain…"

He took a shuddering breath as if he were on the verge of crying. Issai's gaze flickered down from haunted eyes to the hand Keison had unconsciously twisted into his shirt over his heart, as if telling them about the pain had made it reappear.

"I wanted to die," Keison continued, his voice now raw with distress. "I was on the ground begging for him to kill me, but the bastard just stood there looking down on me with the most insufferable smirk I had ever seen, watching me like I was nothing more than a twitching bug he had just stomped on! It probably lasted only a few moments, but I swear it felt like he'd stood watching me screaming and writhing on the ground past several hour-lines before he squatted down and opened that curled fist. And just like that, between one scream and the next, the pain was gone like it'd never been. I mean, I didn't even feel an echoing ache or anything!

"Then as calmly as if he's merely commenting on the weather, he told me his name, that we were beings called 'Old Souls,' and that he was my new master. He said that if I didn't obey his every word, I'd suffer the same agony again until my mind broke.

"As he was talking, he grabbed something out of the air between us that I couldn't see and made a gesture like he was pulling a rope towards him, and that's when I felt it. It was like he'd wrapped an invisible chain around my heart and was currently tugging on it. Before I could get my head around that, he yanked really hard, and it was like he was ripping my heart out all over again. The pain didn't go away so easily that time."

He frowned down at his hands. "He left me there just like that, crying on the floor with only a warning to not leave the city and a cryptic 'see you later' following him out the door. He didn't even tell me to keep our meeting a secret. Well, I guess it wasn't like anyone would've believed me, anyway. I'd only heard about Old Souls in fables my mom used to tell me when I was little."

Keison lifted his head and met Issai's eyes apprehensively. "You were right to suspect me," he blurted, the words running together in his haste to get them out. "None of our meetings were coincidental. The day before I met you for the first time, an Old Soul named Ina came to see me at my boarding house. She said that Soujin had sent her to give me a task. I was to keep my eyes open for you three as well as any other potential Old Souls that may've entered the city. She said that I'd be able to spot an Old Soul easily, that the way we moved immediately gave us away."

The smile that stretched his lips was more grimace than anything. "And she was right. None of you move quite right, like a performer's practiced movements or something. Even him." He pointed to Korin, who jerked, looking completely flabbergasted. "You may be the 'Korin the Watcher' from legend, but I knew that you were an Old Soul from the moment I saw you walking towards me on the street. Ina has never mentioned you, but I'd be surprised if Soujin *didn't* know you were an Old Soul, too."

"I knew it," Hahri muttered, sounding exasperated. "No wonder those damned *Shi* had no trouble picking us out of a crowd."

Keison pursed his lips in confusion. "Shee?"

"Never mind," Hahri waved him off quickly. "Go on…"

Still frowning a bit, Keison said, "Well, imagine my shock when I saw you two coming through the city gates during one of my deliveries to a tavern in the Traveler's District. I figured if a man as evil as Soujin wanted you, then I was damned sure gonna try to mess up his plans." He nodded towards Hahri. "Since I was already going in that direction, I decided to follow you when you split up. I'd hoped for a chance to talk to you without all the prying eyes. But then that slaver attacked you, and at that point, all I could do was try to find your friend."

"Then why didn't you tell me about Soujin right then and there instead of playing the innocent bystander?" Issai demanded angrily.

Keison waved his hands frantically in front of him as if to ward off an attack. "I was going to! I swear I was! But then I felt Soujin tug on those invisible chains I told you about earlier, and I had to get as far away from you as I could before he found out I had seen you! That demon has many powers, and I couldn't be sure if he was back in the city or that he wouldn't be able to see you through my eyes!"

It was Issai's turn to flinch at the blond teen's words. That sounded awfully familiar, frighteningly so… A wave of shock flowed through his body for a couple of beats; apparently he wasn't the only one who had been discomfited, but he dared not look at Hahri and needlessly arouse Keison's curiosity.

Then Issai stiffened abruptly in alarm. "How do you know he's not doing that right now?"

"He doesn't have to," Keison replied grimly. "He already knows you're here."

In an instant, Issai had a handful of the other's shirt,

lifting him off the bed in sudden fury.

"The gods curse you twice, why didn't you tell us that first!" he snarled, shaking the blond sharply with every word.

"Senn, you should not..." Korin fretted, placing a hand hesitantly on the arm that held the teen.

Issai didn't even spare the ancient monk a glance.

"He's not in the city!" Keison gasped, hanging in Issai's grip as limply as a ragdoll. "I wouldn't have dared approach you otherwise! Ina came to me last night and told me some of Soujin's spies had spotted you in the city a few days ago, so I was to focus solely on finding unknown Old Souls. I saw her leaving the city at first light, so I figured this was my best shot to not only warn you, but to also ask for help!"

"I can't even begin to guess what he did to you," Hahri said pointedly. "What made you think we could help you at all? Having you anywhere near us would be like lighting a beacon straight to us!"

"What choice did I have?" Keison cried in anguish. "It's not like I could ask the Temple or the City Guard for help! They would think me either a lunatic or possessed! Or worse, some of them would be Soujin's spies! What little I know about Old Souls is what those demons allow me to know and what I've managed to find out by secretly watching them. That's why no matter how slim my chances were, in this, I could only ask another Old Soul that was still free of Soujin's chains!"

With a huff, Issai allowed him to fall back onto the cot. "How many Old Souls have allied themselves with Soujin?" he demanded.

Keison shrugged as he absently straightened the front of his shirt. "There are two others that I know of, both men in their thirties. One is Ina's 'partner,' Noll. The other, Anzal, is still looking for his. Ina has hinted that Soujin still hasn't found his partner either, but I can't be completely sure. I'm supposed to be looking too, but after a few things I saw last night, I have a feeling that I'd be better off not finding them. Last night was the first time I saw Anzal and Noll. All three stayed with me in my room at the boarding house."

"Are they serving Soujin freely or being forced as you are?" Korin asked.

Keison shuttered. "Anyone who enjoys watching me while I'm being tormented with my invisible chains as much as those three don't need to be threatened into submission. Demons, all of them! Plus, Ina worships Soujin like he's a god. The way she talks about him, you'd think he hung the stars and lit the sun."

"You said she had a *partner*," Saiya spoke suddenly, almost making Issai jump. She had been so silent during the entire interrogation that he had completely forgotten she was even in the room. "What has she told you about that?"

Issai almost hissed at her in irritation. He had also picked up on Keison's emphasis on the word earlier and had wondered if the teen meant something like the bond he shared with Hahri. Still unsure if they could completely trust this stranger that willingly spilled such a treasure trove of information, he didn't want to give away any of their own secrets if he could avoid it. He had worried that the monk and his free tongue would say something completely unnecessary, so why did Saiya have to pick *this* moment to finally speak up? This obsession with breaking her bond with Korin was quickly becoming a thorn in all their sides.

Worse, Keison was now looking at Saiya with a speculative gleam in his eyes. "So there *is* something more to all of that 'partner' business," the blond said, the excitement in his voice now tangible. "The way Ina went on and on about me finding my partner as soon as possible and Anzal being all pissy about not having his yet, I knew there was more to it than having someone to watch your back while doing Soujin's dirty work. I thought Ina was the only one who could do it, but now…"

"Do what?" Hahri interjected with interest.

"Huh? Oh—that's right. I never told you. Ina has some powers that are just as scary as Soujin's. Remember what I said about the invisible prison? Well, Ina's the one who created it. She showed me it this morning before she and the others left the city. I say 'showed,' but it wasn't like there was anything to see. She took me about a hundred strides beyond the city gates and told me to continue walking on my own down the road until she said otherwise. I only made it about another hundred strides before my face slammed into something cold and as hard as stone. It's like the very air had become solid, but no matter how much I squinted, it looked no different than before.

"She said it was a barrier, an invisible wall of her making that she had erected around the entire city. She claimed that once inside, no Old Soul would be able to leave without Soujin's permission, and only if she, herself, opened a doorway."

"What!" both Issai and Hahri exclaimed nearly in tandem.

Saiya looked ready to explode with rage.

"You are saying that *none* of us can leave now?" Korin asked in disbelief, glancing worriedly at Saiya when it looked as though the pseudo-child was about to draw her sword.

Keison nodded slowly. "Yeah. It's what she claimed anyway—but I wouldn't test it if I were you!" That was directed at Hahri who had started to suggest that very thing. "She also claims that she can tell when an Old Soul touches it, and no doubt it would send her running back here."

"How convenient," Issai couldn't help but mutter suspiciously.

Keison turned wide eyes to him. "I swear I'm not making it up! I know it sounds crazy, but that's not even the freakiest thing she can do! Just last night, I saw her soul leave her body and enter Noll's!"

Once again, something vital seemed to get stuck in Issai's mind. It was insane; what the boy was saying was completely insane, and before yesterday, he would have happily slit the blond's throat for spinning them such an obvious lie and wasting their time. However... An image of his own closed-eyed face flashed in his mind like a slap in the face.

He turned to Hahri and was not at all surprised to see the Old Soul persona looking back. Shit—just what in the name of everything unholy had he *done*?

"No! *Don't!*" he suddenly heard Korin shout.

Issai turned his head in enough time to see Saiya lunge at Keison with her sword as if she intended to skewer him, Korin a half-step behind her reaching desperately for her middle with both hands. Then impossibly, Hahri was between them and twisting Saiya's arm away from her target before Issai could even start to gasp in shock.

"Let me go, you bastards!" Saiya shouted, trying to jerk her arm out of Hahri's grasp as well as twist away from Korin, who had somehow managed to grab her around the waist despite all her flailing. "He's playing us all for *fools*! He's one of your *Shi*! I'm going to cut his heart out for real and shove it and his invisible chains down his throat until he *chokes*!"

"He's not."

The effect was instant. Suddenly Issai, and not an utterly terrified Keison, was the focus of those rage-filled red eyes. It was unnerving, even though she was no longer struggling. Issai was infinitely glad that Hahri and Korin were still holding on to her.

The silence was so encompassing that Issai could swear he felt it seeping into his very bones. The way Keison and Korin were staring at him in something like fear, he was certain they were seeing his true face for the first time. Saiya's expression, on the other hand, became even more dangerous, more—inhuman.

The silence stretched on as no one dared to even breathe, a calm before a raging storm. Issai was determined not to be the one to initiate it.

"I've kept my end of the bargain," she finally said, the sharp lines of her face relaxing minutely. "I helped you find that piece of trash behind me, so unless you want to see his guts all over the floor, you had better hope he tells you something that'll help you keep yours."

Some of the tension in the air seemed to clear as Issai nodded. "He already has."

Both Hahri and Korin cautiously released their hold on the volatile girl and slowly stepped away. Saiya sheathed her sword and made her way to the door, settling against it.

Well, that was subtle, Issai thought dryly as Korin hurried over to Keison and reached out a comforting hand.

The blond teen looked as though he was afraid to even blink, staring at Korin's hand with the wide, terrified eyes of someone who was a breath away from fainting.

"Give him some room, monk," Hahri scolded. "He's

eyeing your hand like you're about to put it through his chest. One heart failure per day is enough, I think."

Looking stricken, Korin immediately dropped his arm and hastily stepped back a few paces.

"Sorry about that, kid," Hahri addressed Keison with a somewhat sheepish grin. "Sometimes she can have quite a bite." He clasped his hands behind his back and leaned his weight a bit onto his heels, affecting an air of casualness.

"I-I'm not l-lying—I'm not!" Keison stuttered, his hands gripping the edge of the cot between his legs so tightly that his hands were bone white as his eyes flittered erratically from one person to the other.

He looked so small and pathetic in that moment that Issai was starting to feel a little sorry for him. He imagined the teen was immensely regretting his decision to follow them at the moment.

"Don't worry. That last bit you told us about Ina proved it. At least to us two," Hahri assured him, gesturing to Issai. "That's not something one goes around telling their enemies. You really shouldn't have even told us, but no matter."

The auburn-haired boy shrugged as if it really wasn't a big deal, but Issai could feel how shaken Hahri still was about that particular revelation. His emotions quivered around Issai's own like a swarm of nervous butterflies. He just hoped Saiya's unexpected display of violent insanity didn't dry up this newest well of information for good.

Korin looked stunned. "Can you two do that? Transmigrate your soul into another body without having to die first?"

Issai and Hahri shared a *Look*. Now wasn't that the question of the millennium...

"Maybe..." Issai hedged.

It was Keison's turn to look stunned. "Even I wasn't completely sure that I hadn't dreamed the whole thing, or that the other Old Souls hadn't messed with my head," he admitted. "All I know is that Ina laid down on my bed, and a few moments later, something that looked like a reflection from a sundrenched lake slowly took shape next to the bed. It began to sort of glide, sort of—ripple across the room towards Noll. To tell you the truth, it looked and moved exactly how I imagined the lost spirits in my mother's tales would.

"I was curled up against the wall with my eyes opened only a sliver, pretending to sleep, so I didn't get a good look at it until it passed right by me. I swear to all the gods that it had Ina's face! It just floated right by and disappeared straight into Noll's chest! He just stood there and let it go right into him like it was something he did all the time! Then Noll turned to Anzal, who was sitting in a chair right next to me, and said 'watch my body' before leaving my room."

"So—what you're saying is that Ina—*possessed* him?" Hahri ventured, looking intrigued despite himself.

"I—guess?" Keison replied tentatively.

Issai had to admit, that sounded a lot like what had happened when he had seemed to be looking out of Hahri's eyes and controlling his movements. Minus the floating, of course.

"And you can do this?" Korin asked incredulously, looking back and forth between Issai and Hahri.

Hahri shook his head. "Not intentionally, I think." He looked questionably back at Issai who nodded thoughtfully.

"—and not to such an extent," Issai added and paused.

He looked first at Hahri's expectant face, then at Korin's still astonished expression, to Saiya's look of sharp interest. Perhaps it was time to roll the dice just once and let fate decide the numbers. He had a feeling this was an opportunity for shared information he could not afford to pass up because of earlier misgivings with Korin and Saiya.

"It was an accident really," Issai continued. "I was trying to heal Kye's arm, and when I succeeded, I found myself staring out of his eyes at my own face."

"No wonder you both were so distressed afterwards," Korin said. "Such an uncanny experience would rattle anyone."

"You mean 'dangerous,'" Issai warned, looking at Saiya pointedly. "I could have hurt him—damaged our souls. I can see the wheels turning in your head. If you intend to pursue this in your quest to break your bond, then only do so with Korin's full cooperation. Otherwise, there's no telling what might happen."

Saiya sniffed in utter disdain but otherwise did not refute his words. Issai almost laughed; that snobbish expression looked so ridiculous coming from such a childish face. He completely expected Hahri to, but when he turned to look at his companion, the auburn-haired boy was looking at Keison instead with an unreadable expression.

The blond Old Soul was looking at them both with, not the fear Issai had half-expected, but with something that looked like hope.

CHAPTER SEVEN

"What does Soujin look like?" Hahri asked, leaning back onto his hands where he was perched on top of a small desk adjacent to the cot.

Issai had opted for the sole wooden chair while Korin sat with Keison on the cot. Saiya had not moved from her sentry-like position against the door.

Keison hugged his knees tightly against his chest, fear taking up residence in his eyes once again. "I only saw him that one time, so I might be a bit hazy on the details," he warned. "Plus, I only had one lamp lit in the shop, so it was pretty dark. He was really tall—taller than even you," he nodded to Korin, "and you're tall even by Kairashian standards. His hair was dark and a little wavy, about as short as mine. I think he had light eyes, but again, it was just too dark to know for sure."

"What about the time after you ran away from me?" Issai asked. "You said that you felt someone pulling on those invisible chains of yours. Was it not Soujin?"

"Huh? Oh—well, it probably was him. I mean, I'm

not sure if anyone other than Soujin can even pull on them. No one ever came to me that day, but I don't think he or any of the others were actually in the city at that time. Apparently, he can do it from anywhere. He tugs on it several times a day, probably just to torment me, so I'm never sure when any of them might pop up."

"Which means it's totally useless to us as a preemptive warning," Hahri said with a sigh of disappointment. "Until you can point him out to us, we'll just have to keep clear of anyone that fits his description."

"Honestly, I don't think what he looks like is really all that important," Keison said softly, looking down at his knees.

Issai narrowed his eyes. "How so?"

The blond teen shut his eyes and buried his face into his knees as if wanting to escape some horror that only he could see.

"Believe me," he muttered, "if Soujin was close enough for you to see him, then you'd know it was him even if you had no idea what he looked like. From the first moment I saw him walk into the shop, my brain was screaming to me that something was utterly wrong with that man, but it's not like I could point to anything specific. He was just—wrong. That's why I tried to get rid of him quickly instead of trying to squeeze out one more sale for the night. I don't think he could look normal no matter how hard he tried."

"And Ina?" Issai questioned.

Keison raised his head. "She's totally different," he replied with a frown. "Unless you're paying attention, she blends in pretty well within a crowd. Her features are common of half the young girls who live in the southern cities—long, dark brown hair and eyes, golden skin, a sharp nose. There's nothing about her that would catch your eye except the way she moves sometimes. Not even she can completely hide that sense of *otherness* all the time, I guess."

That description immediately brought to mind the tale Rahzon had spun them about the sixteen-year-old girl Soujin had supposedly made immortal in his presence. Had that been Ina? Had the slaver lord merely been fooled by some Old Soul ability, or was it possible that some Old Souls never aged and died? Or—could Soujin really make an ordinary person immortal? The thought was earth-shattering to say the least.

"Both Noll and Anzal are redheads," Keison was saying, "and like Ina, nothing about them really stands out except Anzal has a strange accent; at least *I've* never heard anything like it, but that may be because I've never been to another city."

"Huh?" Hahri exclaimed, nearly falling off the desk in his haste to sit up. "You're telling me that you've been reborn over and over *only in this city*, and you've never left *once*? How is that even possible?"

"Reborn?" Keison echoed in a strangled voice, staring at Hahri as though he had sudden grown another head. "I don't know what you mean. Old Soul or no, there's only one Watcher, isn't there? Why would you think that I'm like Brother Korin?"

Issai exchanged an incredulous look with both Hahri and Korin. How in the name of the gods did he come to *that* conclusion?

"Okay, back up," Hahri said. "I think some pretty big assumptions have been made on both sides that need to be clarified before we go any further." He looked at Keison thoughtfully. "I have to admit, there is one thing that's been bothering me about your story that I'd like to address right now. Earlier, you said that you'd heard about Old Souls from stories, and yet you didn't know you were one until Soujin told you. I don't understand how you *couldn't* know."

"Of course I didn't," Keison replied bemusedly. "In the stories, Old Souls are said to have the knowledge and experience of eons. I most certainly don't, and I sure as the three hells don't have any kind of power like Soujin and Ina. Unless you count constant exhaustion and having a weak stomach, there's nothing special about me at all!"

"I think I'm starting to see where your misunderstanding is coming from," Hahri said slowly, "especially the bit about Korin."

And suddenly, so could Issai. "Could it be that this life is his first?" he posited to Hahri.

The other boy nodded. "Either that or Soujin made a huge mistake. It's the only thing that makes sense."

"A new Old Soul," Korin remarked with awe.

Even Saiya had dropped her perpetual scowl and was now staring at the blond teen in something like disbelief.

Keison jumped to his feet. "Wait—wait—are you saying that *all* of you have lived more than one life!"

"That's the part your stories failed to mention," Hahri said with a gentle smile. "Old Souls are not born with the experience of eons—we have it because we *lived* it, retaining all our previous memories from rebirth to rebirth."

Keison's eyes were in danger of popping out of their sockets. "But—but—just how many lives have you *lived*?"

"Hundreds," Hahri said with a shrug. "I've long since lost count. Hell, back during my earliest lives, we hardly bothered to mark the passage of time beyond acknowledging night and day and the seasons. No two civilizations kept track of the years in the same way, and their methods were less than accurate. It wasn't until the Temple started to preach the Word across various kingdoms that a calendar became standardized over a wide area. Even then, it wasn't until the monks figured out how many actual days were in a year that they started to tack on that extra tenday at the end of every five years just to divide a year into tendays evenly. You know how the Sons of the Temple love everything orderly, even if it confuses the hell out of everyone else."

Hahri smiled at Korin indulgently. "That being the case, I can only say that I have walked this earth for *around* six thousand years or so. Now Senn's lived—what was it again—" He looked over at Issai. "—377 lives?"

Issai nodded. "It's been around five to six thousand years for me as well. I only kept track of the lives, not the years."

"The shame," Hahri teased with a wide grin.

They all looked over at Korin, who shook his head. "I thought of each life as starting anew, so I did not bother to keep track of the accumulating years beyond the end of each life, much less how many times I have been reborn. However, if I were to estimate, I probably have lived somewhere from five thousand to six thousand years."

Hahri looked surprised. "I thought out of all of us, you would be the one to have an exact age. So how old is your current body? You never told us."

"Eighteen."

Hahri snorted. "Seriously? I thought you were way older—like twenty-five. Senn and I are both fourteen. How about you, kid?"

"I'm sixteen," Keison said faintly, still looking a little shocked. "I can't even begin to imagine what it would be like to've lived so long."

And nor should you want to, Issai thought grimly.

"What about you, Saiya?" Korin asked, his expression openly curious as he turned to look at her. "You said you have lived several thousand years as well, but you never told me your age in this life."

Issai unconsciously stiffened as he turned his attention to the silent girl as well. Asking questions was usually like trying to navigate a field of thorns without getting scratched with this Old Soul, provided she bothered to answer in the first place.

However, this time Saiya merely shrugged and replied in a disinterested voice, "Like I said before, I don't bother to count, but it's probably around twelve years."

Then she unexpectedly fixed Issai with a hard stare that immediately made his heart clench in dread. Crap. He had hoped to have some time to assimilate the troubling things Keison had inadvertently revealed, then discuss them privately with Hahri before having to deal with Saiya's demands, but it seemed that once again, Fate wanted to be a bitch.

"Now that he's had his say," Saiya said, "I do believe you three idiots have a bargain to keep. I've waited long enough."

"And you'll just have to wait a little longer," Hahri retorted. His smile was all teeth. "We have a little conundrum to take care of first."

"Which is?" she all but snarled, murder in her eyes.

He turned to Keison, all mirth gone from his expression. "What to do about you," he said.

And just like that, the fear was back in the blond's eyes.

Hahri shook his head. "Don't misunderstand, kid. I'm talking about your problem. Those invisible chains you described are most likely connected to your soul. Which means that unless Soujin, himself, releases you, they won't be coming off anytime soon. That makes you a huge liability to us. Plus, even if we did let you stay here with us, I don't think even the Temple will be able to shield you from such a man for very long."

Keison's shoulders slumped in misery as he all but collapsed back onto the cot. "Then it's hopeless," he said dully. "That's what you're saying, right?"

Korin placed a comforting arm around the boy's shoulders, blasting Hahri with the full brunt of what was now becoming a very familiar frown of utmost disapproval.

"Not at all," Hahri chided. "I'm merely stating the facts. And there lies the real problem. At this point in time, there are just so few facts to be had that we might as well be walking blind. What we need is time."

Hahri glanced meaningfully at Issai, and that's when he finally understood where the auburn-haired boy was going with all of this. Just like when it was Saiya who was asking—no, *demanding*—the same thing of him, Issai could only feel a sense of dread.

What they needed was time to *experiment*.

"So you'll help me?" Keison asked, the look of sheer relief on his face potent enough to crack through even Saiya's hardened emotions, least of all, Issai's.

"We'll *try*," Issai emphasized. No use sugar-coating it when the odds were so stacked against them.

"...but not today," Hahri finished. "There are many things that Senn and I will have to muddle through before we can even *think* about how to approach your problem. Not to mention that we have a prior obligation to attend to first." He threw a grin to a still murderously glaring Saiya. "In the meantime, I have a favor to ask of you."

"Okay..." Keison replied a bit uncertainly.

Issai was glad to hear that note of hesitation in the boy's voice. It meant that even in his desperation, Keison was still unwilling to completely throw caution to the wind. The last thing they needed right now was a reckless idiot.

"We really need you to go back to your room at the boarding house and continue your life as if this meeting never happened."

"What! Why?" Keison cried.

"Because Soujin is collecting Old Souls, and I really want to know why," Hahri answered wryly.

Keison visibly gulped. "You mean spy for you."

Once again, Hahri's smile was all teeth. "Smart kid."

The teen nodded slowly, his eyes worried. "I usually come to the midday service most days if the pottery shop isn't too busy. If any of Soujin's spies have been watching me over the last couple of tendays, then I should be able to come here without anyone getting suspicious. Besides, Soujin probably knows that I think he's a demon, so he might even expect me to come here a lot."

"Then it's a plan," Hahri said, looking pleased. "Now, maybe we can get a little food in here before we send you on your way..." He looked at Korin hopefully.

As far as Issai was concerned, that was the best idea he'd heard all day. It felt as though he hadn't eaten in forever.

"Of course," Korin said, jumping to his feet. "Those offered Sanctuary here usually dine with the monks, but given the circumstances, I think it best we stayed out of sight for now. I shall return shortly."

The sound of a sword being drawn had everyone immediately looking at the door. Saiya was currently poking the tip into Korin's robes at gut-level as the ancient monk stood frozen with a dumbfounded look on his face.

"No one's leaving this room until I get all the answers you promised me," Saiya hissed, flashing each of them a nasty look in turn. The one she threw at Hahri could have probably melted steel. "I don't care if it takes all day. You've brushed me aside long enough, so unless you want to find out how your knives would hold up against a master swordswoman, then I suggest you start talking."

Issai sighed wearily in his mind. Yes, Fate really was a bitch.

CHAPTER EIGHT

"I swear, that little girl needs a good kick in the head," Hahri groused once Saiya and Korin had left the room. He jumped off the desk and plopped himself down onto the cot.

True to her word, Saiya had grilled Issai and Hahri about every last detail regarding the Bond until she was satisfied that they had held nothing back before allowing Korin to go fetch them food. Even then, she had insisted on going with him to the temple kitchen as if she were afraid he would try to sneak off.

Her only concession had been to allow Keison to leave before their discussion had begun. Hahri had pointed out that the temple's midday sermon had likely already finished, so it was best their young spy returned to the potter's shop to avoid rousing suspicion.

Issai had been relieved. He still wasn't convinced that they could completely trust Keison, and Hahri had given the boy a sound reason to leave them without seeming as though they were trying to get rid of him. The last thing he wanted was for Soujin to know just how little they knew about their own natures.

"Leave it to the monk," Issai warned. "I have no desire to know what it feels like to be cut in half." Hahri chuckled and Issai leaned forward in his chair with a frown. "I'm completely serious. You saw Korin's bandages, didn't you? It's like an unfathomable rage is always simmering at the edges of her emotions ready to boil over at the slightest provocation. If you weren't so preternaturally fast, then I have no doubt Keison would be dead now."

Hahri raised an eyebrow and looked pointedly at the knife Issai still had in his hand. Even after Keison had left, he had not felt the need to put it away—or more accurately, he had not felt that he *could*. At least while Saiya had been glaring at him with the promise of violence swirling in those uncanny, red eyes.

Issai smiled wryly. "I know. I'm the last person who has any right to criticize another about their temper, but when *she* snaps, it's like she *becomes* the rage. I look at her and can't help but think I'm seeing the Old Soul with all the layers of humanity that we clothe ourselves with stripped away. Somehow, that rage has become her true essence. I'm not sure I want to know what kind of experiences can make a person harbor that much rage and hate within their soul that even a creature like me, who has experienced innumerable unspeakable torments over the millennia, cannot understand it."

Hahri made a face. "When you put it that way, my actions towards her do seem a bit reckless in hindsight. You really think she's that hopeless of a case?"

Issai shrugged. "If it were me, alone, who had to deal with her, then I'd have to say yes. Luckily, that nightmare didn't happen. I think you confuse her enough to keep her relatively stable in the short term, but Korin on the other hand...well..."

His companion nodded. "Yes, she doesn't seem to hate his guts as much as me—and to a lesser extent, you—so that's something, at least. Also, the monk is like her complete opposite, so maybe some of that gentleness will naturally temper a bit of her sharp edges as they spend more time together."

"For his sake, I hope so," Issai said, frowning at the door thoughtfully, "because after everything we learned from that boy today, I have a feeling that the bonds that formed between us won't be something that *can* be removed."

Hahri leaned forward, eyes brightening with interest. "Go on..."

Issai shrugged uncomfortably. "Before today, we've only had Korin and Saiya to compare ourselves to, so even if they experienced a connection similar to ours, we couldn't definitively say that this connection was something that would happen to all Old Souls. But now..."

Hahri grinned. "Now, Keison's information more than doubled the number of Old Souls in our awareness and confirmed at least one other pair that are possibly connected to each other just as we are."

For a moment, Issai stared down at the knife he had been unconsciously twirling in his hand. "All this time, I've been thinking that this connection manifested between us as a consequence of something we did wrong out of ignorance when we met in the forest. Now, I wonder if it's something that's naturally supposed to happen between Old Souls."

"Makes sense. Only—that then begs the question of why the Bond didn't happen between us back when we lived among the Vorn."

Issai sighed and raked his free hand through his hair in frustration. "That's why I still have reservations about it. If only we knew more about *how* we are connected. I think at this point, it's more important than the *why*."

"Then let's find out," Hahri said determinately.

Issai's hand stilled. It wasn't hard to figure out what the other boy was proposing.

"Are you sure you want to risk it?" he said slowly. "If I screw up even once, we can end up worse than dead."

"Something tells me that the same could happen to all of us if we *don't*," Hahri replied grimly. "I can't even begin to hazard a guess of why Soujin wants us, at least not one that I'm completely pulling out of my ass. We need to learn everything we can, as fast as we can, if we ever hope to protect ourselves from him because I for one don't want to find out his plans for us the hard way."

Issai grimaced. "I see your point. However, I think we should let Korin know we're going to be tampering with things in case something goes horribly wrong. That way, if he finds us both dead in here, at least he'll know why."

"If I were superstitious, I would be very worried right now," Hahri quipped, shaking his head. "He and Saiya should be back with our meal any moment now. We should probably eat something first."

As if on cue, a soft knock sounded at the door before Korin entered, carrying a tray loaded with cheese, bread, slices of what Issai hoped was venison, a clay pitcher, and two cups. He raised an eyebrow when he realized the monk was alone.

"Lose someone?" Hahri asked, mirroring his thoughts.

Korin shook his head and smiled sheepishly. "She went on ahead to the room next door. Saiya was anxious to begin examining the connection between us, so she had us eat a little something in the kitchen."

Cerulean eyes instantly narrowed. "I know what you promised her, but don't let her dictate everything, Korin, no matter how mad she gets. I don't think she really understands how dangerous it can be, and even if she did, I don't think the threat of damaging your souls would stop her from getting what she wants. Death could be the least of your worries. Also, keep in mind that you'd be no use to anyone, least of all her, as a baby." He glanced at Issai and his smile became wry. "We'll do the same on our end. There's nothing I hate more than wasting time on growing up."

Korin stared back at Hahri, looking slightly discomfited at the other's uncharacteristically serious tone, before nodding, his expression just as serious. He quietly walked over to the desk and set the tray down.

"I'll leave you to your meal."

He started to walk back towards the door before abruptly pausing for a few beats. His eyes were conflicted as he hesitantly turned to look at both of them again.

"Saiya is not the only one I wish to help," he said. "If I may ask—what is it you two are hoping to find in all of this?"

What indeed. Issai exchanged a long look with Hahri before turning his gaze back to the ancient monk. "Answers. Just answers," was his firm reply. "And you?"

"Just one answer," Korin said with a faint smile, some of the tension draining from his shoulders. He had probably expected them to brush him off again. "I wish to understand my purpose for being."

"As far as I'm concerned, keeping Saiya from killing us all is purpose enough for you to exist," Hahri said with a grin. "The rest we'll hopefully figure out soon. Now go before she decides to storm the room and lop off all of our heads. We're gonna experiment a little ourselves after we eat."

After the monk left, Issai scooted the desk and his chair parallel to the cot so they could both eat off it comfortably.

"So what do you think about Keison?" Issai asked as he poured himself a cup of what turned out to be water. He made a face; he had been hoping for at least cider, but it seemed the Temple had their guests eat as simply as the monks.

"Completely unexpected," Hahri admitted. "I don't know whether to thank or curse the gods for throwing such a trouble-laden kid into the mix at such a crucial point. Of course, I mean the trouble he brings can come from either direction. He *seemed* like he was telling the truth, but the thing that makes me hesitate is that he doesn't have the air of an Old Soul *at all*. I mean, even in my first life, everyone always said that there was something *off* about me."

Issai crammed a slice of meat into his mouth to hide the sudden stiffness Hahri's words involuntarily invoked. He really hoped that he had been more successful at keeping any emotions from leaking across their bond. He didn't want to think about his first life, much less talk about it right now, and Hahri would definitely pick at him about it relentlessly if he thought Issai was deliberately hiding something from him.

"If this is his first life," Issai said, "then it's possible that he just hasn't discovered a special ability. It was several lives before I even knew I could heal myself, after all."

"Well, it's all speculation at this point, anyway. Better to let time sort him out and concentrate on the things we can do right now."

"Yes, we can always grill him again tomorrow," Issai agreed.

After a few moments of eating in companionable silence, Hahri picked up the conversation again. "You know, talking about all our ages today made me curious about a few things. What's the oldest you've ever lived to?"

"Thirty," Issai replied promptly. That was one question he didn't need to think about at all.

Cerulean eyes widened in surprise. "No kidding..."

Issai shrugged. "Not for the reason you're probably thinking. Even if the *Shi* never managed to murder me during a life, once I hit thirty, it was only a matter of days before I would suddenly weaken to the point where I couldn't even get out of bed and only a few more after that, that I'd wake up as a newborn somewhere else. The gods only know why."

"I think we should probably talk to Korin and Saiya about this," Hahri said slowly, a strange look in his eyes that had Issai immediately on edge.

"Why?"

"Because I've never lived past thirty either."

Issai dropped the piece of bread he had been about to eat and stared at the other boy mutely for a long moment as the implications of what he had said sunk in. "No way that's a coincidence," he finally said, feeling some of the stiffness that had entered his face start to ebb away.

Hahri nodded. "Either our connection started farther back than we thought, or—"

"—it's an Old Soul thing," Issai finished. He sank back into his chair and sighed wearily. "Truthfully, I never thought much about it. I always figured that it was just the gods screwing with me."

"I always thought it was somehow connected to my

speed, that perhaps it was consuming my life more quickly than everyone else as a consequence." Hahri looked towards the door. "I almost want to go ask them about it right now, but interrupting Saiya would probably result in someone bleeding on the floor."

"And with my luck, it'd probably be me," Issai said sourly. "We'll just ask them at dinner. We should probably get experimenting ourselves."

Hahri crammed one last bite of cheese into his mouth and nodded. "Move the desk and chair back against the wall and come sit on the cot with me. You'll be less likely to fall and crack your head open here if something goes wrong than sitting on that chair."

Issai gave him a dirty look before complying. Then he settled himself onto the cot facing Hahri in the same position they had used back in Rihott.

"How do you want to approach this?" Hahri asked.

"Give me your hands," Issai instructed. "For now, let's just do what worked before. Concentrate on giving me your strength again, and I'll also do exactly what I did—but minus the healing."

Issai took a deep breath to steady himself and closed his eyes. Maybe it was the familiarity of the action, or Hahri's uneasiness about the whole thing, but Issai was almost immediately able to tap into and essentially wrap himself in the other's essence like a cloak.

Then slowly, he opened his eyes.

A shiver washed through his entire being the moment he saw his own face, even though he was half-expecting it this time. It had been so easy—so easy, in fact, that it was more than a bit disturbing. Whereas the other times had been accidental and could be attributed as a fluke, this time seemed to insinuate that transmigrating into another's body was one of an Old Soul's natural abilities.

That is, if what he had done was indeed move his soul from his body into Hahri's. At no point had Issai felt as though he had moved spatially.

Swimming in a mixture of Hahri's sudden excitement and his own apprehension, Issai slowly looked down with Hahri's eyes at their joined hands, wondering if he would remain in control of the other boy's body if he pulled Hahri's hands away. The urge to do it suddenly became almost overwhelming, and he found himself opening Hahri's hands before he had consciously decided to do it.

He watched, fascinated despite himself, as his own body's arms flopped down lifelessly onto his thighs, making the rest of his body sag forward as if it would topple over. Issai reached Hahri's hands out instinctively to catch it, but his body did not fall any farther.

For a long moment, he stared at his own body. He had not felt his arms hitting his legs, nor any of the vertigo of his body falling slightly forward. It was as if he had no connection to it at all, but even so, the body still breathed normally, looking as if he had merely fallen asleep sitting. Frankly, the more he stared at it, the more freaked out he was starting to feel.

Issai wrenched his eyes away and took a deep, shuttering breath. He had a fleeting thought that maybe he should try to walk around in Hahri's body, but then immediately shot that idea down. Perhaps they had experimented enough for the day. His body may still be breathing, but there was no telling what effect, if any, all of this was having on it. What if he stayed too long and ended up trapped inside of Hahri's body!

Now more freaked out than ever, Issai turned to grab his own hands again—and nearly bit his tongue as his mind was abruptly invaded by a series of distorted images that flashed by as if they were a landscape he was seeing while running at top speed on Hahri's back, followed by a stomach-clenching sensation as though he had fallen into a dark, bottomless chasm for a period that could have been hours or only a few beats.

Then just as quickly, the nauseating feeling of his stomach being left behind somewhere far above ceased, and Issai found himself kneeling on a dirt floor in a small, poorly lit room of earthen walls, staring at a thin arm nearly completely marred with bruises and cuts in varying stages of healing.

What the— was all his disoriented mind had time to think before he felt himself bring the arm towards his face and his teeth savagely ripped into the wrist.

Searing pain rushed up his arm like a hot poker burrowing through soft tissue and nerves, followed by a gush of liquid warmth, and still he could feel his teeth ripping down through flesh until all resistance was gone. An almost overwhelming flood of anguish and hatred seemed to cry out from his very soul as he watched the blood gushing from the ghastly wound he had made in the wrist from eyes blurred by tears of pain.

Hate! Hate! Hate them! Hate her!

Issai violently wrenched back away from the pain, away from the hate that was eating into his soul like an acid, with everything in his being until he fell onto his back with a gasp. He was suddenly cold, painfully so, as if he had just fallen through the ice of a frozen lake, and his arms automatically hugged his own shivering body even as his eyes flew open wildly.

"Dammit! What in the three hells just *happened?*" Hahri swore, his legs knocking against Issai's as he struggled to get up.

In some small, still relatively sane part of Issai's mind, he noted that he was back in his own body. Then Hahri was shaking him by the shoulders, and he forced himself to focus on the other now hovering over him with an expression probably as wild as his own.

"Come on! Get up!" Hahri was shouting. "We have to *go*!"

Go? he thought fuzzily. *Go where?*

And that's when he heard the screaming.

CHAPTER NINE

Issai sprang up so fast that he almost knocked heads with Hahri, the other flinching back just in time and nearly falling off the cot for his trouble. Hahri grabbed his arm as the smaller boy staggered onto his feet, pulling at it urgently.

"Come *on*! It's Korin!"

Issai stumbled onto his feet as well, hastily grabbing onto the other's shoulders as a wave of vertigo threatened to send them both pitching to the ground. He shook his head roughly and tightened his grip. Damn it! They didn't have time for this!

"Go!" Issai managed to grit out through clenched teeth, allowing the other to almost drag him out of the room.

Hahri all but knocked the door down as they stormed into Korin and Saiya's room, the door slamming against the stone wall with all the sound of a battering ram. They both nearly tripped on the small body lying crumbled on the floor about a stride from the door. Hahri released his almost crushing grip on Issai's arm as he dropped to his knees beside Saiya's unmoving body.

Issai took one look at her face frozen in a rictus of pain, mouth open in a silent scream, and instantly started scanning the room for the source of the screams. Gods, she had looked dead... His eyes latched on to a figure lying in a fetal position on the floor next to a cot, and he immediately stumbled over to him.

Korin was screaming as though he was slowly being gutted, his eyes squeezed shut so tightly that no more tears were able to escape through the already dampened lashes. Unlike Saiya, the blond monk was still active, his body shaking so badly as he curled protectively around his left arm that it appeared as if he were having a seizure.

Issai dropped to his knees as well and reached a hand to Korin's shoulder, to touch him, to shake him, he didn't know.

"Brother Korin!" several unfamiliar voices shouted frantically behind him, and Issai's hand froze before he could touch the monk, his head whipping around towards the voices as if pulled by a string.

"No! Don't come in here!" Hahri all but snarled over Korin's screams to the small group of monks filling up the entryway.

He had his hand beneath Saiya's head and looked to be in the processes of trying to sit her up. The pseudo-child's arms flopped against her sides like a ragdoll's, though her terrible expression had not changed.

The monks ignored Hahri as they began making their way towards Issai and Korin.

"We don't—dammit! You might be affected as well, so *get the hell back*!" Hahri shouted angrily even as Issai turned in preparation to ward them off.

The monk at the forefront froze as his eyes locked

with Issai's, his look of frantic concern instantly melting into something like terror as the three monks behind him ran into his back with a shout of surprise.

"Go," Issai said warningly before turning back to a still-screaming Korin without waiting to see if they would obey. The ancient monk's voice was almost gone at this point.

Issai grabbed Korin's shoulders and shook him hard. "Hey! Snap out of it!" he commanded sharply, but the older man's body flopped around just as unresponsively as Saiya's.

Korin hadn't even opened his eyes; it was as though he didn't even know Issai was there. What in the name of the gods had happened? Once he had touched him, Issai could feel the pain and anguish rolling off the ancient monk as keenly as he could Hahri's current anxiety through the Bond. Had Saiya managed to break the Bond, or... His fingers tightened unconsciously on the other's shoulders as a terrible possibility dawned on him.

"Is she dead?" Issai called over his shoulder, his voice tight with dread.

"No," Hahri answered, and he almost fell over with relief—a relief that was short-lived when the other boy added, "though that might've been better."

He turned to his companion, noting that the monks were now standing just outside the room looking as if they had just been told the world was about to end. "Do you think she broke it?" he asked, mindful of their audience.

Issai was surprised when Hahri shook his head. "I think they might have made it worse, gone too deeply. Or perhaps only Korin did since he's over there screaming the temple down and she's completely catatonic. That vision we had—"

Violet eyes widened. Thinking back, the arm he had bitten into had been small and slender. "Shit—that was Saiya, wasn't it? One of her memories?"

Hahri grimaced. "Probably. I've tried smacking her face, but it didn't even make her blink."

"Well, *I* haven't," Issai growled, and he turned to Korin and smacked him hard with open palms in rapid succession across both cheeks.

He heard a chorus of gasps behind him and would have laughed had the situation not been so dire. No one had probably ever dared strike the legendary Watcher. But then he heard a gasp that sounded like a bull's death rattle and all amusement instantly drained away as Korin's eyes flew open, the expression on his face something Issai had never seen on another human being's face.

"Ahhhhhhhhhhhhhh!" Korin wailed, curling into a ball of misery as Issai was hit with a wall of emotional pain so heavy that he let out a cry himself.

He fell back onto his butt and shoved himself away from that inhuman wailing even as he saw Saiya violently jerk away from Hahri's grip and scuttle back on her behind like a crab until her back hit the wall hard, her eyes wide and feral like a cornered beast's. Her hand was frantically reaching for the scabbard at her side, but thankfully it was empty.

Issai sat frozen as his senses were completely overwhelmed with Korin's anguish and his and Hahri's combined panic. He had spent thousands of years running away from his emotions, embracing indifference as though it was the very air he needed to live, so much so that this sudden onslaught of the worst ones was a blow strong enough to cause his psyche to begin to crack.

"Help—me—" he managed to grit out, looking at Hahri pleadingly.

That seemed to snap the auburn-haired boy out of his own shocked stupor, and Hahri immediately crawled his way over to Korin, grabbing the keening blond around the shoulders and shaking him for all he was worth. "*Saat!* You're gonna lead us all into madness, monk! Your Brothers are probably all having heart failures out in the corridor! *So! Get! Ahold! Of! Yourself!*"

Yet Issai could clearly see that the monk was beyond hearing any of them, not even ceasing the sobs being ripped from his throat when Hahri began slapping him hard across the face. Korin's emotions had begun to seep into Issai's being even more strongly the moment Hahri had touched the blond. A few more beats of this and Issai was going to break!

He forced his paralyzed limbs to move towards Korin and Hahri. He shoved his partner out of the way with more force than he had intended, and as the other squawked indignantly, Issai smashed the side of his hand into the sensitive nerves at the back of the monk's neck.

Korin let out a choked gasp, followed by a silence so complete that it was almost something physical. Issai sagged against Hahri and took a deep, shuttering breath, trying to regain control of his runaway emotions. Strong remnants of the monk's despair still lingered within. He was not away from the cliff's edge yet, but the fact that Hahri seemed to be trying to block off his own emotions from trickling across the Bond helped immensely.

Issai could see the group of monks tittering in the doorway out of the corner of his eye, but none of them appeared to want to move any closer. Their fear was written so plainly across their faces that they might as well have been shouting it. At this point, not even the Lord of Light, Himself, would've probably been able to get them to enter the room willingly.

"I should've just done that in the first place," Issai muttered blackly.

"Yeah," Hahri said, leaning back against Issai just as wearily. "I never knew a man could scream for so long without breaking his voice, but then again, this is *Korin* we're talking about. We should all be thankful he didn't unleash his Gods' Voice on all of us during all that madness."

Issai felt all the blood drain from his face. He had completely forgotten about the monk's troublesome ability. By his own admission, Korin had not even used a fraction of the power he was capable of when he had flattened them back in Rihott. This time, he could have screamed until he had leveled the entire city!

"What in the name of the gods is going on in here?" a voice suddenly boomed from somewhere out in the corridor, distracting him from the frightening direction his thoughts were taking.

The two Old Souls turned to see the Prior of the temple, still dressed in his midday vestments, pushing through all the other white robes clogging the door. The Prior was a stocky man in his late sixties or early seventies, hair thin and gone completely white. Issai wondered if one of the monks had run to fetch him after everything had gone south, or if the whole temple had been able to hear Korin wailing.

"Entertainment for the gods," Hahri replied dryly, and Issai could have kicked him. Now was not the time for snark.

However, the Prior looked so perplexed that Issai couldn't help the smile that briefly stretched his lips. The old man looked them both over with a stern eye before hesitantly making his way over to them and kneeling a bit stiffly at Korin's head. His hands twitched as if he longed to reach out to the other man but did not dare.

Korin was still lying curled up on his side, but at least his face was no longer pinched with pain, though his expression still looked far from peaceful. His hair at his temples was soaked with sweat from his ordeal, and you could clearly see the damp tracks his tears had painted down his still-reddened face.

"He's just unconscious," Issai felt obliged to tell the man.

The Prior's eyes turned to him, and the old man instantly flinched back with a small gasp. "You're just like him." There was a touch of awe in his voice. "A Watcher."

"There's only one Watcher," Hahri scoffed. "We are the same, but also something altogether different. Let's just leave it at that."

A slight sound behind him had Issai instinctively turning his head. Saiya was on her knees across the room, lifting her sword from beneath a second cot. Issai doubted that Saiya had purposely placed it so far out of her reach, so Hahri must have had the foresight to slide it away earlier.

Her hand trembled as she tightly clutched the hilt and slowly, stiffly, rose to slightly unsteady feet. When she turned around and Issai finally saw her eyes, all he could think was, *Oh shit!*

Then, between one blink to the next, she shot towards them like a loosed arrow, her sword extended before her in a position of attack.

"Get out! Get *out!*" Saiya shrieked at the top of her lungs, slicing the air with her sword with every step as if she had every intention of cutting all three of the kneeling men in half.

"Shit!" Issai snarled as he jumped to his feet, flicking

his knives into his hands even as he tottered on unsteady legs. He jerked away from a lightning-fast swing at his midsection and brandished both knives threateningly at the out-of-control Old Soul. He felt Hahri rise beside him as the Prior belatedly cried out in alarm. "Get Korin and the Prior out of here *now!*"

Gripping the handles of his knives so tightly that his knuckles turned completely white, Issai hastily backed up after the rapidly retreating bodies towards the door, actually praying to the gods that he wouldn't be forced to kill her because he damn sure wasn't going to let her kill him. That was a disaster he did *not* want to be responsible for.

Saiya slashed at him again, and he barely managed to dodge sharply to the side, keeping his arm from being cleaved off at the shoulder. Her eyes were so dilated black with fury that he could barely see the red of her irises. With a sick feeling, Issai wondered if the one she saw before her now was him or someone else from a memory.

Releasing a string of curses that should have had all the gods descending down on him for the insult of uttering them inside one of Their temples, Issai managed to grab the doorknob before she could raise the sword again and pulled the door shut as he jumped back across the threshold. He jerked back with another curse and nearly fell on his ass as a couple of finger-lengths of Saiya's sword shot through the door towards his chest.

Issai scrambled back even farther, crouching down a bit into a defensive position as the blade was pulled out of the door with an animalistic cry of pure rage. The silence and utter stillness that followed was so unnerving that Issai only realized that he had stopped breathing as he stared hard at the door when his chest began to burn.

When it became apparent that Saiya was not going to

come barreling out the door at him, Issai straightened stiffly and quietly stepped backwards to the opened door of his and Hahri's room, still unwilling to turn his back on her even if there was a thick door separating them. Hahri and the Prior stood just inside, a still unconscious Korin held up between them. The other monks were conspicuously absent, which raised their intelligence quite a bit in his eyes.

"Well, look on the bright side," Hahri said with a weak smile, sagging under the larger man's weight as he attempted to adjust Korin's arm around his shoulder. "At least you're not bleeding on the floor."

"Yeah? Well, don't blame me when we both wake up as babies tomorrow," Issai growled. "That damn well nearly gave me heart failure! Those two will be the death of us, just wait."

"Gah! Quit saying such unlucky things!" Hahri complained with a shudder. "Now put those away and come help us with Korin. We need to try to wake him up so he can explain what the hell just happened."

Issai hesitated, clenching his knives a little more tightly before the look of blatant fear directed at him from the Prior had him reluctantly slipping the blades back into their sheaths. He then took the Prior's place as the old man hastily stepped away from them. They laid Korin onto the cot, then Issai pulled the chair over and practically collapsed onto it. Hahri sat on the edge of the cot beside Korin's legs.

"Gentlemen, if I may," the Prior spoke tentatively as he stepped up beside Issai's chair. He looked down at the blond monk with an anxious frown. "Can you tell me what happened to Brother Korin?"

"We don't know exactly," Hahri replied with a weary smile. "Heard his screaming, did you?"

The Prior winced. "Yes. I was just coming to see him when the screams started. It sounded like a man was being tortured down here!" He looked fearfully towards the door. "Did she—"

"No, no," Hahri cut in. "That's just her way of letting the world know she's upset."

Issai snorted as the Prior looked at Hahri as if he was crazy.

"I don't know how much Korin told you about her, but it's best you don't think of her as a little girl but more as a mountain that can blow its top at any moment. In fact, it's probably best that none of you go near her at all. Korin is trying to sort her out, but it's gonna take some time."

The Prior sighed. "Once again, it seems Brother Korin has overburdened himself."

Hahri shrugged. "He has his reasons. I can't say much more than that since it isn't my place to go blabbing all of his business, even to you."

"Of course," the older man said at once. "The will of the Watcher has always been known only to the gods. My only concern is for his continuing wellbeing. Should I call for a healer-monk?"

Issai grimaced at the tone of awe infused into the word "Watcher" by the Prior. Awe was the last thing he felt should be directed at creatures such as Old Souls. The sadness he had glimpsed in Korin's eyes as the other monks looked at him in much the same way as the Prior was now looking at all of them told him that the ancient monk would likely agree with his assessment.

"Just leave him to us for now," Issai said. "We'll let him decide if he needs a healer when he wakes up. Once everything is sorted out, we'll send him to speak with you."

"Thank you for your kindness. Tell him I'll be in my chambers up until the evening service," the Prior said, sending Korin one last worried look before nodding to both of them and leaving the room.

"I honestly expected him to demand more answers," Hahri said with a frown. "Some of the Priors I knew in the past were not so benevolent." He looked over at Korin thoughtfully. "Maybe it's due to his influence. This Prior truly did seem to believe in Korin the Watcher's 'divinity.'" He rolled his eyes to let Issai know what he thought about *that*. "Oh well. If it keeps a few more bastards away from the seat of power, then who am I to correct them?"

"Sounds like there's a few stories buried in all of that," Issai said, interested despite himself. Maybe it would explain some of Hahri's antagonistic attitude with Korin.

The grin Hahri directed at him had enough teeth to make him instantly stiffen. He had a sinking feeling that he had just inadvertently stepped into a snare.

"Just as many as in your first life, I'd wager," the conniving little bastard shot back, his eyes daring Issai to deny it.

Issai stiffened even more. Why did he ever think he could hide *anything* from someone who practically had a window into his soul, anyway?

"Probably," Issai said flatly, staring back at the other just as challengingly.

If anything, the other boy's grin became wider. "Should make for some interesting bedtime stories later on don't you think?"

"I suppose," Issai agreed grudgingly, wondering how every conversation seemed to end with Hahri poking at one of his sore points. It was almost as if the smaller boy could literally sniff them out in a conversation the moment such an opportunity presented itself.

Or maybe he knows them because I already told him, came the unbidden thought, taunting him again with the importance of what he may have lost in less than a blink of an eye. Damn—they really needed to get to the bottom of that.

Hahri looked as though he wanted to say more, but a soft groan from the cot had both of them immediately jerking their heads towards the sound. The monk's eyes were starting to flutter open. Hahri leaned over and smacked the blond soundly on his cheek. Issai had to bite his lip hard to keep from laughing at the startled squawk that Korin let out as his eyes flew completely open.

Hahri pulled back his hand with a look of pure satisfaction. "Excellent reaction. Welcome back to the world of the sane, monk."

"Wh-what?" Korin stuttered, wide, dark eyes now looking back and forth between the younger teens with the most bewildered look Issai had ever seen on anyone's face. He tried to sit up, but Hahri reached over and pushed him back down firmly.

"I think it's best you stay right where you are for now," Hahri said cheerfully. "You've already had quite enough excitement for the day."

"What are you—" Korin started to say in a horribly raspy voice but then cut off with a wince, his hand going to his throat.

Issai silently got up to pour him a glass of water. Korin downed the contents in one gulp and smiled at him gratefully.

"Perhaps it's better if we do most of the talking for now," Hahri said, flashing Korin a sympathetic smile. "You're probably wondering why your throat feels like you just swallowed a cart full of glass shards. I'm actually impressed you can talk at all, seeing as how you spent a good quarter-hour screaming your throat raw while Saiya lied catatonic on the floor. We'd hoped that you'd be able to shed some light on that."

Korin's eyes were now widened to impossible lengths. "Is Saiya all right?" he rasped, the panic in his voice distinguishable even then.

"Well, right now she's next door doing her damndest to imitate a rage monster, so I'm not sure 'all right' qualifies, but after the way she chased us out of the room slashing at us with her sword, there's no way in hell I'm going back in there to ask her. At least she's no longer catatonic."

Instead of sputtering in shock and dismay as Issai fully expected, Korin suddenly paled. "It's because I saw," he whispered hoarsely, covering his eyes with both hands in consternation.

"You saw her killing herself," Hahri said just as quietly, the mirth completely gone from his expression.

The blond started and dropped his hands from his eyes. "How did you know that?" he asked roughly, his eyes once again wide with shock.

"Because we saw it, too," Issai replied.

"But—but—*how*?"

"That's the question of the day, isn't it," Hahri answered. "What we'd like to know first is how the whole thing came about in the first place? What were you two doing exactly?"

Korin frowned thoughtfully. "We were trying to sense each other's emotions the way you described, Senn. Saiya was getting really frustrated, then angry when all of our attempts failed. I tried to calm her down a bit, but the more I said, the angrier she seemed to get."

"Imagine that," Hahri muttered sarcastically under his

breath, rolling his eyes. Issai shot him a Look.

"That is when I felt it," Korin was saying, oblivious to their byplay, "or thought I felt something. I could not be certain that it was not my own frustration, so I concentrated my entire being on that one sensation. That is when it happened. I was suddenly on my knees in a dark room with walls made of dried mud. My entire body throbbed and burned terribly as if I had been dragged behind a horse and then beaten afterward. My legs were bound tightly at the ankles with a thick rope and tethered to what looked like a wide tree stump in the middle of the room."

Korin shuttered. "I could feel everything so keenly—the discomfort of the small pebbles in the dirt I was kneeling on, the biting cold in the air that seemed to freeze my breath with every gasp, the throbbing of my eyes from crying for great lengths of time, the burn around my ankles from the rope having already embedded itself deeply into the flesh. I could even smell the stench of unwashed bodies and human waste. The only thing I could not do was control my body. It was just as Kye described when you took control of his body briefly, Senn.

"That is when I realized that it was not me kneeling there but Saiya, a Saiya that was a bit older than she is now. I realized that what I was experiencing was one of her memories. Of course, I instantly tried to wake up, to pull myself out of the memory, but I just could not."

"No, you pulled *us* into the memory instead," Hahri said grimly, "just in time to experience the joys of tearing through our own wrists."

Korin flinched. "She was in such agony," he whispered brokenly. "More than the physical pain, her soul was drowning in hate, anguish, and anger, so much that my own soul was being crushed under the weight of it. Over and over we experienced that same scene of agony for more times than I can remember."

"Hence the screams," Hahri said. "It's no wonder. For a soul that has never been tortured, I imagine it was a harsh lesson. Luckily Senn was able to pull us out of it relatively quickly. *All* of us."

"And for that, an eternity will not be enough to thank you properly," Korin said to Issai, who merely shrugged uncomfortably. "The suffering you all have endured at the hands of the *Shi*, I was naïve to think I could ever understand it."

"And you should never wish to!" Issai admonished sternly. "There is nothing to gain by courting such an understanding."

For a long moment, Korin was silent, staring up at the rafters as if he could somehow find all the answers within their shadows. The sight of the monk absently wringing his hands even as they rested on his abdomen was oddly reassuring to Issai, just as Hahri's teasing had somehow become the bane to his melancholy.

"Perhaps I should go talk to her," Korin said finally, struggling to sit up.

Instead of pushing him back down again, Hahri reached over and pulled him up by his upper arms until he was seated. "Your voice still sounds shredded," Hahri said pointedly. "It needs rest. Maybe one of your healer-monks can fix you up an herbal tea or something to soothe it. Plus, I think you should give Saiya her space for the time being. She really lost it this time, and you'd be doing more harm than good by confronting her when she might still be less than sane."

Korin's shoulders sagged. "I cannot seem to get anything right when it comes to her."

"Don't beat yourself up too badly about it," Hahri chided. "It's not like she's exactly making any of this easy on anyone. She seems to purposefully court conflict. Maybe it makes her feel more in control. Can't say I really blame her if what occurred in that vision was indicative of a lot of her lives."

"Yes, that memory," Korin said, worrying his bottom lip. "I cannot fathom how I could have drawn both of you into her mind with me when I could not even sense Saiya's until that moment."

"It might have something to do with the fact that my mind was controlling Hahri's body at the time," Issai interjected. "Perhaps our presence to you was more— prominent because of that."

Black eyes flashed with excitement. "So what Keison said is true. Old Souls *are* capable of transmigration while still alive."

Issai shook his head. "You're getting ahead of yourself. My soul didn't float out of my body or anything like that. For all I know, we merely connected our minds."

But even as he said that, he remembered the creepy sense of dissociation he had experienced when he had been staring at his body right before Saiya's memory had invaded his mind. It was quite possible that his soul *had* left his body and entered Hahri's.

"True," Hahri added thoughtfully. "Once I felt you take control of my body, I was merely observing. It wasn't like I tried to take control back from you or any-thing. Not to mention I was watching you up until I started to feel your emotions more prominently within me, and I never once saw anything like Keison described leave your body. Maybe next time I should try to take back control."

"I'm fine with it; only...let's not try again until tomorrow."

Hahri tilted his head curiously. "Did something happen differently this time?"

"In all the excitement after I pulled us out of Saiya's memory, I haven't really had a chance to think about it, but when I felt myself back in control of my own body, I was freezing. I never felt cold after the other two times, so I wonder if it had something to do with how long I spent in control of your body."

"Or it could mean that your soul really did leave your body," Korin said tentatively. "We of the Temple have long believed that a body cannot survive long without the soul."

"I wondered about that, too, at the time," Issai admitted.

Hahri frowned. "If there's even a small pinch of truth to that, then maybe we should wait to talk to Keison again before we try it again. We never did ask him how long Ina remained outside her body." He turned a critical eye on Issai's face. "You're not really looking any paler than usual, which is saying something considering how close you came to being split open a few moments ago. Are you still feeling cold?"

"No, and I can't really tell you when I stopped." He smiled thinly. "I was a little distracted."

Hahri snorted. "Yeah, screams and rage monsters have a tendency to do that." He looked at Korin sharply. "That's why there'll be no more experimenting for you and the brat. At least not until Senn and I are able to figure out the Bond a little more. It's simply too dangerous for you to have another accident like today's. Imagine what could have happened if Senn had not been able to break you out of that memory and you had gone insane—

screaming."

Korin suddenly looked so horrified that Issai felt certain that city-leveling possibility had never even occurred to him.

The smile Hahri directed at the monk didn't reach his eyes. "Exactly. I don't think that purpose you are searching for is to become the new God of Destruction, so if Saiya gives you shit about it, tell her exactly that. I don't think even she fancies being ripped apart by your voice."

Issai winced. Well, that was certainly blunt, but given his own experience with the monk's stubbornness, sometimes being excruciatingly blunt was the only way to make him understand.

"And on that bright note," Issai said sourly, "I do believe the Prior wants to talk to you before the evening sermon. He said he'd be in his personal chambers. You can show us where the kitchen is on the way since right now I'm hungry enough to eat a whole cow. We can talk more after."

CHAPTER TEN

The door before Korin could have been the portal leading to the first hell and the thought of walking through it still wouldn't have filled him with as much dread as he was currently feeling. He had more than one reason to fear what he would see beyond the door. Taking a deep breath, he balanced the tray of food he was carrying on one hand and rapped on the door lightly with his knuckles.

"Saiya?" he called, wincing inwardly at the obvious wariness in his voice. "It's Korin. I have your breakfast. Is it all right if I come in, or do you wish for me to leave the tray by the door?"

He waited for several tense moments before deciding to take her silence as permission to enter rather than something more sinister. Swallowing nervously, Korin slowly opened the door, his eyes immediately sweeping the room until they locked on the small figure standing against the opposite wall, her sword pointed straight at him. The expression on her face immediately set off every warning bell in his head. He could practically see his own death in those narrowed eyes.

He stood frozen at the threshold, unsure of whether backing out of the room would cause more harm than good. He had hoped that leaving her alone overnight was enough time for her anger to run its course, but apparently he was just as naïve as both Senn and Kye accused him of being when he had told them of his intentions of bringing Saiya breakfast. Even though she was no longer rampaging, Korin could practically taste the fury radiating from that rigid body.

"I shall—just—leave this here," he said cautiously when it became apparent that she was waiting for him to make the next move.

Korin had just started to slowly bend down to put the tray on the floor between them when Saiya abruptly brought the sword down to her side. The monk's heart leapt into his throat as his body instinctually flinched back, nearly causing him to pitch forward onto the tray. He immediately straightened and stared at her with wide eyes. His hands gripped the ends of the tray as though they were the edges of a cliff he had unexpectedly stepped off.

The fury in Saiya's eyes had not dimmed in the slightest. "Where are the other two?" she demanded sharply, leaning a bit of her weight on the sword as though it was a cane.

It took his still panicking mind a moment to understand what she was asking. "Oh! Ah—they are next door eating," he answered hastily.

"Close the door." She gripped the hilt of her sword more tightly and pointed her free hand at the cot to her left. "Sit there. You're going to explain everything to me *right now*."

Korin blinked at her in surprise for a couple of beats before reaching behind him to push the door shut, not wanting to turn his back to her just yet. He slowly walked over to the desk adjacent to the cot and set down the tray before seating himself, all the while maintaining eye contact with her.

He was suddenly grateful for the few hours of rest he was able to get last night as the three of them had each taken a shift to "watch over things" while the other two slept. This was definitely a conversation he didn't want to have while his body was both traumatized and sleep-deprived. However, he wasn't so blind that he didn't realize that Senn and Kye had suggested the shifts because they had been worried that Saiya would decide to murder them all in their sleep.

"I'm sorry," Korin began tentatively. "I understand that what I did to you is unforgiveable, but I wanted to say it anyway. It grieves me that the ignorance of my actions caused you so much pain. I—"

The blond's words were instantly lost somewhere in his throat when Saiya suddenly moved towards him and raised her sword until the point pressed firmly into the center of his abdomen, slightly above his bandages.

"You have two beats to tell me exactly how you entered my mind before I drive this into your gut and pin you to the wall," she hissed, her voice deep and rough with barely contained fury.

Korin blanched. Kye had asked him that very question earlier, and he doubted an answer of "I have no idea" would earn him the same benign eye-roll here.

He swallowed thickly. "I—just think it was—an *accident*." A muscle in her jaw ticked, and he quickly raised his hands up in an effort to stall the attack that was probably a breath away. "You were really frustrated," he rushed to explain, "and for a moment, I thought I had felt it, too. I concentrated hard on that feeling, and the next thing I knew, I was kneeling in a dark room."

Korin's breath got stuck in his throat as he abruptly felt the tip of her sword pierce his skin, but he didn't dare move away, didn't dare to even blink. Thankfully, that small prick was all he felt.

"You would really let me do it, wouldn't you?" Saiya accused, sounding even angrier than before.

"Do what?" Korin asked against his better judgment.

She flashed him a disgusted look and pulled the sword away from him, jamming the tip into the floor again. "I felt you—*all* of you in my head."

Korin wet his lips nervously and slowly lowered his hands onto his lap. "That was my fault as well, I believe. When I realized that it was not me in that room, that I was likely experiencing one of your memories, I tried to pull my mind away, but nothing I did seemed to work. Senn and Kye believe that I unconsciously sensed their minds and tried to latch on, which was why they were drawn into the memory as well. Senn was controlling Kye's body at the time, so Senn thinks that may have been the reason I sensed them and not any of my Brothers. If it hadn't been for Senn, then I think we all would still be trapped within that memory."

He wanted to ask why—why *that* memory—but his chances of having it answered were practically non-existent so he kept quiet. The only thing it would accomplish was to fuel the fire of her anger, and he had already done too much of that this morning.

"Senn? What did that bastard do?" Saiya demanded suspiciously, her hand tightening on the hilt of her sword as if moments away from attacking.

Korin sent a silent prayer to the gods that she was

not.

"Once he pulled himself and Kye out of the memory, they both ran to us, and he slapped me back into reality," he replied with a wry smile. "Rather hard, I might add. My cheeks are still a little sore this morning."

He thought she might smile a little at that, but other than a blink, Saiya's expression remained hard and unchanged.

"It was enough to break apart our minds. Kye said that they found you lying catatonic on the floor, and you only 'woke up' when the connection was broken."

That, more than anything, was what drove him to see her this morning. He had been worried that the incident might have done more than make her feel that they had violated her mind. More than her wrath, he had feared finding her collapsed on the ground from some damage he had inadvertently caused to her soul.

"Saiya," Korin continued cautiously, "I think we should let Senn and Kye do all the experimenting with the Bond. If anything, yesterday proved that neither one of us has any kind of control over any of it. We both could have been driven mad; I could have accidentally invoked my Gods' Voice and killed everyone in this city. I might have even shattered our souls with it."

For a long moment, they stared at each other silently. Saiya's eyes still burned with barely contained fury, and had he not been looking so intently at them, Korin would never have seen it, but it was there. Buried deep beneath the rage, beneath all the violence and the cutting language was a large amount of fear.

Even so, he was still shocked when she nodded curtly in agreement.

"Keison should be coming to see us around midday. Senn and Kye want to ask him more questions about the

Old Soul, Ina, and her bond with Noll. Do you wish to listen in?"

Saiya shot him a look as though she thought he had just asked something incredibly stupid before sheathing her sword and turning her attention to the tray of food on the desk. Apparently, their conversation was over.

Korin sat silently and anxiously watched her eat. She had not told him to leave the room, so perhaps that was a sign that her anger was subsiding. Maybe she would even talk some more to him after she finished. Even if all she did was berate him, it was still infinitely better than shutting him out completely. A negative connection was still better than no connection at all.

After Saiya finished eating, she sat down on the edge of the other cot across the room, her toes barely brushing the floor, and just stared back at him with a hard frown. Korin could almost see the wheels turning in her head. However, she didn't say another word until the temple bells signaled the half-hour warning before the midday sermon, and only to bark a curt "let's go" to him as she headed to the door.

She abruptly paused with her hand on the doorknob and turned sharply towards him before Korin could even rise. He froze and stared back at her a little apprehensively. She opened her mouth as if to speak, but then just as suddenly closed it until her lips were pressed into a thin line. For a half-beat, bewilderment replaced the anger in her eyes before she turned away sharply and yanked the door open so roughly that Korin was surprised she had not torn it from its hinges.

Maybe he *was* naïve, but Korin couldn't help but think that things were starting to look a little less hopeless between them.

***

Issai turned sharply to the door as a knock sounded, the door opening before either he or Hahri could say a word. He relaxed when he saw that it was only Korin. However, he was not at all prepared for the small figure that pushed past the ancient monk into the room. He instantly stiffened and was a beat away from drawing his knives before he realized that she was moving away from all of them to the opposite side of the room.

"I thought Keison would be here by now," Korin said, oblivious as always to the ripples of unease he had just caused.

"He may not come at all today, you know," Hahri pointed out.

Although Hahri was calmly looking at Korin, Issai could tell that his companion's attention was really on Saiya. For once, the other boy was as tense as he was.

The monk frowned worriedly. "I hope that is not the case. It would mean at least one of the other Old Souls is currently in the city."

"Not necessarily," Hahri said. "It could also mean he's ratted us out to Soujin and we'll never see him again."

Korin shook his head. "I do not believe he would do that. His fear was not an act."

"No, it wasn't," Issai agreed, glancing surreptitiously at Saiya from the corner of his eye.

That she was sitting on the other cot and watching them all with more interest than suspicion was hardly reassuring. Not that he believed for a moment that they all weren't one tantrum away from a sword in the gut, anyway. He doubted he would ever feel anything but on edge in her presence.

"That's why it doesn't matter if his intentions are honest or not," Issai continued. "The threat of betrayal is high either way. We'll just have to be careful about what we say to him, or better yet, just assume that whatever he hears will likely be repeated to unfriendly ears."

"But—were we not going to help him?" Korin protested.

"Whether or not we *can* help him still remains to be seen," Hahri reminded him. "We'll cross that bridge later. Right now we need to concentrate on wringing all the information about Soujin and these other Old Souls out of him if we ever want to leave this city again. I'm still not sure I believe him about Ina and that barrier or whatever, but we also can't afford to discount it either."

"So we wait here," Issai cut in, "out of sight, for a couple of days. If he doesn't show, then we'll decide whether or not to look for him again or try our chances against this 'barrier' and leave the city."

Korin nodded thoughtfully. He started to head towards the cot Hahri occupied, then paused for a breath before turning and heading towards Saiya. Issai nearly fell off his chair. Just what in the three hells was that damned monk *doing*?

However, instead of drawing her sword as Issai expected, Saiya silently watched the ancient monk advance with the sharp eyes of a predator ready to strike the prey that had so wittingly wandered into its territory. Korin sat on the edge of the cot and turned back to the two teens as nonchalantly as if what he had just done was as normal as breathing.

For her part, Saiya sat so rigidly that she looked like a statue of a child, staring at Korin as though she expected *him* to attack.

Issai felt an insane urge to laugh at the absurdity of

what he was seeing. *Saiya* was actually afraid of *Korin*.

"I have something I want to ask you two," Hahri said suddenly, nearly making Issai jump out of his skin. "What's the oldest you have lived to?"

Korin blinked at him in surprise. "I once made it to one hundred, although I would say I average out around eighty-five years or so. Why do you ask?"

Issai was relieved that Hahri's random question had broken the mounting tension in the room. He exchanged a grateful glance with Hahri before reluctantly looking at Saiya. If the question weren't so important, he would've been just as happy to let her remain silent, but...

"And you?" he asked, ignoring the monk's question for the moment.

Her eyes moved from Hahri to him. "Why do you care?"

"Because it could be important," Hahri answered before Issai could even open his mouth. "Senn and I wish to confirm something before speaking to Keison again, something that we don't want him to know and are hoping won't need to be asked. Korin's answer only muddied the waters. Your answer will be the final decider on the matter."

The suspicion was back in her expression for a moment before her features smoothed into something like indifference. "I've never died of old age if that's what you really want to know," she said flatly. "The gods made sure of that."

"What do you mean?" Korin asked, startled.

Saiya turned to the blond and laughed nastily. "Your precious gods made sure to send every lowlife ever conceived across my path no matter where I turned. Need I spell it out for you?"

A startled burst of emotion flared up throughout his

body, and Issai knew that Hahri was just as stunned about Saiya's unexpected admission as he. Was she really implying that she had been killed in every single one of her lives? Suddenly the depth of her hatred and madness made perfect sense.

This time, even Korin was struck speechless as he stared at Saiya in a strange mixture of horror and sorrow.

"Senn and I have never made it past thirty," Hahri said into the ensuing silence. Korin jerked his head towards the younger teens, and if anything, his expression seemed even more stricken and bleak.

"Thumb your nose at the gods one too many times, did you?" Saiya shot at Hahri, though there was surprisingly no real heat in her tone.

The auburn-haired boy chuckled. "Maybe, but who can say that's the real reason why. If we aren't killed beforehand, then once we hit thirty, we start to weaken and are dead within a tenday. We wondered if the same was true for all Old Souls."

"I see," Saiya said. She stared at Hahri for a few more beats before adding, "I've lived into my forties a handful of times."

Hahri sighed. "Well, there goes that theory out the window. The next option would be to blame it on the Bond, but since you two don't seem to have the same problem, even that explanation is a bit shaky. Damn. We'll probably have to ask Keison about it after all."

"But—is this not Keison's first life?" Korin said.

Hahri nodded. "If what he's told us is the truth, but it's the other Old Souls' life experiences that I'm after, not his. If he truly isn't deceiving us, then maybe he's overheard something useful."

A soft knock sounded at the door, and they all froze.

"Well, if that's not one of your Brothers, then things

might not be as boring as I thought today," Hahri quipped.

CHAPTER ELEVEN

The blond boy on the other side of the door looked like shit.

Issai could hardly believe that this was the same boy that had followed them into this very room only yesterday. His skin was so sallow that he looked like a day-old corpse, the area beneath his tired eyes darkened to the point where Issai would have believed they had been bruised by fists. His entire body trembled as if he was terrified, but that didn't match the real smile that stretched his now colorless lips as he looked at Hahri.

In short, the boy looked one step away from collapsing.

Hahri hurried him over to the empty cot, then pressed the remains of his by now lukewarm mug of cider into Keison's trembling hands. "Drink that. You look like someone who's dying of the plague."

Keison made a face. "Th-thanks."

"That or you had some visitors last night," Issai said, watching the boy's face closely.

Keison's eyes immediately fixed on him as he slowly lowered the mug to rest on his lap. His hands squeezed the now empty mug tightly as if desperately trying to draw warmth that was no longer there.

"Not visitors—exactly," the blond teen replied with a grimace. "Soujin just decided that he'd rather torment me than sleep last night, I guess. He kept pulling on that invisible chain around my heart until I thought the damn thing was really gonna be ripped out! When he finally stopped early this morning, I tried to sleep some before I had to get to the shop, but then the nightmares started."

"He give you those too?" Hahri asked dubiously.

Keison sighed wearily and rubbed a fist over his eyes. "I don't think so. They're nightmares I've had on and off again for as long as I can remember, long before I ever met Soujin. But—" His eyes suddenly widened. "Wait! Come to think of it, they *have* been getting worse ever since the first time that demon hurt me! I used to only have them once every two or three moons, but now it's almost every night! Especially when he—"

Keison dropped the mug and grabbed his head in anguish. The sound of it breaking on the stone floor seemed abnormally loud.

"Does that mean he really *is* in my head?" the blond teen cried, fingers pulling agitatedly at his hair. "Has he *always* been in my head? My dreams..." He suddenly jumped to his feet, his eyes wild with fear. "He could already be in the city! We have to get out of here! He'll know *exactly* where to find all of us now! He'll know that I've *betrayed* him!"

Hahri was instantly up off the desk and grabbed Keison's arm before the panicking boy could even take a step towards the door.

"Hey—calm down!" Hahri commanded sternly,

squeezing the teen's arm until the other winced in pain and stopped trying to pull away. "Even if you're right, it's way too late now. Soujin already knows we're in the city, remember?"

Though Issai watched them, still and seemingly without concern, the boy's words were an uncomfortable reminder of things he'd rather not think about. They *all* had just been within Saiya's head yesterday. He, himself, had easily taken over Hahri's *entire body*! Considering all of that and what the mysterious Old Soul had allegedly already done to the teen, it would be no real shock if Soujin was capable of all Keison had just accused him of and more.

They *really* needed more information.

"But he could already be coming here!" Keison insisted frantically.

"Here or somewhere else, we'll all have to deal with him eventually," Hahri said with a shrug. "The best thing you can do for us right now is to tell us everything you can about all of them before that inevitability happens."

Hahri slowly released his arm, and Keison immediately collapsed back down onto the cot as if his legs no longer had the strength to hold him. Whatever rush of energy his panic had injected into him seemed to have left him all at once.

"We have questions about Ina and Noll," Hahri said, nodding towards Issai.

"Specifically, about the conscious transmigration of their souls," Issai added. "Have you ever seen Noll's soul enter Ina's body?"

Keison blinked at Issai in surprise. "Noll? It never even occurred to me that he could since before talking to you yesterday, I thought it was just one of Ina's scary powers. I've only seen Ina do the possessing thing that one time, and none of the three have ever talked about Noll or Anzal being able to do it in front of me, not even when they thought I was asleep."

Issai frowned in disappointment. That was the one thing he had really hoped the boy would have an answer for.

"How long did Ina stay within Noll's body?"

"She was gone half the night—four or five hours maybe."

"And did she complain of any adverse affects when she returned to her body?"

"Not really, no, but then she didn't leave the bed afterwards either. She just told Noll to keep watch while she slept and as far as I know, went straight to sleep."

"Which doesn't really prove anything either way," Hahri noted with a sigh. "I guess personal experience will have to answer that one for us. Now, about those night-mares you mentioned…"

Keison immediately stiffened. "What about them?" he asked warily.

Hahri snorted. "Don't worry, kid. I'm not trying to accuse you of anything. I just think it's important to know whether or not Soujin is screwing with your head, or if your nightmares are the result of something else entirely. I just want you to describe them to us."

Realization washed over Issai. Of course! Maybe Kei-son's dreams were connected to the boy's as of yet un-discovered Old Soul abilities.

Keison ran his hand nervously through his limp hair. "That's easy enough 'cause there's really not a lot to tell. Most of the time, the dreams are nothing but darkness and pain, like my whole body's covered in the worst burns you can imagine and the wind is blowing hard over me. It's enough to drive a person mad within a few beats."

His expression was bleak. "Sometimes I see things like I'm looking out of a muddy window—the walls of an unfamiliar room, a weedy field, a cracked window, different people I don't recognize. Sometimes there are voices, but they're so soft and muddled that I can't understand what they're saying. The only thing the dreams all have in common is that the pain is always there. My mom—" He broke off abruptly and something like fear flashed in his eyes. "Never mind."

Hahri raised an eyebrow at Issai then looked meaningfully at Korin before turning his attention back on the fidgeting teen. Issai was almost shocked that the monk took the hint and went to sit next to Keison.

Korin gently placed a hand on the boy's shoulder. "It's all right. You can tell us."

Keison swallowed thickly. "I—my mom—she thought that someone had cursed us. First my father dies in a freak accident while I was still in her belly, then I'm born small and sickly a whole moon too soon. She said that I used to scream and scream in those early days like something was flaying me alive. She took me to the temple, but even the healer-monks could give me no relief because they had no idea why I was so sick. After a while, even they thought I was being tormented by bad spirits."

Korin started. "You are Elly's son!" he blurted, looking completely flabbergasted.

Keison flinched as though the monk had suddenly taken a swing at him. Fear had replaced the weariness in his eyes. "How do you know that?" he demanded in a tight voice, edging away from the older man.

The ancient monk was suddenly looking at the blond teen with barely contained excitement. "The monks told me about you when I first entered the temple here," he explained eagerly, oblivious to the boy's discomfort, "although, they referred to you only as 'Elly's child.' They said that your mother just one day stopped bringing you to the temple. They assumed Elly had either left the city, or you had died and she had been too ashamed to ask for the proper rites for your burial. I looked for you, but none in your community seemed to know where your mother had gone."

Keison smiled bitterly. "I bet they didn't tell you that she left because they drove her out. They thought, as the monks did, that I was possessed by demons." He laughed a bit hysterically. "In the end, I guess they weren't wrong."

"We don't know that for sure, kid," Hahri said quietly. He looked at Issai briefly, his eyes contemplative, then continued, "We all feel various forms of pain just as you do. I'm pretty damn sure it's because of our Old Soul bonds and not because we've been taken over by demons or men who might as well be. Right now, you're only in pain when Soujin feels like torturing you, right?"

Keison nodded hesitantly. "My mom said that eventually I stopped screaming. I don't know if it was because of pain or something else—like the nightmares— that had me screaming as a baby. I don't remember feeling any pain at all when I was little; I was just always kinda sick. But I never really grew out of the weakness I was born with. Even without Soujin keeping me awake at night, I always feel tired, even if I sleep all day."

"Where is your mother now?" Korin asked, excitement melting into concern. "If she's still in this city…"

Keison lowered his eyes. "She died of lung-fever two years ago."

Korin's eyes softened with sympathy. "I am truly sorry."

"At least she's beyond Soujin's reach now," the boy said softly, looking down at the hands he had fisted tightly in his lap.

Issai shifted uncomfortably. Perhaps it was time to steer the conversation to less emotionally loaded topics. The heaviness in the air was starting to strangle him.

Issai coughed purposely. "I didn't get a chance to ask you yesterday," he said once all eyes had turned to him, "but how did you manage to run across Saiya when she was being chased by those four 'guardsmen'? Considering everything you've told us, that's one coincidence I still have a hard time believing."

Even though his words held a note of suspicion, the slight relaxation of Keison's shoulders seemed to say the teen was, at the very least, glad for a change of subject. "I really did have no idea who she was," he insisted. "Like with you two, I was on my way back to the pottery shop after a delivery when I saw them chasing what I thought was a little boy. I was pretty close to the shop, and I figured if I could somehow lose them, I could double back and hide him in the shop. So I grabbed her when she ran by and headed down the first alley I came to. I'd never been down that way before, so I had no idea it was a dead end."

"You never did say why you feel so compelled to help any child targeted by the slavers," Issai interjected.

The look on the blond teen's face suddenly made him seem every bit the child the boy had thought Saiya to be, like a child overwhelmed when he realized for the first time the true size of the world. "Like I told you before, slavers kidnapping children is something that's plagued this city all my life, and nobody seemed willing to do anything about it past warnings of its existence. After a while, you learn to spot them. You *have* to.

"Then Soujin suddenly shows up, and the Mahze seemed to be *everywhere*. That the slavers immediately went after Kye from the moment you two stepped into this city, and then Saiya a few days later, I started to wonder if Soujin was the true power behind the slavers—for the Mahze clan at least. I've never heard of the Norin clan 'hunting' in this city, but that may just be a territorial thing."

"That has never stopped either of those clans before," Korin interrupted suddenly. "A few days ago, both slaver clans were seen in Aideya."

Keison nodded. "That's why I'm not really sure about the Norin, but to me, it makes sense for someone who is trying to find Old Souls to use slavers, a group whose sole purpose is to snatch and sell children, to also keep an eye out for Old Souls."

"If that's true, then it's only a recent partnership," Hahri said slowly. "This is the first time Senn and I have ever run afoul of slavers who had targeted us just because we were Old Souls and not 'children.' Plus, the slaver lord behind our capture had a personal bone to pick with Senn. It's possible Soujin may have learned about it and recruited the Mahze then, though from what we were able to get out of the bastard, I don't really think 'capturing' was Soujin's true agenda."

"What do you mean?" Keison asked.

"It's only speculation on my part," Hahri replied, waving the topic off, "and at this point, not something we should be focused on when we're still missing so many parts of the whole." He stood up from the desk and stretched. "Looks like Senn and I have our work cut out for us. As for you, you still have a quarter-hour or so before the sermon is over. You look like someone two moons too long since your last good meal, so you should have The Watcher there take you to the kitchen before you go. Beg off work for the rest of the day if you can, too. Even Old Souls need sleep, kid, so get as much as you can, when you can. We need your mind as sharp as possible for when Soujin or his pets come knocking at your door again. Hopefully your next visit here will bear better fruit from both sides."

"You should also have one of your Brothers escort him out, monk," Issai added. When Korin flashed him a confused look, he elaborated, "If some of Soujin's spies happened to attend the midday sermon today, then don't you think they would wonder about Keison's absence? If he's seen talking with a monk on his way out, then they'll only think he came here for some one-on-one guidance. After all, we have no proof that Soujin knows you are talking to us, and I think we should continue to behave as if that's true.

CHAPTER TWELVE

Does she have swords for eyes? Issai thought sardonically as he tried, in vain, for the second time to take control of Hahri's body while a certain brat was doing her best to bore a hole through the side of his head with her gaze alone. *I can't concentrate, dammit!*

Feeling his irritation ready to boil over, Issai opened his eyes and turned his head sharply towards the offender. "Can you stop staring at me so hard!" he snapped at Saiya, in that moment not caring in the least if he pissed her off. "I can practically feel you trying to dig into my skull, and the last thing we need is a repeat of yesterday's accident!"

Korin immediately stiffened and looked warily at a stone-faced Saiya before shooting Issai a pleading look. He and Saiya were currently sharing opposite ends of the second cot, practically guaranteeing the monk would be her first victim by sheer proximity should she suddenly go berserk again.

Saiya sniffed, her face contorting as though she suddenly smelled dog shit before turning her face away to stare at the door instead. Issai was shocked that she didn't at least try to bite his head off. Maybe the incident yesterday scared her a lot more than she had let on—at least to Hahri and him.

Korin had spent an hour with her this morning, so who knows what they had talked about, what she had admitted, if anything. They really needed to have a long, private conversation with Korin about Saiya and soon, but for now, he'd let the monk worry about her. He had too many things on his plate as it was.

Issai turned his attention back to Hahri, who was pressing his lips firmly together as if he was, for once, trying not to laugh. He sighed. Things were definitely dire if even Hahri was making an effort to behave himself. "Let's try this again."

With all external distractions removed, Issai found himself looking through Hahri eyes within beats. He took a moment to just stare at his own body more closely than he ever had before. Although his chest was rising and falling steadily with breath, there was a stillness about the rest of him that did not look natural. If someone were to ask him why, he didn't think he would be able to point to anything specific. There was just something *wrong* about his body's entire demeanor, something that perhaps only his subconscious mind could see.

Issai noticed that the hands within Hahri's felt limp and heavy. He slowly released them and watched as his body's hands flopped lifelessly to his lap. As before, breaking the contact between their bodies did not cause any adverse effects to his own body's breathing. He breathed a sigh of relief using Hahri's body, and noted that his own didn't so much as twitch. Once again, he felt completely disconnected from his own body.

Issai hesitantly reached one of Hahri's hands towards his body's face and ran the fingers down one of his cheeks. The skin felt warm, normal, beneath Hahri's slightly damp fingertips. He frowned. Had the bone-chilling cold he had experienced last time been purely mental?

"Did it work?" Korin's voice abruptly cut through his thoughts, making Issai jump.

He had completely forgotten that the other pair was watching.

Issai turned Hahri's head towards the monk and said a little irritably, "Yes."

It felt strange to hear Hahri's baritone instead of his own deeper voice.

Korin jumped to his feet excitedly. "And you are completely in control of his body? Can you walk?"

Issai felt a shiver of unease wash through him at the other's words, but he was fairly certain it was all his own. He could strongly feel Hahri's excitement underlying his own misgivings. "Let's find out." Perhaps the best way to go about this was to just step off the cliff and hope he could fly.

He unfolded his legs and stood up just as if he was in his own body, and Hahri's body complied as naturally as if it *was* his own. He walked to the door and then pivoted back towards the desk next to the cot he had just vacated. Although walking in Hahri's body didn't feel completely normal—the auburn-haired boy *was* a little shorter, after all, and Issai noticed the difference right away—the gait was totally his own.

"I can tell it's you, Senn, by your movement alone," Korin said, echoing Issai's thoughts as he stepped up to him. "Where Kye's movements are always smooth and fast, yours are very calculated and precise." The ancient monk stared into his eyes for a long, uncomfortable moment. "I can see your soul looking back at me through his eyes," he continued with a satisfied smile. "You are definitely inhabiting this body."

"Did you actually *see* my soul leave my body?" Issai asked.

The monk shook his head. "No, nothing like Keison witnessed with Ina. It was a very silent occurrence. Nothing even like the extreme pressure I felt in the air during your healings. However, there *is* a noticeable heaviness in the air surrounding us right now."

Issai frowned. As far as he could tell, his hyper awareness of the movements of those all around him was no different than when he moved with his own body. The air seemed no heavier now than it did before they had begun experimenting.

"It feels the same to me."

"Perhaps it's my proximity," Korin said thoughtfully. He walked back to the cot where Saiya still sat silently watching them with sharp eyes. "Yes, the heaviness is almost gone now."

"Well, whatever you're feeling it's not because of anything I'm doing consciously," Issai said, absently starting to run a hand through his hair in agitation before his fingers suddenly met with the unexpected resistance of hair pulled taut against his scalp.

For half a breath, he was confused before he remembered that Hahri wore his hair pulled back in a tail. That very physical proof he was in fact inhabiting his partner's body instantly made him anxious to get back into his own. However, Korin was approaching him again, beckoning Saiya with a hand as he walked, and the opportunity was lost.

"Can you please come and stand beside me, Saiya?"

the monk entreated.

Issai even felt a burst of shock from Hahri when the normally volatile Old Soul once again did as the monk asked without so much as a sneer in the older man's direction. Issai was beginning to wonder if silence was just her way of communicating interest.

Saiya made it to within a pace of Korin then abruptly froze, her eyes widening in what looked like shock. "That damn buzzing inside just got *worse!*" she exclaimed, but instead of accusing them of some deliberate malfeasance against her, the red-eyed girl backpedaled so fast that she almost got tangled up in her own feet.

Issai was so busy staring incredulously at Saiya that he would have completely missed Korin's reaction had the man's own sudden jerk backwards not succeeded in landing him on his ass and drawn his attention.

"What? You too?" Hahri's voice sounded almost shrill. "That's it! Experiment's over!"

Issai all but ran back to his body and snatched up his hands without bothering to sit back down onto the cot. He received another shock when he realized the hands he held felt as if they had been dipped into a snow bank. Panic started to squeeze his throat, making it difficult to breathe. *I have to get back inside* now!

A burst of raw emotion from Hahri suddenly washed through him, stopping his tidal wave of panic in its tracks as effectively as if the other boy had physically doused him with cold water. Issai closed his eyes tightly and through sheer will, forced himself to calm down until Hahri's heart was no longer threatening to tear out of his chest and the invisible hand squeezing his neck completely relaxed its hold.

Even Hahri's presence seemed to grow smaller as if the other boy was making a conscious effort to be as emotionless as possible, to be unobtrusive. Only then was Issai able to concentrate enough to begin trying to sense his own body's heartbeat.

Unlike when he was trying to take control of Hahri's body, in a body absent of emotion, the heartbeat was the only tangible thing Issai could still sense from it and thus, try to latch onto. Yesterday, his reentry into his body had been purely mindless and instinctual, an action born of sheer panic as he had torn his and Hahri's minds from the prison of Saiya's own. This was the first time he was consciously trying to move back into his body.

He focused on feeling the tiny, but distinctive reverberations of each beat that he usually could sense from anyone around him if he concentrated enough. Once he had identified the faint ripples from all the other usual sensory noise he was receiving, he concentrated on gravitating towards their source with his entire being.

An eternity later, a blast of cold suddenly engulfed Issai's entire body like a million knives stabbing into every piece of skin all at once. His eyes flew open with a gasp of startled pain to find the auburn-haired boy looking down at him with a concerned frown. Issai had never been happier to see the other boy's face in his entire life.

He immediately let go of Hahri's hands and wrapped his arms tightly around his own trembling body. Gods, he felt colder than a corpse in winter!

"Here," Hahri said, draping the cot's sole, thin blanket around his shoulders and then sitting down beside him.

"Your lips are bluer than an afternoon sky. I don't suppose you monks keep any wine around here, do you?" he asked, turning to look at Korin, who had wandered over to them sometime during all the drama and was watching them with wide eyes. Apparently the monk had recovered from whatever had happened to Saiya and him earlier. "He could use a heated mug or two. Hell, so could I."

"The healer-monks keep a few bottles for medicinal purposes," Korin replied. "I shall go fetch one. Do you need anything else, Senn? Something for pain, perhaps?"

"N-no," Issai answered through chattering teeth. "N-nothing h-hurts. I-I'm just r-really c-cold."

"Some woolen blankets then," Korin decided, eyeing them both worriedly. "Are you cold as well, Kye?"

"No. In fact—" he suddenly laughed. "I actually feel really energized, but that could be just because of all the excitement. Don't worry about me."

"I'm going with you," Saiya suddenly announced, moving towards the door.

She had been so silent that Issai once again had forgotten that she was in the room. Her face was curiously blank as she regarded all three of them from the threshold.

Instead of looking pleased, Korin's eyes reflected even more worry, but he merely nodded and followed her out of the room without another word.

"S-sorry I f-freaked again," Issai said with a wry smile as soon as they were alone. "I k-know I p-promised not t-to, but t-to be honest, t-this whole j-jumping into b-bodies thing s-scares the c-crap out of m-me."

Hahri grinned. "Completely understandable. I could feel your hands, too, remember. Speaking of—give them here. Maybe I can rub a little warmth back into them before the rage monster and monk get back."

"We s-scared her."

"A lot," Hahri agreed, looking up from their hands, "and before you ask, I don't think I was doing anything that might've caused all those weird things, either. Or it's more correct to say that I *couldn't*. The only thing I had control of the whole time was my mind and emotions, and even then I was only watching. I didn't actively think or try to do anything."

"And I did n-nothing different t-than what I normally do while in my own b-body. Gods—that s-sounds really weird."

Hahri chuckled. "Given the hornet's nest we just ripped open, my guess is that saying things like that will become the norm and not the exception. At least your hands are starting to warm up. How are you feeling now?"

"Cold, but n-not painfully cold anymore," Issai replied.

"Well, your teeth aren't chattering as much as before, so that's definitely something. You really don't feel sick or have a headache or anything like that?"

"Shockingly, no. Right now I feel no worse than I w-would after wandering around outside when it's freezing without a c-cloak. It's starting to look l-like I panicked for nothing. Maybe I'm supposed to feel c-cold. After all, we d-don't know if this happens to Ina when she d-does it."

"Yeah. Remind me to tell Keison to touch her skin next time she leaves her body behind in his room," Hahri said with a grin. "Imagine the look on his face."

"S-sometimes I think you're having way too much f-fun with all of this," Issai remarked, shaking his head.

"Without fun, then what's the point of living?"

Issai opened his mouth to retort, thought better of it, and instead, just shook his head again. "I can't believe I'm about to say this, b-but you may have a valid argument th-there."

A strange emotion flashed within Hahri's eyes for a beat. However, before Issai could attempt to grasp its meaning, cerulean eyes blinked and the usual spark of mischief and wide grin had replaced it.

"There's hope for you yet, my friend," Hahri teased.

Both boys started violently as the door was suddenly kicked open, and Saiya, followed by a very chagrined Korin, entered the room instead of the dozens of *Shi* Issai had half-expected. Saiya carried a small metal bucket that faintly smoked with the corked neck of what was presumably a wine bottle visible above the rim while the monk carried a tray of mugs and a couple of thick blankets. A white cloth small enough to be a hand towel was draped over one of his arms.

"I thought this might be faster," Korin explained at their questioning looks. "I packed hot coals all around the wine bottle rather than take the time to heat it over the kitchen hearth. The walk back should have given the wine long enough to warm."

Issai's eyes flitted from Korin to Saiya, wondering if it was such a good idea to allow something like hot coals anywhere near such an unpredictable girl. He was relieved when she set the bucket down onto the desk without looking at either of them and headed back towards the cot across the room.

Korin set down the tray next to the wine bucket and then handed the two blankets to Hahri while keeping the hand towel. While Hahri fussed over him with the blankets, the blond pulled the cork from the bottle and used the towel to lift it out of the bucket. Within beats, Issai had a warm mug in his still-chilled hands.

He made a face as the warm, acrid liquid hit his tongue. To call the drink vinegar would have been an insult to all vinegar makers, but that's what the taste most resembled—if the vinegar had been made over a thousand years ago.

Flashing him a curious look, Hahri grabbed his mug

and stole a sip. "Bleah! Where did you find this bottle, monk? Buried beneath an ancient cesspit?" he demanded. "I think some of the filth may have seeped into it."

To their surprised, the ancient monk's expression was amused rather than insulted. "The monks produce it here in the temple. I did tell you that the healer-monks use it for medicinal reasons—as a base mostly to dissolve their herbs and powders—and when have any of their potions ever tasted good? Efficacy and not flavor has always been their main concern."

"In that case, I think I'll pass," Hahri said, handing the mug back to Issai.

Issai eyed it sourly, but then held his breath and downed the rest of it in one gulp. He really did need the warmth, and he could already feel the heated liquid slowly blanketing the cold within. He accepted the mug that Korin had already poured for Hahri without comment, but he did not drink it, wanting its warmth for his hands for the time being.

"So, do you want to tell us what happened to you two there at the end?" Hahri asked, looking at both Korin and Saiya.

Korin shifted nervously, his dark eyes once again reflecting worry. "For a few beats there, when Saiya was so near, the trembling within my soul changed. It became so violent that it was painful, excruciatingly so. Then I realized that it was not the only thing that had changed. That strange heaviness I had felt had grown so strong that it was like a large hand had wrapped around me and was slowly squeezing my body.

"I tried to step back, but it was like there really was something physical holding me there. That is when I jerked away with everything I had in me and ended up on the floor. My whole body stung like I had just ripped off a bandage that had become stuck to the wound."

Issai exchanged a sharp glance with Hahri. That description sounded awfully familiar. Looking thoughtful, Hahri suddenly climbed onto his knees and slid behind Issai, grabbing the dark-haired boy around the middle, blankets and all, and hugged him tightly against his chest.

Issai stiffened. "What the hell are you doing?" he growled, looking over his shoulder irritably at the other boy.

"Testing something," he murmured into Issai's ear. Hahri lifted his head. "Korin, come stand directly beside us," he instructed. "Tell me if you feel anything weird."

Issai turned to look at the blond. The monk stood frozen on the other side of the desk, looking as if Hahri had asked him to approach a hungry tiger. Issai felt a burst of amusement through the Bond.

"We're not gonna do anything, monk," Hahri said. "I just want to know if the heaviness you felt was because our souls were in the same body or just because you were so near both of us."

Still looking a little wary, Korin did as Hahri asked.

After a long moment of silence, Korin said, "Yes, I can still feel something—barely. It's noticeable only because I am paying particular attention to the way the air feels all around me."

Issai could feel the smaller boy nod at his back. Then Hahri released him and got off the cot, walking over to the door.

"How about now?"

Korin frowned, closing his eyes for a moment, before turning back to Hahri. "It's completely gone now."

Hahri walked up to the monk until they were toe-to-toe and just stood silently for a few beats. "Me, I still don't feel anything other than the usual proximity pain I always do around Senn," he said finally.

"And all of that proves *what* exactly?" Issai asked as the auburn-haired boy plopped down next to him again.

Hahri shrugged. "That maybe the Bond does a lot more than tie two Old Souls together. Especially if it's affecting more than one other Old Soul outside the Bond. We should really test this on Keison the next time he comes, ask him if he sensed anything similar around Ina and Noll when they both inhabit the same body."

He turned to Issai. The hesitation in the other boy's eyes immediately told him that he would not like what Hahri was about to say.

"How are you feeling now? Still cold?"

"A little," Issai replied slowly. He had a sinking feeling that he knew where his partner was going with this.

The expression on Hahri's face had gone from hesitant to deadly serious. "Do you think you're up to another transmigration attempt right now?"

He sighed. "What do you have in mind?"

"I want to try to gain back control of my body while your soul is still within me," Hahri said.

Issai was surprised—and relieved—that Hahri didn't want to try something more outlandish. "I'm fine with that."

"Korin, you and Saiya should probably stay as far away from us as you can while we do this from now on. At least until we understand all of this better."

"You mean 'if,'" Issai warned as the monk quickly joined Saiya on the cot. "There's no guarantee that we'll ever understand it."

"That sounds like a bet," Hahri said, his eyes lightning up.

Issai shook his head. "You're incorrigible." Then he smirked. "But why the hell not. You can tell me the terms later."

Once again, that strange emotion flitted across Hahri's eyes, but no matter how close he paid attention, Issai felt nothing of it through the Bond. He wondered why the unfamiliarity of it bothered him so much when he had never really cared about the emotions of others before beyond a threat assessment.

"You should probably stay wrapped up in those blankets," Hahri said as Issai absently set his mug down onto the desk, his mind still pondering the incomprehensibility of his bond partner. "Might keep you from feeling like such a corpse this time."

"Thanks so much for that pleasant reminder," Issai snarked without any real heat.

"One other thing—if I do manage to take back control from you, don't be surprise if you start feeling a little sleepy."

"What do you mean 'a little sleepy'?" Issai demanded in alarm.

Hahri shrugged, looking unconcerned. "Just that I had the feeling that if I hadn't purposely kept my mind so focused and alert on what you were doing that I could've easily fallen asleep."

Now Issai was really alarmed. "That sounds dangerous."

"Maybe," Hahri allowed, "but I admit I'm a little curious to see what would happen if I just let myself drift a bit."

"Well *I'm* not, so you better not do it!" Issai warned. "A little curiosity is *not* worth the very real possibility of you erasing yourself permanently!"

Hahri huffed. "I don't think that would happen."

"...says every fool right before their gruesome death," Issai grumbled.

"Fine, fine," Hahri relented with a sigh. "At least stand up once you have control of my body. I'll try to take back control then."

Issai could feel the other boy's exasperation with him keenly once he had completed the transmigration. He had a feeling that Hahri was doing it on purpose. He just couldn't understand why the auburn-haired boy didn't seem as bothered about having his body taken over so easily as Issai thought he should be.

Issai stood and walked to the center of the room, pointedly ignoring Korin and Saiya as this time, they were both determined to stare a hole into the side of his head. He wondered what it was they were trying to see.

He took a deep breath. "All right, Kye. Try to push me out."

Almost immediately, Hahri's presence seemed to swell to twice its size within his psyche, and for half a beat, the world violently tilted on its axis. Then Issai could feel his eyes blinking rapidly as the room abruptly came back into focus, and he realized that he was not the one doing it. He tried to turn his head towards his body, but Hahri's body refused to obey him.

"Well—that was easier than I thought," he felt his mouth—or rather *Hahri's* mouth—say with surprise. Hahri turned towards the other pair. "I thought for sure his soul would return to his own body, but I can still feel his presence within me. Hey—you still aware in there, Senn?"

Issai released the emotional equivalent of an "of course" retort in a strong burst.

Hahri winced then let out a rueful chuckle. "Yeah, he's there all right. We must've just switched drivers to the carriage, so to speak, and Senn's now the passenger." He started to walk around the room in circles. "Everything feels normal. Even the proximity pain is the same as when you're controlling my body."

"Do you think you can switch control again?" Korin asked, his eyes swimming with fascination.

"Good idea. Rather than relinquish control, why don't you try it this time, Senn? Just concentrate your entire being on the desire to move. That's all it took for me."

Gladly, Issai thought with a sense of relief. Being able to sense everything but not able to move at all was beginning to remind him of that joyous time he spent trussed up in a sack on his way to the Mahze compound. He was starting to feel more than a little claustrophobic.

He focused on a desire to walk back to his own body and instantly found his world turning on its head again. He was already taking a step towards the cot even before his vision cleared.

"You're right, that was almost as easy as breathing," Issai said, continuing on to the cot and sitting next to his body. "Other than the initial vertigo from the transition, I don't feel any adverse effects at all." He reached over to his body and clasped one of his hands. It was already starting to feel like ice. "You felt that, right, so I think it's time to return to my b—*whoa!*"

Issai nearly fell off the cot when a white hot burst of energy unlike anything he had ever experienced suddenly thundered into his entire being with all the power of a raging storm, and the entire room was enveloped in erratic streams of colored particles of light like something out of a fevered dream. Then before his stunned mind could even begin to try to make sense of what was happening, what he was seeing, Issai felt the energy leave him with a sensation virtually identical to what he experienced after a healing. The color streams also seemed to fade in tandem.

Issai clutched the edge of the cot so tightly that his hands shook. "Kye!" he practically bellowed. "What the hell did you just *do*?"

CHAPTER THIRTEEN

"I *told* you not to do it!" Issai snarled, so furious that he barely registered the cold.

Hahri sat facing him with a sheepish smile. "It wasn't *that* bad. So we saw some interesting lights, and I suddenly felt like we could take on a whole army alone. The important thing is that at no time did I feel like I wasn't in control of my own mind. Until you pounded my senses with a huge dose of shock, it was a rather exhilarating and peaceful experience."

"Peaceful?" Issai repeated in disbelief. "Exactly how can being hit by a lightning bolt be described as peaceful? Because that's exactly what being hit with that wave of power felt like. It was so intense that it was almost painful!"

"I really did expect to just fall asleep," Hahri insisted. "I just thought it might be good to know whether or not one of us could rest our mind while the other was fully alert while sharing a body. You never know if something like that might come in handy sometime in the future should we find ourselves with one body and in need of a sentry during the night."

"What was it that you saw exactly?" Korin asked. This time, the ancient monk didn't even attempt to approach them.

Issai blew out a frustrated breath. "If neither you nor Saiya saw anything unusual, then it's quite possible that it was just something screwy that happened to Kye's brain as a result of all that excess energy that was released from the gods-only-know where."

"Then why don't I at least have a headache?" Hahri asked. "Hell, I don't even feel the least bit weak, or dizzy, or even particularly jittery. In fact, I feel so wide awake and energized that I'll probably have trouble sleeping tonight." He looked pointedly at Issai. "Do *you* feel any worse than last time?"

"No," Issai admitted reluctantly.

Instead of rubbing it in, the other boy just flashed him a gentle smile. "Don't think that I don't appreciate how much you worry about me," he said. "It may not seem like it, but I really am doing these things carefully. That's why I pulled back immediately when things got so weird."

"You really don't think it was a hallucination do you?"

"I don't, and I'll tell you why. I meant what I said when I told you I felt peaceful—because for the first time since the forest outside of Daisha, the pain of being so near to you almost disappeared."

Issai's eyes widened even as Saiya let out an involuntary gasp of surprise. "You're kidding!"

Issai hadn't noticed any difference in his own proximity pain, but then again, it was already so faint when he had control of Hahri's body that it was possible he wouldn't have noticed any differences unless he was paying particular attention to it.

"That's why I think we should do it again," the other boy insisted. "I believe that whatever it was that happened definitely had something to do with the Bond. At the very least I would like to see if it was just a one-time fluke or something that's supposed to happen."

"You really enjoy playing with fire, don't you," Issai griped. "At least let me warm up a little more first."

Hahri jumped to his feet. "I'll get you some more wine."

Issai shot Hahri a dirty look. "This better be the last time today. I don't think my stomach can take much more of that shit."

"This is the last time, I promise."

A quarter-hour later, Issai was back in Hahri's body. Moving his soul between bodies was so easy now that he barely had to exert any effort to do it. He didn't know whether to be relieved or more worried about that fact.

"Whenever you're ready," he said to Hahri, bracing his back against the wall in case he experienced the same overwhelming influx of energy as before.

A couple of beats later, he was thankful for the precaution. If anything, the onslaught of power was worse this time around. Issai wasn't certain if it was because he knew what to expect this time or because it was stronger.

As the power roared within his being for what seemed like an eternity, a different type of chaos was happening right before his eyes. The streams of light had appeared again, faint and flowing through the air in no one direction or discernable pattern like eddies of a volatile river. They seem to come into and flow out of the room through the walls as if the barriers weren't even there.

This time Issai stared at the ones that flowed particularly close to his face. He saw that they were composed of perhaps millions of extremely tiny pulsating lights in various shades of yellows and greens that reminded him of a smaller version of the sparks coming off a struck piece of flint, but at the same time seemingly as transparent as a sunbeam.

As he watched the colorful currents in an almost hypnotic daze, Issai realized the excess power within him seemed to be equalizing to a point where he no longer felt as though he was drowning in it. He wondered if it was Hahri's doing or something that was occurring naturally.

Issai turned to his body, suddenly worried that these strange streams of light might be affecting it somehow, but none seemed to even flow near enough to touch his body, never mind penetrate it. He stuck his hand through one of the green streams flowing at the level of his stomach and was perplexed when it didn't seem to interact with his hand at all, the flow remaining completely undisturbed. He also could feel no change in temperature around his hand, or even a disruption in air to signify the movement he was seeing.

What in the world could these streams possibly be? Were they merely hallucinations after all?

Issai turned to look at Korin and Saiya and nearly bit his tongue as he abruptly jumped to his feet in shock.

"You're both glowing blue!" he exclaimed in bewilderment, watching in a combination of horror and fascination as tendrils of a blue, fog-like substance as different from the other light streams flowing through the room as water was from wind undulated around their bodies like blue flames.

"What!" Korin said, jumping to his feet as well. The blond monk immediately began scanning his body before turning to give Saiya the once over.

The so-far silent girl was looking at Issai as though he'd suddenly gone insane. "Now I know you broke something in there," she scoffed.

However, Issai barely heard her through the rapid beating of Hahri's heart as he stared down at the exact same shade of blue emanating from the arms he had extended that had most definitely not been glowing just a few moments ago. No—not the same. The glow of light particles coming off Hahri's arms looked a little more substantial, denser, than what he was seeing coming off the other two. A closer look at the pair confirmed that the chaotic glow coming off Saiya was not quite as dense as Korin's.

Issai cautiously touched Hahri's arm as if he expected it to burn, but as with the green particle stream he had tried to touch earlier, he felt nothing other than the normal warmth of Hahri's skin. His fingertips didn't even tingle.

He turned to look at his body again, but he still didn't see even a hint of a blue glow coming from it. Was that it then? Issai turned his gaze to the monk who was now frowning with concern. Could he possibly be seeing a manifestation of the Old Soul Bond?

"I do not see anything," Korin said slowly, sounding apologetic.

"Because he's hallucinating," Saiya insisted, though she didn't sound as confident as her words.

"I don't think so," Issai told them. "I see the blue glow coming from everyone except my body. If I were merely hallucinating, then wouldn't it be strange that only my body was excluded? No—I think it could very well be the Bond I'm seeing."

"You mean what's causing the buzzing within me?" Saiya demanded, her eyes lighting up with excitement. It was the first time Issai had ever seen that type of emotion in her eyes.

He nodded cautiously. "I obviously can't confirm anything at this point, but it's as likely an explanation as any. Kye, take control of your body and let us know if you are seeing the same thing as me."

Issai knew the very moment Hahri took action. The extra energy he had been enjoying began to rapidly bleed away and the rivers and flames of color began to fade as Hahri's presence got larger. By the time Issai was relegated to observer only, the room had returned to normal, and no one was glowing.

"That was the most fascinating thing I have ever seen," Hahri commented the moment he was able.

"So you saw the blue glow as well," Korin intuited.

"Oh yes," Hahr replied with a grin that Issai was sure he had never felt on his own face. It was almost uncomfortable, as if someone was stretching the corners of his mouth into a parody of a smile. "There were rivers of colorful light particles flowing everywhere. It was quite beautiful. Although I can no more tell you exactly what it was we were seeing than I can tell you what the gods are thinking, I do think Senn could very well be right about the blue glow. It definitely looked like it was emanating from all of our bodies—*except* for Senn's."

"It appeared as if Senn was trying to touch the phenomenon," Korin said. "What did it feel like?"

Hahri's brows drew together. "Nothing," he replied. "It gave off no discernable heat, nor did it seem to be interacting with anything at all. I could see that some of the light streams were moving through the walls and the floor, but the stones didn't disrupt the streams at all. It was like they weren't even there." A burst of excitement abruptly surged through Issai's being. "Senn—what do you say about taking back control and going for a little stroll around the temple? I'm really curious to see if only

Old Souls have that blue glow. If so, then it'll at least confirm whether it has to do with our Old Soul natures or not."

Issai immediately pushed his presence to the forefront and walked over to his body as soon as he was able. He grabbed one of his hands. It was cold, but still not as cold as they had felt the first time he had left his body. His body also still looked to be breathing normally, his lips pale, but not yet tinged with blue.

"Okay," he said in answer to Hahri's proposal. He turned to Korin and pierced him with an intense look. "I'm trusting you, monk, to watch over my body while we're gone."

Korin nodded solemnly. "No one will enter this room," he promised.

Issai flashed his motionless body one last uneasy glance. "I don't think I should be away from my body for very much longer, so this'll just be a short trip."

Issai had hoped that they would run into some of the monks in the narrow hallways so they wouldn't have to stray too far from his body, but that wing of the temple seemed empty at the moment. Cursing inwardly, he headed towards the main atrium. He was relieved to see a couple of monks at the entrance greeting everyone as they trickled in. There were already a dozen or so people inside the room on their way towards a pair of doors to the right, perhaps to seek personalized council.

Issai stood in the doorway leading to the monk's wing of the temple. "All right, Hahri, do your thing. We'll get to see both monks and regular people here."

He leaned his back against the doorframe and braced for the onslaught of energy. He kept his eyes closed until the worst of the rush had leveled out.

The streams of color were even more spectacular in

the voluminous atrium. A stormy ocean had replaced the thundering river he had seen back in the room, currents of different colors pulsating and flowing from what was seemingly a thousand different directions. It was enough to make him dizzy.

It took Issai a while to find and fixate on the people moving obliviously through that blinding maelstrom, but even as far away as he was from them, he could clearly see that their bodies were engulfed with the glow of that writhing blue phenomenon. He could sense Hahri's surprise as he stared at all the moving bodies with narrowed eyes. The glow was much, much fainter than even the one surrounding Saiya, but it was definitely present.

He fixed his eyes keenly on the two stationary monks at the entrance. The densities of their glows were similar to each other's but definitely not identical. He tried to compare them with the people walking past them through the doors, but they were simply moving too fast for him to make a good comparison.

Oh well, he had seen enough, anyway. They could always stand and watch people in the marketplace or attend one of the temple services later to be absolutely sure, but right now Issai was more concerned with the implications this newest discovery raised about his body and its lack of a blue glow. He really wanted to get back into his body *right now*.

"That's enough, Hahri," he whispered.

Issai waited until he could no longer see the streams of light before heading back to their room.

"Saiya's definitely not going to be happy," he muttered.

He barely remembered to announce himself before opening the door, nearly bowling over Korin in his haste. The monk had probably been standing guard at the door.

"Let me return to my body; then we'll talk," Issai said before the other pair could say a word.

He was relieved to feel that his hands were no colder than before they had left. That relief lasted only as long as the moment he reentered his body and the now familiar needles of ice stabbed into him. Issai was completely caught off guard when a wave of exhaustion also washed through him. He clumsily threw out a hand onto the cot to catch himself before he toppled over.

Hahri immediately grasped his shoulders to steady him. "What's wrong?"

"I think my body's had enough for t-today," Issai said, trembling. "Just help me prop myself up against the w-wall and pour me a cup of that goat piss, and I'll be f-fine in a moment."

Hahri chuckled and complied.

"Well?" Saiya demanded impatiently as Hahri was handing him the warm mug of wine.

"Everyone has it," Hahri said without preamble. He climbed onto the cot and made himself comfortable next to Issai.

Korin looked both crestfallen and intrigued. "So I take it the blue glow has nothing to do with our Old Soul bonds..."

"Probably not," Hahri agreed, "but I do have another theory. As I watched all those people walking through the atrium, it made me think of something Keison said about Ina, about how her soul seemed to 'ripple' when it moved through the air. Even though its movement reminds me of dancing flames, I realized that the blue glow could also be described as 'ripples of water.'"

"You mean our souls," Issai said quietly, turning to look at the other boy thoughtfully.

"Yes. It would explain why you didn't see the blue

glow around your body. Your soul had left it."

"And it looks the same with everyone?" Korin asked.

Issai shook his head. "No. The density of the glow is much stronger in us than regular people, but no one's is identical as far as I've been able to see. Saiya's glow is a little less dense than yours, monk, and while I shared Hahri's body, the glow was at least twice as dense as yours."

"Which would make perfect sense with two souls occupying the same space," Korin said with a nod.

"We should totally take a look at Keison the next time he shows up," Hahri said. "We can see if his glow is as dense as Korin's or Saiya's."

"If that proves to be the case, then I wonder if it was Ina and Noll that pointed Soujin to Keison," Issai added. "If they can see the same things as us while sharing a body, then it wouldn't take much for them to come to the same conclusions. Maybe we can use it to our advantage as well, find any other Old Souls before they do."

"But then, that begs the question of why Soujin would leave Keison here with the sole job of finding Old Souls if he has a pair of more loyal minions that would definitely yield better results?" Hahri pointed out.

"That's assuming the boy has been telling us the truth," Issai warned, rubbing his eyes wearily. Gods, but he could sleep for a tenday. "I still haven't made up my mind about him."

"So far, I've heard nothing but assumptions," Saiya said derisively. "The likely outcome of all of this is that you're all full of shit, and I'm just wasting my time." She stood up and made her way to the door. "If that brat shows up again, come and get me. Otherwise I don't want to see any of you idiots for the rest of the day."

She slammed the door behind her, followed a couple

of beats later by the door to the adjacent room. Another beat of silence and Hahri practically exploded with laughter. "'That brat,' she says. If I didn't have to worry about being sliced in half, then I would tease her mercilessly."

Whatever else the auburn-haired boy said was lost as Issai finally lost his battle with sleep.

CHAPTER FOURTEEN

Issai watched Keison enter their room through Hahri's eyes.

The two were seated side-by-side on the cot, backs against the wall and touching all along one side of their bodies. Issai's body had his arms loosely crossed against his stomach and his head down with his eyes closed as if he were meditating or dozing.

Upon Issai's suggestion, they had found that Issai could still transmigrate his soul easily without clasping Hahri's hands as long as their bodies were still touching somewhere. A quarter-hour before the midday sermon, they had done so in preparation for a possible visit from Keison. They wanted to observe the boy while they could see the energy streams without letting on that Issai was in charge of Hahri's body.

Seeing the dense, blue glow surrounding the teen's thin frame as Keison closed the door behind him was somewhat of a relief. From what Issai could recall, the cloud of particles was probably as dense as Saiya's, definitely much denser than those he had witnessed in the atrium around the two monks and the temple patrons passing through the room. If Hahri's speculation about souls was correct, then it was the first tangible evidence that Keison was truly an Old Soul and not just some hapless kid that Soujin had sent to toy with them.

Issai quickly dug Hahri's nails into his hand, the signal for them to resume control of their own bodies. His body was still cold even though he hadn't been gone for very long, but he did his best to keep from visibly trembling as he opened his eyes. He hadn't realized just how huge of a difference being wrapped in blankets from the start made until now as his limbs felt like useless blocks of ice.

Korin greeted their new arrival warmly, and ushered him into the wooden chair beside the desk. He pressed a warm mug of cider into the boy's hands, and then made a big show of refilling the empty mugs on the desk and offering them to Issai and Hahri.

"Why don't you two have some as well while I go fetch Saiya," the monk said a little too cheerfully, which had Hahri biting back a snort of amusement.

At least this little show of hospitality would give Issai time to recover without hopefully clueing in Keison that something was amiss.

"She's off sulking in her room," Hahri explained with a smirk at Keison's questioning look. "She'd probably kill us if we all started talking without her."

Issai took the opportunity to down the entire contents of the mug while the blond teen's attention was focused on Hahri. Thankfully, it really was hot cider this time and not that liquid atrocity posing as wine. At this point, he would rather swallow Saiya's sword than choke down another mug of that vile concoction.

"At least you look more rested today," Hahri noted,

passing Issai his steaming mug without comment.

Issai clutched it between his hands, grateful for the warmth.

"Yeah," Keison muttered nervously, staring at the thin wisp of steam rising from his own mug. "Soujin left me alone all night."

Hahri frowned. "You don't sound too happy about that."

The boy shrugged. "It just makes me wonder what he was doing that he didn't have the time to torment me."

"Something worth worrying about for sure," Hahri said with a nod just as Korin returned with Saiya skulking behind him like some disgruntled child.

"Ina and Noll showed up at the shop yesterday right as I was leaving," Keison said as soon as the monk and brat were settled on the empty cot. "They waited until we were back in my room at the boarding house to start with the questions. They were particularly interested in whether or not I had seen any new Old Souls. I told them I hadn't, that I still hadn't even seen you three, but instead of getting mad, she just waved it off, saying that I shouldn't concern myself with you three anymore. She said that you were now solely Soujin's business."

"Did she say whether or not Soujin knew that we were still in the city?" Hahri asked.

Keison shook his head. "That was the only time she even mentioned you. It was almost like she couldn't be bothered with me, like she was in a really big hurry and was only talking to me 'cause Soujin had told her to and she needed a place for her and Noll to stay. Well, at least for Noll's *body* to stay."

"Wait, wait!" Hahri exclaimed, leaning forward. "*Noll's* body? So he can move his soul after all?"

Keison nodded. "Yeah, I was really shocked, too.

After Ina finished with me, he just laid himself down on my bed, and his soul left his body and entered Ina's in exactly the same way. Then Ina threatened to have Soujin yank on the chains around my heart until I begged for death if I did or let anything happen to Noll's body while they were gone, and I could swear it was actually Ina making the threat and not Noll talking through her. I watched her as she left the room, and she moved the same as she always did. Whatever the reason Noll's soul went into her body, it wasn't to possess her like she had him."

An image of the colorful particle streams of light instantly entered Issai's mind. Was Ina able to see them too with Noll's help?

"Did she say where they were going?" Issai spoke for the first time.

"No. She never does. However, this time they stayed out until just before sunrise."

"Noll stayed out of his body that long?" Issai asked, startled.

Keison blinked at him in confusion. "Is that a bad thing? His body did feel a little cold, but I thought it was because I had run out of firewood and my room was freezing last night."

"So you touched him?" Hahri said, looking pleased.

Keison squirmed in his seat, his face flushing lightly with embarrassment. "Anzal wasn't there this time, and I wanted to see if it looked or felt like a corpse. Other than the cold, he just looked like he was asleep. He was still breathing, and his skin was soft."

"Did Noll look sick or anything after he reentered his body?" Issai cut in.

"He cursed a lot and demanded I use one of my chairs for firewood, but he didn't seem weak or wanting to puke or anything—just cold. In fact, they only stayed for another hour before heading out again. Ina said they were going to Toridas for a few days. She's never told me any of their plans before, so I don't know if it's true or not."

"Maybe a couple of us should go to Toridas as well," Hahri mused, "see what they're up to."

Keison immediately shook his head. "You won't be able to get past Ina's barrier, remember?"

Hahri's brows drew together. "Damn! I completely forgot about that. Are you sure it's still there?"

"I—I think so, but..."

"Right," Hahri scowled. "The perfect trap, one that cannot be verified unless sprung. I'm almost willing to try it anyway. If those Old Souls are truly headed for Toridas then it's the first real chance we've gotten to get the jump on them."

"That's a lot of 'ifs,'" Issai said. "Too many for my piece of mind. We should probably poke around here a little more before we go chasing hares."

He stared meaningfully at Hahri, willing the other boy to read between the lines. Keison had just given them a treasure trove of information, and he wanted to explore as much of it as they could before even thinking about borrowing more trouble.

"Are you all trying to find the Old Soul Ina keeps hinting is in this city, too?" Keison asked curiously, misunderstanding his words.

"We're trying to do a lot of things," Issai hedged.

"Too true," Hahri said with a sigh that sounded completely fake to Issai's ears. "After all, we did promise the kid to look into his little invisible chain problem, and he's more than held up his end of the bargain."

A loud sniff sounded across the room, and Issai turned towards the other pair. Saiya was glaring at Hahri as though his very presence was offending her. He could only guess that she had been reminded about how little progress they had made in understanding the Old Soul Bond as they had promised *her* and was pretty sore about it.

For his part, Hahri didn't even acknowledge that he'd noticed her ire, which was probably for the best. For a child throwing a tantrum, sometimes the best course of action was to simply ignore them.

"Have you discovered anything yet?" Keison asked, his eyes suddenly lighting up with hope.

That pitiful look made Issai instantly change his reply from a definitive "no" to, "It's hard to say for sure right now. I know that's not what you wanted to hear, but we did warn you that it may take quite a bit of time, if we even find a solution at all."

The blond teen looked so crestfallen that Issai had to look away in sudden discomfort.

"If Ina's to be believed, we still have a few days yet before they contact you again," Hahri said gently. "A lot can happen in that time."

"Yeah, like Soujin coming for me, himself," Keison returned miserably.

CHAPTER FIFTEEN

"Who would've ever thought that *you* of all people would've made friends with that little novice?" Hahri quipped, shaking his head in mock incredulity.

"I didn't 'make friends' with him," Issai repeated for what seemed like the tenth time. "I only said that he had been useful to me and had a good eye for things. It's not like I even know his name."

They were currently waiting for Korin to return from speaking to the little blond novice that had attached himself to Issai when they had been looking for Keison in the Merchant District. Issai had never gotten around to telling Hahri about the helpful boy, and now he was starting to regret ever bringing him up at all.

Keison had informed them that he planned to go back to his boarding room before returning to the pottery shop. The master of the shop had given him a set of dishes and a large, rather heavy vase to deliver after he attended the midday service. Since both delivery destinations were in the southern part of the city and the temple in the north, he had decided to leave them in his room rather than lug them all the way up to the temple and then having to trek across almost the length of the whole city afterwards to complete the errand.

That had suddenly given Issai an idea. The fact that the kid was starting to get under his emotional skin bothered him quite a bit, and he wanted to find out once and for all if Keison was telling them the truth. The problem was that they had no idea which boarding house the teen lived in, and the last thing Issai wanted to do was outright ask him and raise unnecessary suspicion.

That's when Issai had thought of the eager novice. The boy knew what Keison looked like. If they could just stall Keison for a bit, long enough for Korin to find the little monk-in-training and explain what they needed of him, then the novice could follow him back to the boarding house. Luckily for him, the solution had come in Korin's offer of food. Issai had jumped at the chance once Keison had accepted the meal, telling the monk that he would accompany him to the kitchen.

Issai had received a short burst of bewilderment from Hahri through the Bond, but the auburn-haired boy didn't so much as give him an odd look. A sharp look at Korin stalled any questions from that direction, but he had been worried that Saiya would say something that would make Keison suspicious.

However, either she had realized that he wanted to speak with Korin away from the blond teen, or she really was as uninterested as her bored expression suggested. Either way, Issai knew he could count on Hahri for misdirection should it become necessary while he was gone.

On the way to the kitchen, Issai had presented his plan and the reasoning behind it. Though initially reluctant to involve one of the novices in such a potentially dangerous task, Korin had relented after only a minimal amount of persuasion and had taken him to a large chamber where at least a hundred novices were in the midst of a lesson.

The novice had been just as excited and eager to help him as Issai had expected. The plan was for the boy to wait at the main entrance as if he were a greeter and follow Keison as discreetly as possible. Then he was to report back to Korin, who would be waiting for him at the door to the monks' living quarters.

When they had returned, laden with food trays, Issai could tell that Hahri was near bursting with curiosity even without the Bond. He had watched his partner up until Keison had left with some amusement as Hahri's body became stiffer and stiffer with the effort of keeping quiet. Keison had barely closed the door before Hahri had turned to him demanding answers.

Issai was certainly paying for making the other boy wait with all the incessant teasing that had followed.

"Well, if your 'useful' novice comes through for us, then I take it we will be the spies tonight?" Hahri asked, the mischief on his face melting into a more serious expression.

"That's the plan," Issai replied, "but until then, I have a few things I'd like us to experiment with today."

"Oh?" Hahri said with interest.

"That's the smartest thing you've said all day," Saiya spoke up suddenly. "I was beginning to wonder if today was going to be another waste."

"Says the girl who does nothing but stare and growl," Hahri retorted with a grin that was all teeth. Apparently Saiya wasn't the only one whose patience was wearing thin today.

"*Anyway*," Issai interjected forcefully in an effort to

stave off the coming eruption, "as I was saying, I want you to try to take control of my body this time."

"Because of what Keison said about Noll?" Hahri hazarded, looking intrigued.

"Yes. Maybe it's something all Old Souls can do rather than just a select few," Issai surmised, glancing at Saiya.

Red eyes immediately narrowed. "Don't you think for even a beat that I would let any of you try to possess me!" she snarled.

"Don't worry," Issai muttered as Hahri snorted in amusement. He would rather be flayed alive than ever share such an intimate connection with the "rage monster."

A knock abruptly sounded at the door. "It's Korin," the monk announced as it swung open.

Issai could tell from the excited look on his face that the novice had been successful.

"That was certainly quick," Hahri commented as Korin went to sit down beside a still murderously scowling Saiya. It was a testament to how used to seeing that expression on his bond partner's face he had become that the monk didn't even deem it worthy of mention.

"Devin did not have to follow him far, as it turns out," Korin said. "He said Keison went straight to the boarding house, a modest two-story building named White Meadows located just two blocks outside the Merchant District right off the main road. His room is on the bottom floor, last door on the left. Devin watched until Keison emerged again just to be certain, and he assured me that Keison was indeed carrying a large vase and a wrapped package when he left."

"Good. I was afraid we'd have to scale the roof," Hahri said.

"Are you planning on watching him all night?" Korin asked, looking concerned.

"Depends on what we see," Issai replied with a shrug. "Or hear if his room doesn't have a window. Odds are we'll have to watch him for more than the one night."

"And if the boy proves to be a liar, what then?" the ancient monk asked carefully, gazing back at Issai in an almost challenging way.

Hahri raised an eyebrow at Issai, an echo of his own surprise. It was the last thing he had expected the blond to ask, especially when he, himself, hadn't really thought past just watching Keison.

"We'll worry about that when or if there's something *to* worry about," Hahri said with an air of finality, staring down Korin until the monk's gaze fell to his clasped hands. The auburn-haired boy then picked up the two woolen blankets at the end of the cot and proceeded to wrap them around himself. "Right now, let's see if I can take control of Senn's body this time."

The pinched look immediately vanished from Korin's face. "If you really think it's possible, then maybe Saiya and I should—"

"Touch me and you'll have to finish this life with only one hand," Saiya hissed, scooting over as far as she could from Korin, her hand on the hilt of her sword.

"But..."

"Let it go, monk," Hahri warned. Saiya looked about half a breath away from drawing her blade, and once again, the monk was exhibiting a poor sense of self-preservation. "You'll have plenty of time to discuss it later, but right now I need to concentrate. I don't have the same sensitivity to various energies as Senn does, so this'll be hard enough without all the inevitable screaming in the background as she slices you open."

Issai smirked at the affronted look Korin shot Hahri as he accepted the other boy's hands.

"I'll try to send as much emotion as I can down the Bond," Issai said. "Try to focus on that and my heartbeat."

"How will I know if I managed to transmigrate?"

Issai frowned thoughtfully. "When you open your eyes and see your own face looking back," he replied with a shrug. "It's not like I felt my soul move or anything like that. Just open your eyes when you feel my presence around you as keenly as you did when I was within your body."

Hahri nodded and closed his eyes. Issai did the same.

For a long while, the only sounds in the room were their soft exhales and the thumping of his own heart. Issai tried to emote his desire for Hahri to succeed as hard as he could, hoping it would be enough of a beacon for the other boy to latch onto. He avoided paying too much attention to Hahri's presence; he didn't want to accidentally move his soul into Hahri's body instead.

An eternity later, Hahri's emotions suddenly surged into him as if somewhere a dam had finally broken, the foremost, a deep sense of frustration. At that point, Issai expected his eyes to fly open, but other than Hahri's emotions swirling within him as chaotically as the winds of a hurricane, his body still remained in his own control as evidence of Hahri's hands tightening around his own.

Maybe he doesn't have the ability after all. Or... Issai paused in sudden realization. *...or it's* me *that's the problem.* He allowed Hahri's growing aggravation to flow through him without restriction while willing himself to relax his body even more.

"Why can't I do it!" Issai's mouth suddenly shouted at the same time his eyes opened to the sight of Hahri's completely placid face.

A short burst of shock rocked his senses, and then Issai's lips stretched into a wide grin before letting out a *whoop* of triumph. "Holy shit, I actually did it!"

Issai's mind was suddenly in real danger of being consumed by his partner's excitement. He frantically released the mental equivalent of a kick in the head and was relieved when Hahri's excitement almost instantly tapered down until it was replaced with sheepish concern.

"Sorry Senn," his own voice said contritely, sounding even stranger than when Issai had heard himself speak with Hahri's voice for the first time.

His hands slowly let go of Hahri's as the other boy took a few moments to stare at his now inert body just as Issai had the first time. "You're right; that's creepy as all hell," Hahri announced before slipping off the cot and turning to the other pair with a wide grin and a surge of almost child-like wonder.

Korin stared back at them with an expression that looked like alarm. "Seeing Senn grin like that gives me the shivers," the ancient monk admitted.

Hahri laughed in delight, and Issai had to admit that hearing those kinds of sounds coming out of his mouth made him want to do more than shudder at the utter *wrongness* of it.

"I wish there was a mirror in here," Hahri lamented. "I've always wanted to see what Senn would look like drunk and grinning like a maniac!"

Then Issai felt his face contort into what he imagined was that very expression as Korin looked so horrified that you would've thought Issai's body had suddenly sprouted horns, but it was the loud snort of amusement that seemed to have broken free unwittingly from Saiya's ostensibly impenetrable stone façade that was the last straw.

Outrage exploded through his entire being, and then Issai nearly fell over as the swiftness of the change of control of his body jolted his equilibrium for a few beats. He staggered a couple of steps, then turned to glare at the stationary body of his partner before remembering that the blasted jokester wasn't even in it.

However, his irritation instantly melted once he noticed the streams of pulsating lights swirling around Hahri's body, and more importantly, the absence of an undulating blue glow around it. He whipped his head around to look at Korin and Saiya. Their bodies were surrounded by the blue light particles exactly the same as before. Issai looked down at himself and the pulsating blue glow was just as dense as it had been when they had shared Hahri's body.

"Kye, get back into your body," he commanded without preamble, walking over to the other boy's body and clasping his now significantly cooler hands, resting his thumbs on Hahri's pulse points. "Just concentrate on feeling your heartbeat, and will yourself to merge with it. That's what worked for me."

Although not as quickly as he, Hahri managed to successfully reenter his body much more swiftly than it had taken him to leave it. It seemed he was starting to get the trick of it.

"*Saat*! It really does feel like my insides were starting to freeze!" Hahri griped, gripping the blankets more tightly around his visibly shivering body.

"You were only gone for a few moments," Issai scoffed, noting the lack of chattering teeth. "Just wait until it's an hour or so, then you'll really know pain."

"Did something happen?" Korin asked.

Issai nodded curtly. "When I took back control of my

body, I saw the streams of light again. Kye's body was no longer emitting the blue glow, but the rest of ours were, same as yesterday."

"That's probably because your soul beat mine down into submission after you got so irritated at me," Hahri said. Issai met his gaze, completely unrepentant. "It was the same feeling as when I withdraw myself consciously and cede complete control of the body to you. I could still see the light streams as clearly as I could while you were in control of my body."

"Did anything seem different when you were in control, or were you too busy playing the puppeteer with my body to notice?"

Hahri chuckled. "Consider me sufficiently chastised, but I wasn't being completely irresponsible. I did notice that the air felt strange as I walked around, denser, like I was trying to walk against a strong wind." He paused, scrunching up his face thoughtfully. "No—it was more like the pressure I feel when I'm running at top speed. Senn! Let me in again. I want to try something."

Issai stared back at him for a moment, then nodded and sat back down onto the cot. He thought he knew what the other boy was up to.

Several breaths later, Hahri was once again in control of Issai's body without any of his earlier difficulties and heading for the door.

"Where are you going?" Korin called after him as Hahri crossed the threshold.

"Just to the hall," Hahri assured him. "Wait here for a moment."

Hahri turned to look both ways down the long hall and then closed the door behind him after muttering, "Good, it's empty."

Then without warning, Hahri shot off to the left, and

in the blink of an eye, Issai's body jolted to a halt before the wall at the end. Then his body turned, and in the space of another blink, he was stopping in front of the wall at the opposite end. Both times, it felt as if his body barely even moved, as if he had only taken a couple of steps in either direction at the most.

Hahri's excitement flooded his being as Issai tried to make sense of what had just happened. He had figured that Hahri had wanted to see if he had the same incredible speed while using Issai's body, but what his partner just did had not felt like running at all. Except for those first couple of steps, the distance traveled had felt almost instantaneous.

Grinning that wide, uncomfortable grin, Hahri reentered their room. "I wanted to see if I could still run at the same speeds while in Senn's body," he told Korin before the curious blond could even open his mouth.

Hahri absently gestured across the length of the hall towards Korin with one arm as he spoke, and the ancient monk suddenly went flying backwards into the wall as if Hahri had shoved him hard. For a half-beat, they all froze in shock, and then Saiya jumped to her feet and drew her sword, wielding it threateningly at Issai and Hahri.

"Calm down!" Hahri cried, taking a step back from her. "That *wasn't* on purpose!" He looked back at Korin, who was still sprawled out awkwardly where he had fallen onto the cot, but didn't attempt to move closer. "*Saat*! I'm sorry! Are you all right?"

"I'm just—surprised," Korin assured him as he struggled to sit up.

Saiya's eyes darted over to the blond briefly then back to Issai's body. She watched them warily with unblinking eyes, both hands clutching the hilt of the sword so tightly that it quivered. Issai could sense their mutual relief that she had not yet attacked them, and with a startled realization, he wondered if a wound would appear on Hahri's body while his soul was away if she managed to cut him.

"You can put that up anytime," Hahri said as he cautiously stepped backwards towards the other cot, not daring to take his eyes off her. "I'm going back into my body now."

That utterly unexpected incident had rattled Hahri up enough that he had more trouble returning to his body this time. Issai was pretty rattled himself.

"Explain," Issai demanded as soon as he could move his limbs again.

Hahri tightened his grip on the blankets and met his gaze with an unreadable expression. "I'm not sure I can. I was just thinking about running down the hall when it happened. Just—talking," he finished helplessly.

"I did not see anything unusual, either," Korin added. The monk had finally managed to right himself and was seated in his original position on the edge of the cot. "I just suddenly felt like a huge gust of wind slammed into me. It did not hurt, and I did not hit the wall hard enough to bruise anything. As I said before, I was just startled."

"Well, it's not like I can exactly explain how I can suddenly see those streams of light when we're merged, either," Issai pointed out. "Maybe this is something like that. Also, when we were running down the hall, it didn't feel the same as the times when you carried me on your back."

Hahri frowned. "It did to me. What was it that you felt differently?"

"After the first step you took, I couldn't really feel us move at all," he replied. "Whereas the previous times, we were moving so fast that I was being pressed down against your back so hard I could barely breathe."

"Huh. No wonder you freaked out so much the first time I did it. I don't feel the pressure quite so badly, especially for that short of distance."

"That explains a lot of things," Issai said dryly, "namely how you could even run at all and for so long without your lungs collapsing with the strain to breathe. You weren't straining them at all."

"I wonder if what I just did to Korin is something I can do even when it's you who is doing the possessing?" Hahri mused. "I mean, you were in control of my body most of the time, and I doubt you just sat back and completely relinquished control to me when you weren't."

"No I didn't," Issai agreed with a wry smile. "That being said, until we figure this out, you might want to keep your gesturing to a minimum when we're within the same body. Korin was lucky you didn't take his head off."

A loud *click* had all three immediately looking at Saiya in alarm. Thankfully, it was just the sound of her sheathing her sword.

"I can't believe you don't see it," she said, looking at them all with an unreadable expression. At their blank looks, she added impatiently, "I would've thought what happened in that courtyard in Rihott was something that had seared itself permanently into what little brains you have."

Korin stiffened instantly, guilt clouding his eyes for a couple of beats at the memory, before the enormity of what she had said sunk in, and his eyes widened comically large. "You mean my Gods' Voice!"

Suddenly Saiya's violent reaction made perfect sense. Once upon a time, she had faced the power of Korin the Watcher's Gods' Voice, too. It wasn't something you wanted to experience twice.

"Can you only blast people with your voice?" Hahri asked, his eyes glittering with way too much excitement for Issai's piece of mind.

"No," Korin answered slowly. "It's sound that is at the core of my power. I tend to use words for the most part out of convenience, but I can just as easily clap my hands or stamp my foot against the ground and achieve much the same results. It's my mind, my will, which augments it into something destructive. However, I can always see the ripples in the air that accompany my release of power, and I did not see any of that as I was knocked backwards just now."

"Neither did I," Hahri said with a shrug. "It's not like I was thinking of hitting you, either. You just flew back without any warning. When you hit me with your Gods' Voice, I was facing away so I didn't see any of the ripples you mentioned, but I definitely *heard* you. I thought my ears were gonna rupture!"

"Your voice didn't sound any louder than normal," Issai informed him. "Nor did I sense any kind of movement in the air other than that caused by your—my—arm."

"Well, speculating can only get us so far," Hahri said. "We'll just have to experiment with it later, perhaps away from the temple so we don't accidentally hurt anyone."

At least their conversation seemed to have relieved some of the tension from Saiya. She was once again sitting on the cot and watching them all expressionlessly.

Issai got up and poured a mug of hot cider. Hahri blinked in surprise when it was handed to him.

"We still have a long time before we need to set out to Keison's boarding house," Issai responded to the question in those cerulean eyes, "and I have a feeling you'll

want your body to be completely recovered for what I
have in mind next."

CHAPTER SIXTEEN

"Are you sure you want to do this?" Hahri asked as Issai bundled himself in the extra blankets he had asked Korin to fetch for him.

A tinge of worry echoed along the Bond, and Issai looked back at the deceptively calm façade of the other boy in surprise. Something must really be troubling him for Hahri to feel enough worry that it was leaking through. After all the excitement he had been expressing earlier, it felt out of place.

"Do you want to tell me what's bothering you?" Issai said, ignoring the other's question for the moment.

Hahri made a sour face. "I didn't think I was being that obvious about it." His eyes flickered over to Korin and Saiya briefly. "Remember back when we were locked up in those cages?" he asked quietly.

"It's about ten thousand years too soon for me to forget," Issai replied dryly, wondering where the other boy was going with this. If he was reading his partner correctly, then this was something he was not comfortable talking about in front of the other pair.

Hahri's answering smile did not reach his eyes. "Remember what I was worried about then? It worries me even more so now."

Issai felt something tighten in his chest as some of Hahri's words from that time, forlorn and muted, surfaced in his mind. *"While I was certain we would be together in death if you were the one dying, the same is not necessarily true if I die first."*

"I take it you're worried that our souls will suddenly fly off once they are outside a physical body?" he assumed.

Hahri's lips thinned unhappily. "That's part of it, yes, but I'm more worried that it'll be because of something *I* screw up rather than the act of moving beyond the body, itself. I'm not as good at this transmigration stuff as you are. I could end up reborn on some island on the other side of the world that's impossible to leave, or perhaps not even able to be reborn at all!"

"Then I, alone, will try this first," Issai said firmly, staring back at Hahri challengingly.

The auburn-haired boy studied him for a long moment. "You really believe that this is something we have to do," he said finally.

"Unfortunately, yes," Issai replied despondently.

The corners of Hahri's lips turned up minutely. "Then I don't mind handing you my fate. If it's one thing I've learned in these past tendays, it's to trust your instincts."

"You shouldn't think so highly of me," Issai muttered uncomfortably, flashing the other a pained look.

They had discussed the possible methods at length earlier and had agreed that using their emotions might be the key. Issai closed his eyes and concentrated on his strongest emotion, currently his anxiety, while Hahri was hopefully clearing his mind and body of all thought and emotion that could potentially distract him through the Bond. He ignored the feel of his clothes against his skin, the scratchiness of the wool blanket clutched in his hands and against the back of his neck, the feel of the cot's hard edge pressing into the backs of his legs, everything that was interacting with his body down to the air he was breathing. Only when Issai had completely become an embodiment of his anxiety did he surge forward with all his might.

He had once had a container of hot wax knocked onto his bare arm. Like the light resistance and sudden release of his skin he had felt as the dried wax had been peeled off, something within his being seemed to peel away from whatever it had been stuck to.

What followed was complete and utter chaos.

Issai had not opened his eyes, but suddenly the darkness behind his lids had erupted into a bewildering world of flashing and shimmering lights that flowed and swirled and coalesced into various shapes like dust particles in a wind storm amidst a dimly glowing background of a startling color he could not name. At least that was Issai's initial thought.

It didn't take him more than a beat to realize how wrong that first perception was when he became conscious of the fact that he was sensing every single point of light and not just their movement. He instantly knew the position of each one simultaneously at each instant of time as naturally as a baby knew how to breathe at birth. He was also sensing the colors he perceived very similar to the way he sensed minute changes in the air when something moved around him. Red caused more of a disturbance than blue but slightly less than purple.

However, it was the perhaps trillions of *very familiar*

glittering particles of blue light that seemed to hover before him to about a pace out from where he stood that had captured his undivided attention. Issai had the desire to look to the left, and his field of perception was instantly pointed in that direction.

The blue light also extended away in that direction for about three paces, and he immediately focused on the inside edge of it where an undulating mix of various-colored light streams seemed to thinly outline a large concentration of countless individual particles of sparkling, golden light. A second, similar concentration of chaotic streams and particles lay closely to its left just outside the expansion of blue light, though its overall shape was a bit longer. That's when Issai finally understood what he was seeing.

Feeling more excitement than he could ever remember feeling throughout all his many lives, Issai willed his perception to the opposite direction and was rewarded with a second pair of the same type of golden concentrations within a cloud of thick, blue illumination like two burning embers stuck in a sea of molasses. That settled it. This was what the others, the room, looked like through the perceptions of a soul without a body.

Issai needed to speak, but as was true whenever he shared a body with Hahri, he could not while in soul form. He needed to get back into his body. As soon as the desire to return had entered his mind, Issai instantly found his soul almost on top of the concentration of light streams and particles that was his body. He willed himself into that golden configuration, wondering if that alone would re-attach his soul into his body. He no longer had hands in which to grip his body, and in this new state of being, he was unsure how to even begin to sense something as corporeal as a heartbeat.

In the space of a heartbeat, Issai found himself surrounded by the golden particles that composed his body. A flash of what felt like "green" had entered his perception, mixed within the golden illumination for the smallest fraction of that same beat, before it seemed to stick to him with all the consistency of a sheet composed entirely of spider silk.

That was when the cold hit him, something so familiar and *real* that Issai could not help but gasp as though it was the first breath taken after nearly drowning. Unlike his previous transmigrations, his heart hurt as if it had suddenly received the worst jolt of fright he had ever experienced. He gripped a tight fist against the center of his chest and bent slightly over it in an unconscious attempt for relief.

"I was beginning to wonder if you were gonna come back," he heard Hahri say through the harsh sound of his heavy breathing.

Only when Issai slowly lifted his head in response did he realize that his eyes were still closed. His lids felt heavy and totally alien as he opened them, his thoughts fuzzy and disoriented. It was as though his equilibrium had been completely thrown off. His vision, however, was sur-prisingly quite clear as he looked back at the very blatant look of worry on Hahri's face.

Focusing on Hahri's face helped to center himself again. "I-I wasn't out *that* l-long," he wheezed.

"Yes, you were," Hahri insisted with a frown. "It's been nearly an hour since I first saw your soul glide out of your body. It stopped in the middle of the room, just shimmering and floating seemingly in midair until a few beats ago when it glided back into your body."

The remaining fog instantly cleared from his mind as Issai narrowed his eyes sharply at the other boy in disbelief. "That's a-absurd! It f-felt like less th-than a q-quarter-hour!"

"I'm sorry, but Kye is right," Korin spoke up hesitantly. "It really has been about an hour."

"Look at the way you're shivering, Senn," Hahri continued. "Your own body can tell you the truth of it better than us."

Issai's gaze immediately fell down to the hands that gripped the blankets tightly closed over the middle of his chest. They were trembling worse than a ninety-year-old with palsy even though the cold, itself, seemed no worse than the first time he had experienced it. The ache still present in his chest was also something he had not experienced before, but he had also never been outside his body for such a long period of time. Rather than a consequence of his soul leaving his body so forcefully, perhaps these new symptoms were simply time related.

"It r-really didn't f-feel that l-long," he insisted weakly.

Hahri shrugged, though his eyes still held a hint of worry. "Maybe for you, it wasn't—in the same way time can seem to stop for me when I'm running."

Issai nodded slowly. "Maybe," he agreed. "Once my s-soul left my body, m-my perceptions of e-everything changed so m-much that I'm n-not even sure I c-can really d-describe it a-accurately."

Hahri's eyes briefly lit up with a burst of excitement, but then he shook his head and smiled a bit ruefully. "As much as I'm dying to hear what it was like, you really need some hot cider first. You're much too pale for my liking. We can fill you in on what we saw in the meantime."

Issai downed one whole mug and was sipping on another before Hahri stopped fussing over him enough to settle himself back down onto the cot. He must have looked really bad. At least the ache in his chest had eased almost completely.

"It really was just like Keison described," Hahri said. "I can see why he had such a hard time telling us about it. It was like looking at the shimmering heat coming off the desert sand in the distance."

"Could you see something of my face?" Issai asked. He was pleased that his voice no longer trembled.

"At times, I could almost make out features like a nose, mouth, or eyes, but not very clearly, and I didn't want to move closer to get a better look. I really didn't want to find out what would happen if I accidentally touched your soul. That seems like a taboo that should never be broken. Anyway, you didn't even have the shape of a man, just a shimmering blob about the size of a torso."

Issai made a face. "That really does sound like something out of all the old myths about spirits and demons. Then again, we Old Souls have been around for a long time, haven't we…"

"That is a good description for what I saw, as well," Korin said, "almost like something that was barely in the mortal plane of existence."

"If so, then I wonder if everyone can see it, or just us Old Souls?" Hahri mused. "After all, some of the old tales say that only those 'touched by the gods' or cursed can see various spirits or monsters." He turned to Korin and grinned mischievously. "Maybe we can glide up and down the halls during the night sometime and see if any of the monks see us."

Korin instantly looked horrified. "You will have the whole of the temple convinced they are being attacked by evil spirits!"

"Would you rather us go out into the marketplace

first?" Hahri countered, the laughter in his eyes belying the seriousness of his tone. "This is something we really need to know."

"That might be even worse!"

"Fine, fine," Hahri said with a roll of his eyes. "A tavern would be a much better place, anyway. A few drunks raving about seeing spirits would hardly raise any eyebrows there."

The relief on the monk's face was almost comical. Apparently, Korin still hadn't learned to recognize when Hahri was deliberately trying to get a rise out of him.

However, the expression on Hahri's face when he turned his attention back to Issai was a lot more serious. "Speaking of gliding, I'm pretty surprised that I didn't see you move around more. What were you doing 'standing' so still for so long? Or was it that you were just having trouble moving?"

Issai shook his head. "I was just taking everything in. If you thought the currents of light particles we saw earlier were confusing and dazzling, then I would say it's infinitely so while in pure soul form. Since I obviously wasn't 'seeing' with my eyes, the best I can say is that my perception of this room and you three was more a matter of sensing everything in a way that's similar to how I perceive movement while in my body.

"By knowing where every single light particle all around me was, my best guess is that my mind constructed an image of what the light streams, plus everyone in the room, looked like based on all my visual memories. Colors had their own distinct 'feel.' There were even some that I had never seen before, that I could never, even if I lived a billion more centuries, hope to describe to you. I wasn't actually 'seeing' anything, per se, just perceptions interpreted by my mind."

"I hope you know that none of that made any kind of sense whatsoever," Hahri said. "I can't even begin to wrap my head around the idea of my sight and my sense of touch or even sense of movement being one and the same."

"That's probably because I'm not explaining this very well," Issai replied with a frustrated sigh. "I mean, what is 'color' anyway? I've known many people over the years that could not see shades of red or green as anything other than gray. Was there something wrong with their eyes? Perhaps it was something gone awry in their brain or even their very soul? Who's to say that you would even 'see' the same thing as I?"

Hahri shrugged. "I've never had that problem, so the gods only know. I guess I'll just have to experience it for myself before I can truly understand. I have a few more questions first, the most important being whether or not you ever felt like your soul was being pulled away from here?"

"Not even once. When I pulled my soul from my body, I actually felt like I had peeled myself away from something or other. It wasn't painful or anything. If you've ever dribbled hot wax on your skin and then peeled it off once it had dried, then the sensation is comparable. After that, any movement was simply a matter of will, of knowing what space I wanted to occupy or what direction I wanted to focus my perceptions on.

"When I wanted to return to my body, I merely had to think of myself within it and my soul instantly complied. Whatever I had detached my soul from when I left my body seemed to cling back onto me without any conscious effort on my part. Only then did I start to feel my body again, to feel the cold."

"Hmm," Hahri hummed thoughtfully. "That doesn't

sound too bad."

"It's just as easy as transmigrating into another body," Issai agreed. "However, actually moving around as just a soul will probably take a while to get used to. After all, we don't even know how far we can safely travel away from our bodies and probably a hundred other things I haven't even thought of yet."

"What did we look like to a soul's 'eye'?" Korin asked.

"I could still 'see' the blue glow for one thing," Issai said, the edges of his lips curving up as he took in everyone's startled looks, "but in much more detail. It made me think that perhaps we were a bit premature in discounting it as the source of the Bond."

"How so?" Saiya demanded sharply. As always, the mere mention of the Bond had the silent girl suddenly remembering her ability to speak.

"It's because I didn't see the blue glow only around you three individually. This time I could see that it was like a single, misshapen cloud of undulating light particles that surrounded Kye and me—my soul, not my body—completely, and another, less dense cloud that surrounded you two. I don't know why Kye and I didn't see that connection before when we shared a single body, but maybe it's as simple as a matter of different perceptions." He absently ran a hand through his hair. "I suppose the only way to know for sure if it has anything to do with the Bond is for me to watch Korin and Saiya move away then closer to each other and see if anything noticeably changes."

Issai turned to Hahri and continued, "When I looked at our bodies sitting on the cot, I was really surprised to see that, other than the blue glow, they looked almost identical. You know how when you look up at the sun in a cloudless sky around midday, you can sometimes see a rainbow of colors along the outer edges of the golden-white illumination? That's what it reminded me of while I was looking at us through my soul's eyes. Only, instead of a clear sky, it was through a thin cloud of blue fog.

"So my question is—am I really seeing the Bond, or did it just appear as if there was a connection because we were all either sitting, or hovering in my case, too close to each other? That's why, Kye," Issai said carefully, in an almost guilty way, "I also want to see you as a pure soul while in the same form."

Hahri's shoulders immediately tensed. "Did you feel any kind of pain while you were over there in the middle of the room?" he asked.

Issai blinked in surprise. That was not at all the question he had expected.

"You mean the proximity pain?" Hahri nodded. "Actually, I don't remember feeling any pain at all. That's not to say that I didn't, what with my senses being bombarded by so many alien things from every direction."

"Believe me, you would've noticed it, regardless," Hahri said with a grimace. "The moment you became visible as a soul, my pain tripled. I've never felt it that bad, not even when we were dying in that cart, and I didn't think anything could top that. It almost felt like you were trying to drag my soul to you by force. The pain didn't go back to normal levels until you were back in your body. I find it strange that the same thing didn't happen while we shared a body. The pain got worse, yes, but no where near the intensity of this time."

"I don't *think* I did anything to cause that," Issai replied, his voice sounding unsure to his own ears. "Are you worried something worse will happen if you and I are outside our bodies at the same time?"

Hahri pursed his lips unhappily. "I hate to be the wet

rag this time, but you have to admit, it's possible."

"Why don't you try moving your soul from your body alone first," Issai suggested. "Let's see if it causes me to feel the same kind of rise in pain and go from there."

Hahri nodded slowly. "That would probably be best. Besides, there's no guarantee I'll be able to do it at all on the first try."

"Take your time. It'll give me a chance to thaw out properly."

It took Hahri three attempts spread out over two hours of increasing frustration and pointers from Issai before he finally succeeded. Rather than emerge slowly from his chest as Issai had expected, the rippling distortion in the air was just suddenly in front of him between one breath and the next. It was just as large as Hahri had described earlier and transparent enough that he could still easily see both Korin and Saiya through it. He thought he could discern the faint lines of a face within the ripples, but nothing really definitive enough to know who he was looking at if he hadn't already known.

For a few beats as he stared at Hahri's soul in fascination, Issai felt a slight surge in his proximity pain, but once he focused all of his attention on it, it tapered down to the barely there ache he always felt when Hahri was that close to him. That small twinge proved that there was definitely something strange happening with the Bond, but he wondered why Hahri had had a much more adverse reaction. The thought made him that much more eager to see his bond partner's soul with a soul's perception.

It also made him wonder if Hahri would be able to hear him speak in that state. He, himself, did not remember hearing anything at all, but no one had even attempted to speak to him. Plus, there was the chance that he *had* been hearing the natural sounds of their breathing or shifting in a way he did not know how to interpret yet.

He really didn't want to wait.

"Kye, if you can hear me," Issai said to the transparent blob hovering before him, "I did feel a small surge in pain for a few beats when you first appeared, but once I focused on it, it leveled off to what I normally feel at this distance from you. If nothing adverse has happened on your end, then I would really like to join you as a soul right now. If you're fine with it, then move over to the door, and if not, then get back into your body so we can discuss it."

For a long moment, Hahri's soul just hovered in the same spot, before finally gliding over to the door. Issai was relieved.

He turned to the other two. "Once I'm out of my body," he said to Korin, "can you speak to me a little? Kye obviously heard me somehow. I want to know what talking sounds like to a soul."

The blond nodded. "Of course."

As an added precaution, Issai scooted himself back on the cot to the far corner. He wanted as much distance between them when his soul emerged as he could manage.

Even though he knew what to expect, it was still a shock to his whole being when the dark world behind his eyelids exploded into the shimmering light world of a soul. He took a couple of beats to reorient himself before seeking out Hahri's soul in the direction of the door.

What Issai "saw" was nothing he could have ever imagined.

Instead of the concentration of golden particles he had half-expected, a smaller, seemingly writhing oval of dense light that was slightly less curved on the left side, shining more white than blue, was nestled centrally within the far edge of the cloud of blue light particles that still surrounded both of them. About the size of a dinner plate, it was a node that seemed to warp the blue particle-filled space around it like a heavy object sinking into a smoothed out sheet, causing the material to wrinkle.

He willed his soul to look back at his own body, then Hahri's body beside him. They both still shined as brilliantly as a pile of gold coins in the sun. Then Issai turned his attention to study Korin and Saiya for a moment before re-focusing on Hahri's soul. As he had thought, he definitely could not see even a hint of that dense, blue-white mass through the golden particles. It reminded him of a fruit pit, unseen until the "meat" was stripped away. In this case, the meat was the golden light particles that constituted their physical bodies.

Upon closer scrutiny, Issai "saw" that it was in fact shining purely white in its center, gradually adding a blue tone as it shined outward until it seemed to meld perfectly into the much larger blue mass of particles around it. He also realized that the flickering concentration of innumerable blue light particles were not moving randomly at all, but clearly moving with a purpose, moving very slowly towards that nucleus of white and blue that was so brilliant he would have surely gone blind with one glimpse had he viewed it with his physical eyes. It was like looking into a million suns.

The closer the blue particles got to that dense nucleus, the more slowly and erratically they flowed until they either were absorbed or destroyed by that brilliant light—Issai couldn't really tell which. They just ceased to exist to what he was coming to think of as his "soul sense."

Wanting a closer look, Issai willed his soul to slowly

move towards Hahri's. Along with the normal lessening of his proximity pain, it also seemed to excite the blue particles a bit, like throwing a small pebble in the middle of a swarm of ants, but it wasn't until he was about an arms-length from Hahri's soul that he saw something that made his whole being freeze in shock. The rippling outer edges along the less curvy left side of that blue-white nucleus had noticeably started to stretch towards him until he could start to make out the individual particles of light that formed it. It looked somewhat like a piece of potter's clay being stretched too thin.

The way some of the particles in that distorted portion of Hahri's soul moved was different than the whole; they looked to be resisting the pull, trying to stretch back into their proper place. Feeling a sense of dread, Issai willed his soul forward a fraction and saw quite a few of the resisting particles lose their battle and begin to stretch towards him again, quivering like a rope pulled too taunt but with not enough force to snap.

Now that Issai was focused entirely on that one area, he noticed that the blue particles in a portion of the space between their souls about the width of his forearm were different, not only moving more languidly, but also a slightly lighter shade.

—and all quivering as if straining towards his soul.

Seeing all of that was the moment Issai finally understood what was probably causing their proximity pain. He had stepped into this plane of existence where souls resided hoping to discover the secrets of the Bond, only to have his worst fears about it confirmed.

CHAPTER SEVENTEEN

"D-did you s-see it?" Issai asked as soon as he saw Hahri lift his head to look at him.

The other boy's eyes were unfocused, his movements lethargic, like someone who was either drunk or had been abruptly awakened in the dead of night. Judging by how spectacularly bad he felt, they must have been outside their bodies even longer than the hour Issai had taken before. Keison had said that Noll had stayed outside his body for several hours. He must have felt as if he had been sleeping under a snow bank all night afterwards.

Damn but he was getting tired of the cold.

"I-I d-did—m-maybe even m-more s-so than y-you," Hahri replied, teeth chattering as well. "I a-assume you s-still w-weren't able t-to see a-anything of y-yourself?" Issai shook his head. "D-did m-my soul l-look egg-shaped, t-too?"

"Y-yes, the c-core of it, a-anyway. At th-this point, I'm p-pretty sure th-that the b-blue glow s-surrounding us is p-part of the s-soul, t-too, if n-not exactly w-why."

216

Hahri nodded. "I think so, too," he articulated slowly, making an obvious effort to control the trembling in both his voice and body. "The reason why I asked about the sh-shape is because part of your 'core,' as you c-call it, looked wrong. It just seemed to b-bulge out too much on the right side, making the whole of it look unnaturally asymmetrical. I d-don't know what you saw exactly, but when you m-moved closer and I saw what was happening to all the b-blue light particles between us, the way they were straining t-towards your soul core, the differences in the p-pain we share suddenly made perfect s-sense."

Issai winced. "Once I g-got a closer l-look, I d-did think that the left s-side of your c-core looked a bit w-warped, and that's w-why I moved even c-closer, just to see w-what would happen."

"And the warping got worse, didn't it?"

Issai just grimaced.

Hahri's answering smile was gentler than Issai thought he deserved. "When you moved away to go back to your b-body, I watched the space between us c-carefully, and sure enough, many of those lighter blue light p-particles began to strain towards *me* right in accordance to the f-fading of my proximity pain. It's no wonder that we can find no r-real relief from it. It's very evident that a piece of my s-soul somehow got stuck to yours, and when it d-did, it didn't completely detach from me. It appears as if we've been b-battling each other over it ever since."

Issai closed his eyes and pinched the bridge of his nose in agitation. "I can't p-possibly see how it h-happened."

"Nor I, but doesn't it remind you of s-something?"

He stared at Hahri blankly for a long moment before his eyes widened in sudden comprehension. "Keison!"

"Yes. Those invisible chains of his may very w-well be

made of pieces of his own soul that Soujin s-somehow has the ability to pull out at will."

"That still d-doesn't explain how a p-piece of *your* soul ended up attached t-to *mine*," Issai said dejectedly, "because I s-sure as the three hells d-didn't reach into your chest, p-pull out a chunk, and s-stick it to my soul like I was p-patching a damn hole in m-my shirt!"

Issai's tirade was cut short by the sudden appearance of a steaming mug in front of his face. He automatically grabbed the mug with both hands and turned to see Korin looking back at him as if he had a billion things to say and was about to burst from the effort of keeping silent up until now.

"Thanks," he muttered, downing it gratefully in almost one gulp as Korin handed a mug to Hahri as well. He shuttered as the warm liquid coated his insides.

The blond looked between them both as they drank with an expression that looked as guilty as Issai felt before he finally said, "If all what you just said holds true, then do you believe that carrying a piece of Kye's soul, how-ever inadvertently, is the only thing that binds you together?"

Issai and Hahri looked at each other with what were probably identical expressions of startlement.

"I don't think so," Hahri answered before Issai could even open his mouth. "You and Saiya don't feel pain, only an annoying vibration, or 'buzzing' as Saiya puts it, within, correct?"

"As long as we are not touching, yes."

"Well, maybe Senn and I would feel separation the same way if the pain of trying to rip out each other's souls wasn't so overwhelming. After all, when I'm far away from him, I still feel a dull throb that, while not par-ticularly painful, is annoying as all hell. Also, at no time did I see that blue glow that encompasses us separate. It was pretty uniform except in the place where our soul cores are connected. Even when Senn moved away to return to his body, it just seemed to expand in the center to accommodate the distance. Our soul cores were pretty much like two yolks nestled within a single eggshell. We'll have to separate for greater distances as well as get a look at you two in your soul forms to be sure, but I think the Bond lies within those blue particles. The how or why of it—your guess is as good as mine."

"So what you're saying is that you *still* have no idea how to rid me of this damn buzzing," Saiya interjected disgustedly.

Issai instinctually stiffened and eyed her warily, wondering if she was about to snap, but thankfully, her hands were gripping the edges of the cot in agitation rather than reaching for her sword.

"I think the better question at this point is whether or not we can somehow detach the piece of Hahri's soul core fused to my own without damaging either one of us," Issai said carefully. "Anything else would be a moot point if we can't even accomplish that."

"Then what are you waiting for?" Saiya demanded.

"My body to defrost, for one," Hahri replied acidly.

"Not to mention you two haven't even tried to transmigrate your souls into each other's bodies, much less move outside of them completely," Issai added pointedly. "We can't do anything if we can't even *see* the whole of your souls."

"I would rather set myself on fire than share the same body with him!" Saiya hissed, pointing at Korin sharply as if she were thrusting her sword into him. "We can just move our souls completely out of our bodies and be done with it!"

219

"Whatever," Hahri said with a roll of his eyes.

She jumped to her feet, her blazing eyes zeroing in on the monk. "We're going next door."

As she stalked to the door, Korin hastily stepped in front of her. "Wait! I have something else to ask them, first."

The look on her face would have made a lesser man soil his pants.

Korin turned to Issai and asked, "Did you hear me speak?"

For half a beat, Issai had no idea what the monk was talking about before he sucked in his breath sharply in sudden realization. In all the excitement, he had forgotten all about his request to the monk. No, he didn't hear him, but he had been so focused on the horror of realizing he actually *had* stolen a piece of Hahri's soul that he doubted anything else would have registered.

He shook his head and turned to Hahri. "Did you hear him, Kye?"

"No, but it wasn't like I heard you either."

Issai started. "What? Then how did you know I wanted you to move to the door?" he demanded.

Hahri pursed his lips thoughtfully. "The same way we can sometimes read each other's emotions—through the Bond—except, while in soul form, it's more like I'm reading your intent rather than just a few of your stronger emotions. I just suddenly felt like I should move to the door, so I did."

"I never sensed anything like that from you."

"That's because I was just watching your soul. I didn't try to communicate with you at any time because I could tell you were really bothered by the soul core thing, and I didn't want to set you on edge any more than you already were."

"That certainly will make things easier," Issai said. "Not being able to communicate properly while in soul form was to getting to be a real pain in the ass."

Hahri glanced over at Saiya, who was glaring impatiently at them all. "It's probably about six lines past midday, so we should probably get something to eat and rest up before going out to spy on Keison," he said to Issai.

"Don't even think about it," Saiya warned, narrowing her eyes at Korin as the monk started to speak. "*You* aren't going anywhere except next door with me."

"Go," Hahri urged him when the monk hesitated, "but remember what we warned you about the other day. I don't want to find myself pulled into another one of her memories mid-bite."

The main road was a lot more crowded than Issai had anticipated as he made his way towards the Merchant District. It was already a couple of hours after sunset and the road was just as crowded with people, carts, and animals as it was in the early morning. He kept to the edges, watching the flow of people carefully from beneath the folds of his black hood.

Issai was even more paranoid about ambushes on this outing than he usually was because this time he carried the soul of his bond partner within him. That's probably why Hahri had been surprised when he had requested it of him. Issai had wanted to observe Keison with his newly discovered "soul-vision," but was not yet comfortable with wandering around the city as just a soul. Plus, he would have an extra ability or two at his disposal should it become necessary to flee from an enemy. Hahri could just take over his body, and they could be back at the temple in a blink of an eye.

Following Novice Devin's directions, upon reaching the boarding house, Issai was pleased to see that Keison's room did indeed have a window, and as a bonus, the area beneath the sill was so overgrown with thick weeds that he would be able to easily conceal himself within them in the darkness. He would also be perfectly positioned to see the street.

The room was still dark; they had beaten the blond teen to the boarding house just as they'd hoped, but with any luck, they wouldn't have to wait for very long for Keison to show up. Issai didn't want to find out what it felt like to have a fidgeting soul within him.

However, it seemed Issai waited within the weeds for half the night before he saw the hunched over figure of Keison slowly walking along the street towards the main entrance of the boarding house, one hand carrying a small lantern and the other clutching at his shirt as if someone had just stabbed him in the chest. A wave of concern washed through him briefly, letting him know that Hahri had also taken note of it.

"We need to see things now through our souls' eyes," Issai whispered.

He braced himself and within a couple of breaths, the night all around him exploded into the by-now-familiar streams of light particles. He was momentarily distracted when he noticed that the weeds all around him were giving off a faint, barely yellow glow, writhing and pulsating just like the blue particles that composed a portion of their souls.

But then the window above him abruptly flooded with an orange glow, and Issai shook himself out of his fascination. They would have plenty of time later to observe the world through their soul-vision.

Keison was currently gripping the edge of a desk tightly where he had set his lantern down as if he had just caught himself before he could fall to the floor. Then the boy lowered himself to his knees with a moan that was audible from where Issai crouched, watching, and he wrapped his arms tightly around his torso, his face a rictus of pain.

Frowning, Issai stared hard at the trembling body, trying to see if anything was different about the blue glow surrounding Keison's body, but it looked no different than it had when he last saw it that morning. Now that he knew what he was looking for, he had hoped to see a hint of Keison's "invisible chains," but either they were simply not there, or it was something that could only be seen while in pure soul form.

Suddenly, Keison shrieked and fell over onto his side like a sack of flour that had been kicked over, balling up into a fetal position. He began to writhe along the floorboards as though he was having some sort of fit, except he was screaming and pulling at his shirt as if the material was burning him.

"Please stop! Soujin please! Please *stop*!" Keison begged, but whatever the malicious bastard was doing to him didn't seem to wane in the least.

Issai completely expected the Old Soul in question to walk into view at any moment from the shadows, but as Keison screamed and screamed, the room showed itself to be truly empty of anyone else. Issai wondered if Soujin could sense the amount of distress he was causing the boy, or if the mere knowledge of what he was doing to Keison was enough to amuse him.

A burst of anxiety through the Bond rocked Issai's senses for a moment, but he shook his head with a grimace and whispered, "There's nothing we can do for him right now."

Not so much as a cricket chirped in the unnatural stillness that had suddenly fallen all around the building once those bloodcurdling screams had begun. The only thing that made sense as to why none of Keison's fellow boarders came running to investigate was that this was not the first or even the second time he had screamed like this. Perhaps even the boy, himself, had warned his neighbors that he would do this on occasion, passing the episodes off as night terrors.

Issai's heart clenched painfully as the hard sobs woven within the screams and pleas for mercy reached his ears. When Keison had told them about the attacks, he had never imagined that they were this bad. He had a fleeting thought of asking Hahri to leave his body to scrutinize Keison with a soul's eye, but then immediately discarded it as fruitless. They probably wouldn't be able to see anything else until Keison moved his soul out of his body, anyway. Issai had seen and heard enough for now.

"Let's go," he muttered to Hahri, trying to convey his feelings on the matter through the Bond, "but stay as you are. I want to watch everyone who crosses our path on the way back. Maybe we can spot the Old Soul Keison seems to think resides in the city before Soujin does."

Issai carefully moved away from the window and back to the street, all the while trying to ignore the screams at his back. Nevertheless, they still echoed keenly in his ears long past the point when distance should have silenced them.

Once back along the main road, the sight of the handful of people still trekking along through the darkness of the moonless night made the hairs on his arms stand up. The way the writhing, blue glow that surrounded each figure and the chaotic streams of light particles that saturated the air looked in the normal gloom of night made Issai feel as if he were watching some eerie parade of the dead as they silently moved passed him.

Although the wind gusted strongly enough to occasionally threaten his balance, it did not seem to affect any of those light streams or the fog-like glow emanating from the night's pedestrians and his own body. Faced with such a contradiction of logic, if not for Hahri's confirmation, Issai could have easily believed that they were the hallucinations of a mind that had finally cracked.

Adding to his sense of dread as he headed back towards the temple were the three illuminated figures he could clearly see hiding behind a partially crumbled perimeter wall of one of the corner properties up ahead. Issai was fairly certain that they would have been completely hidden in the darkness if not for his enhanced vision.

It was times like this that he absolutely loathed having such a small stature. It showed that he was still young enough to be a desirable mark for slavers and perverts and suspicious enough for any *Shi* scouring the crowds.

He had no way of knowing which of the three the ones waiting in ambush were or if they were simply thieves watching for the perfect victim. The only thing he was certain of was that the density of the blue glow around each of them was nowhere near that of an Old Soul, and as far as he was concerned, it was the only point that mattered. He would not play the victim tonight.

A sudden idea had him smirking. "Hahri, take control," he said under his breath. "I think—"

A slight distortion in the air was his only warning, and Issai instantly whipped around mid-word, a knife already in his hand, just as a large body collided with him with all the force of a battering ram. With a startled grunt, Issai's back slammed into the ground hard, the heavy body that fell with him knocking out what little air remained in his lungs. As he gasped for air, wet warmth gushed over the hand caught between their two bodies, fingers still gripping the knife handle tightly.

The body above him shuddered and coughed wetly, warm droplets of what was probably blood spraying like a fine mist across his face. Issai cursed in disgust and struggled to push the flailing, blue-glowing mass off him. A surge of energy suddenly flooded his body, giving him the extra strength he needed to finally shove the body off to the side. He felt the knife jerk in his hand as the momentum tore the blade free from the flesh with a meaty *squish*, his attacker letting out a gurgled scream that sounded as though his head was underwater.

Issai staggered to his feet and quickly backed away from the body convulsing on the road, eyes darting all around for more attackers as he hastily drew his hood back over his head with his free hand. The street was now surprisingly empty, the only sounds coming from his attacker choking on his own blood and the faint whistle of the wind. Even the three people lying in ambush up ahead had stayed put.

His eyes fell back onto the dying man at his feet. A lone wolf, perhaps?

The blue glow surrounding the man seemed to be rippling more wildly than before as if mimicking the panic their attacker was surely feeling as his life poured out of him from the visibly gaping wound going diagonally from chest to the side of his belly that the man futilely tried to staunch with both hands. A pulse of surprise, then rising excitement flooded strongly through Issai's being at that moment. Perhaps Hahri had noticed it as well.

Instead of getting the hell out of there before the

Guard showed up, Issai watched the dying man with uncharacteristic fascination. The blue, visible portion of his soul seemed to be getting discerningly less dense, slowly fading like the fog it resembled. It disappeared completely a few moments later. Yet, the man still continued to weakly suck in a dozen or so more stilted, tortured breaths before his life, too, faded completely away with a final rasp.

Even then, Issai could not tear his eyes away from the now dead body. He had never once seen the various colored streams of light particles interact at all with anyone, even the regular patrons of the temple. They had never come nearer than a hand-span from the edges of the blue portion of the soul, as if somehow repellant to each other. Now the streams seemed to flow into and out of the still body as unobstructedly as they had through the walls of their room. It was as if the dead man wasn't even there.

A slight distortion in the air had Issai sharply looking towards the south.

"*Now* switch with me," Issai muttered as several running forms became visible along the road in the distance. He glanced up ahead to the crumbled wall and was surprised to see his audience of three still had not fled. "This is our cue to 'disappear,' don't you think?"

CHAPTER EIGHTEEN

"Perhaps we should rest a bit," Korin suggested worriedly as he watched his bond partner's face turn increasingly redder with both effort and frustration.

Saiya's eyes snapped open, and she actually growled at him like a feral beast that had abruptly been disturbed. "Unless you want me to remove your soul from your body with my blade, then you'd better get back to it," she snarled.

"It's almost morning," Korin persisted. "Senn and Kye have probably returned from watching Keison. We should at least go to them to ask for further instruction. After hours of trying, I fear I am no closer to consciously transmigrating my soul than when I first began. I simply do not understand how they can so easily become aware of their souls. I do not believe we can do this alone."

Saiya's eyes narrowed angrily, but rather than the scathing retort he had expected, she nodded curtly and headed for the door without a word. She must have been really frustrated to agree to his suggestion without a fuss.

Korin stepped out of the room in enough time to see her kick the two teens' door open with unnecessary force. He winced as it banged rather loudly against the wall, wondering if any of his Brothers would come to investigate. After the ruckus that Saiya had caused a few days ago, Korin had urged them to ignore any further commotion coming from their two rooms, but he was not completely confident that they would, especially if they thought his safety was in jeopardy.

His thoughts were interrupted by the harsh curses coming from the room, and he hurried over in enough time to see Kye on the floor next to his cot still wrestling with the blanket that had somehow become knotted around his legs. Senn was crouched on the other cot, shirtless, with both knives clutched in his hands. His violet eyes were fixed on Saiya, looking a bit wild and dangerous.

Korin was a little alarmed to see a crumpled shirt on the floor beside Senn's cot, stained dark with what looked like dried blood. His gaze darted back to Senn, but the dark-haired Old Soul's chest looked uninjured. Considering Senn's ability to heal, it wasn't as reassuring a sight as it should've been.

"Dammit, kid! That's a good way to get your throat cut!" Kye groused, drawing Korin's attention back to the other boy before he could ask about the shirt. Kye had finally managed to untangle himself, and he dropped back down onto the cot with a sniff of derision.

Korin shot them both an apologetic look as he stepped farther into the room and shut the door. "I am so sorry to have woken you. I would not have disturbed you if I had known."

Hahri shook his head. "No need for *you* to apologize, monk. Is it time for breakfast?"

"No, not for another hour, yet," Korin replied. Out of the corner of his eye, he saw Senn return his knives into the small sheaths strapped to his forearms and slowly settle himself on the edge of his cot. He was relieved. Although infinitely more stable than Saiya, it was times like these that Korin was blatantly reminded that these two "teens" were also considerably more deadly when they chose. "We were coming for some advice, actually."

Kye smirked knowingly. "Still can't move your souls out of your bodies, huh? No wonder the kid is glaring daggers at us."

"That's why I told you to try transmigrating into each other's bodies first," Issai interjected impatiently. "It's much easier to get the feel of it that way."

"*No*," Saiya said forcefully, turning her glare to the black-haired boy, who just stared back at her stoically.

Kye sighed noisily. "If you insist on being so stubborn about it, then at least try to feel out the Bond again; try to sense each other's emotions. It shouldn't be too hard for you, monk, seeing as Saiya seems to be perpetually pissed off. That's one emotion you won't mistake for your own. Then once you get a feel for that foreign emotion, try to move towards it as if you were walking without actually moving physically."

"That is the part I cannot really understand," Korin admitted. "How to move without moving."

Kye shrugged. "Well, it's not something I can properly explain, either. It's more instinct than anything. Senn naturally senses these forces at a higher level than all of us, so for him it was as natural as breathing. By sharing a body with him first, I benefited from experiencing some of that higher sensitivity firsthand."

"The best advice I can give you is to try to do this one at a time," Senn said. "Focus entirely on your own emotions first. Ignore everything else—your clothes rubbing on your skin, your eyes blinking, even your heartbeat. Once you achieve that state, then try to search out Saiya's emotions through the Bond while she focuses on projecting them strongly to you. You are already connected, so just think of it as shortening the distance.

"Remember, once in pure soul form, movement is only a matter of will. Keep it simple. Concentrate on moving *closer* rather than *to her*. If you're too aggressive, then you may very well end up inadvertently entering her body."

Korin winced at the black look Saiya shot them both. To violate her trust in such a way would most certainly alienate her for eternity.

"You should probably eat something before getting back to it," Kye added, "maybe even sleep some. If the darkness under *both* your eyes is any indication, you've been at it all night. It's no wonder you haven't been successful. How can you expect to concentrate when you're tired and sleepy? Don't worry about meeting Keison today. Senn and I'll take care of it."

Korin's eyes widened. "Oh! I almost forgot to ask— did you learn anything during your vigil last night?" he said, looking between the younger teens eagerly.

Senn shrugged. "Just that Keison was at least telling the truth about Soujin tormenting him. He was screaming and writhing around on the floor like his guts were being pulled out through his belly button. Unless I can look at his soul outside the body, there really isn't much I can say or possibly do about those invisible chains of his. For now, I'm just going to focus on detaching the piece of Kye's soul stuck to my own and see if the fracture can be mended somehow with my healing ability. If I'm successful, then we can see about helping Keison with his problem."

"We'll come get you if Keison tells us anything important," Kye promised. Then he suddenly grinned and shared an amused look with Senn before adding, "Oh, and if you happen to hear any rumors about evil spirits or demons appearing along the main road last night, we'd *really* appreciate you passing along the story to us."

"You...!" Korin started to exclaim, once again eying the bloody shirt on the floor, but then he shook his head. "Never mind," he said with a tired sigh. "I have a feeling that I would be better off not knowing."

As he followed a more sedate Saiya back to the second room, he briefly puzzled over the two teens' often contradictory behavior of ancient and young before simply dismissing it as a lost cause. He didn't think an eternity would be enough to understand their motives.

"I hate to admit it, but the brown-haired idiot's right," Saiya said, looking disgruntled as she sat down on the chair next to the desk. "I'm too tired to concentrate right now."

"If you want to sleep, I can go back next door," Korin offered, his hand still on the doorknob.

She scowled. "It's not like I've been able to do more than doze ever since that night in the Aideyan temple. I would rather you go get us something to eat than waste time trying to sleep. We can rest enough while we eat."

"I did not realize the vibrations were so bad for you that they affected your sleep," Korin said guiltily.

"Save your sympathy, monk. I told you before that I don't want to hear it. The only thing that holds any value for me is results, not intentions. I've kept my end of the bargain by doing all of this your way, but if I don't start seeing the results promised me soon, then I'll just try to break the connection *my* way..."

"Yes, likely with your sword through my neck," he acknowledged with a self-deprecating smile. "A good motivator for anyone, even an Old Soul, but you do not need to worry that my determination has waned. I do not forget my promises, even if that promise is something that will cause me pain in the end."

Her disgruntled expression changed to something unreadable before she looked away.

"You're as much an idiot as Kye," she said without any real heat.

Unfortunately, Saiya was only willing to grant him a half-hour respite before ordering him to resume his efforts.

"Make sure you stay out of my head this time," she warned.

Across the room, Korin nodded solemnly and closed his eyes. While eating had seemed to revive Saiya, it had only made him sleepier. He was more tired than he wanted to admit to the ill-tempered girl, but he didn't think he was to the point of collapsing just yet.

He went over all the advice Senn and Kye had given him in his head one last time before trying to put their suggestions into practice. Last night he had tried to approach the problem by going into a meditative trance to clear his mind as was his usual practice when seeking advice from the gods.

This time, he did the exact opposite, filling it with nothing but his desire to help Saiya. He tried to focus solely on that and ignore his body completely, something he immediately found to be nearly impossible once his nose started to itch and his rigid posture started to relax, causing his half-healed cuts to sting as his center of gravity shifted downwards.

Adding to his distraction were the periodic flashes of

impatience he felt that were most certainly coming from Saiya. The first few times, Korin had stopped trying to ignore all the sensory input of his body and attempted to just will himself towards those erratic bursts of emotion like Senn had suggested. That had worked out as well as he had expected—which was not at all.

An hour later, he was beginning to think that Senn was right. They needed to try transmigrating into each other's bodies first. However, more than the problem of Saiya's flat-out refusal was the fact that they needed to be touching for it to work, something that caused excruciating pain to them both. Convincing Saiya to do it would be a moot point if they would never be able to concentrate enough because of the pain to do it in the first place. Perhaps the whole endeavor had been doomed from the beginning.

"I am starting to feel bursts of your emotions every now and then," he felt inclined to tell her, wanting to show at least *some* progress. "I could not even do that much last night, so perhaps it's merely a matter of repetition and time."

"I've been practically screaming my emotions at you for the past hour," Saiya said irritably. "I don't know what more you expect me to do."

Korin sighed wearily. "Perhaps we should switch roles for the time being. Right now, I daresay the level of my exhaustion would be a strong beacon for you."

"Fine," she huffed in annoyance, sitting back in her chair into a slightly more relaxed position.

For the next hour, Korin focused solely on the bone-deep weariness that permeated his body. Every once in a while a burst of anger got through that heavy exhaustion, but other than that and the constant thrum of the Bond, it seemed they were as far apart as ever.

"Korin!"

He heard the shout as faintly as if it had crossed the vast ocean from his lost homeland. He couldn't understand what was happening. What had he been doing? Why was it so dark? Why was someone sitting on his chest, making it very difficult to breathe?

"Brother! Where are you!"

That frantic voice—he knew it didn't he?

Suddenly, light flooded his vision, and he winced away with a startled gasp, trying to raise an arm to cover his eyes, but none of his limbs seemed to be working. A thick cloud of dust invaded his lungs, causing them to seize painfully before he erupted into coughs. More dust immediately followed that first deluge until he felt he would suffocate.

Cold hands grasped his cheeks as that familiar voice once again shouted, "Korin!"

It was only after he was finally able to draw a few clean, though still labored, breaths what felt like an eternity later and his gasping and coughing had subsided that he was able to focus on the tear-blurred vision of the dark-haired figure looking down at him from above. Of course...

"Haydin—what—?" he asked in bewilderment.

"Korin, you stupid bastard!" his older brother raged. "Why the hell didya have to—I could've—!

Korin blinked up at Haydin, his mind still completely muddled. It almost sounded as though the man was on the verge of tears. He tried to raise a hand to brush the other's hands off his face, but he realized that something was blocking both his arms. He looked down at himself, but a jagged, gray stone wall lay just a thumbnail's length from his chin, blocking his view.

He jerked back in surprise and was rewarded with a sharp pain in his chest as if he had suddenly been stabbed with a spear. A gush of warmth seemed to boil up his throat, and then it erupted from his mouth in one violent cough. He tasted salt and bitterness.

"Hay—din—" *he managed to choke out in fear. What in the name of the gods was going on?*

"I don't know what to do!" *his brother cried. This time the tears were evident in his voice.* "You're trapped! The rocks are too big, too heavy for me to lift! Why did you come running to me? I would've gotten out of the way in time! You didn't need to do this!"

As if the fog surrounding his mind had been blown clear by the older man's words, Korin remembered seeing a huge chunk of the cliffside break apart and come tumbling down right above where Haydin had been walking. He remembered dropping the deer carcass he had been carrying and sprinting over to his brother with the intent of pushing him out of the way, and then—nothing.

Suddenly the wall of rock, the weight on his chest, made sense.

"I didn't make it." *His voice sounded strangely plaintive, young, like a child's, even through the wheezing.*

Another coughing fit had him choking on another mouthful of bitter, warm liquid. From the stricken look on Haydin's face, Korin knew that he would not see tomorrow.

"It's all right, Haydin. I'm not in pain," *he rasped, voice barely above a whisper now.*

He felt so tired. His eyesight was starting to fade, and he could hardly feel his brother's calloused fingers framing his face anymore.

"Father will never forgive me," *he heard Haydin whisper back, and then everything went black and numb.*

The blow to his back was as shocking as a clap of thunder in a cloudless sky. Korin gasped and once again found himself choking on a warm, thick liquid in his throat and mouth. His eyes flew open in a panic, and a light as brilliant as a dozen suns instantly assaulted his eyes, as painful as if someone had thrust a flaming torch into them.

It was cold, painfully cold. He automatically tried to wrap his arms around his body, but he couldn't seem to make his arms work.

Vague, dark shapes moved across his hazy vision for a moment before he felt the world sudden tilt upside-down and something soft and hot pressed up against the back of his head. An overwhelming sense of vertigo washed through him as he abruptly felt himself move through the air.

And yet—even though his senses were being assaulted from every direction in a way that he had never experienced, his thoughts were strangely muddled, disconnected, as if he were thinking within a dream.

Something was making a terrible, indeterminate noise that sounded as though he was hearing it through ears full of mud. His thoughts floated along a stream of uncertainty for a long moment before he realized that it was the sound of a baby screaming.

Korin tried to turn his head in an effort to locate the baby, but once again, his body did not seem to want to obey him. Then he felt his back settle into something that was both soft and hard, and he was suddenly being squeezed tightly. Words that didn't make any sense whatsoever filtered through the baby's cries, fast and excited—a man's—followed by the higher pitches of a woman who sounded as if she was speaking through tears.

He tried to speak, to ask what was going on, but all he heard was the wails of the baby and the two voices speaking gibberish. At least his eyes were finally starting to adjust to the light, but everything still remained strangely indistinct no matter how hard Korin tried to focus.

A shadow loomed over him, tall and shaped like a person. The man he had heard speaking, perhaps? Korin tried to speak again but to no avail. The baby's shrieks suddenly increased in volume as if the child was being hurt. A small, blurry fist shot across his vision and back, and his eyes immediately followed the movement to see a tiny arm and shoulder only a finger-length away.

Am I lying on top of the baby? *he thought with alarm.*

Then before he could even attempt to roll over, his entire body started to move from side-to-side like a rope bridge swaying in the wind. What was going on? Was someone trying to move him off the baby as well? Korin turned his head away from the man still bent over him to the other side and was greeted by a shape that was unmistakable, even through his hazy vision. Slowly, his gaze moved higher. No—the surface he was lying on wasn't moving. He was being rocked!

With horror, Korin realized that he was in the arms of a smiling woman he didn't know—and that the screaming baby was him.

Korin blinked and met red eyes as shocked as he felt.

"That was you...?" Saiya asked quietly, her expression melting into something that was, for once, more open and curious.

"I—had all but forgotten that," he replied shakily, still engulfed in the strong emotions of that terrifying moment of realization. "That was how my first life ended. It wasn't until a couple of days after my second birth that I finally remembered being buried beneath the falling rocks, realized what had happened. I had died, but instead of my soul going to the Valley of the Gods like I had always expected, I was somehow alive again. I was an *infant*. All I could think was that because of my sacrifice, the gods had deemed me worthy of a second chance at life."

"Is *that* how you see this unending life? A reward?" she sneered.

Korin smiled wryly. "During my second life, yes; it was the only way I *could* interpret it. I had been reborn into a peaceful culture on the other side of the world, one that had never even heard of my first tribe. I lived for about eighty years with no more conflict than the occasional severe storms and a single occurrence of famine when an infestation of cicadas had decimated more than half our crops.

"I had lived a happy and satisfying life, so imagine my shock when I went to bed one night an old man and woke up an infant again moments after my third rebirth, among yet another strange culture. Had I not already been given my reward? It was a couple more lives, when my Gods' Voice manifested for the first time, before I realized that perhaps the gods had granted me all these extra lives, not so much as a reward, but in order to serve mankind in a unique way. I've devoted myself to Them, to understanding the purpose of this extraordinary existence, ever since."

Saiya turned her face and scowled at the door. "I'm not the same," she said curtly.

"What do you mean?"

"No matter that you think you're fulfilling some divine mission, your words, and the tone of—satisfaction—in your damned voice, tell me you still consider your existence as an Old Soul as some kind of reward. If that's true, then the reason I'm an Old Soul is not even close to yours."

"Why?"

"Because my lives have been about nothing but punishment."

"Punishment?" Korin echoed in bewilderment. "Whatever for?"

When Saiya turned to face him, her face was completely devoid of emotion. "Taking my own life."

CHAPTER NINETEEN

Hahri set the bucket with hot coals piled around a couple of mugs of cider onto the cot against the wall between them.

"It's worth a shot, at the very least," he said with a shrug as he moved back to the edge of the cot where he would be sitting for the duration of their latest experiment.

Issai had already bundled himself up in the wool blanket. "I hope it works because it's really annoying not being able to move normally," he grumbled. He could hear the strain in his own voice.

"It's okay if you can't detach it, you know," Hahri said quietly, making Issai inwardly curse his lack of control over his emotions. Until he had met Hahri, it had never really been a problem.

"It's *not* okay, dammit! This is a piece of your *soul* we're talking about! To have taken something so sacred from you, something that never should've even been *touched* much less fractured in the first place—"

He broke off as Hahri reached over and touched his arm through the blanket, and it took everything within him not to stiffen. "Issai, I've told you a million times that it isn't your fault. I never once thought it was, so there's no reason to blame yourself, either. For all we know, it could've happened because something *I* did, or the gods did it because they thought it would make for a good laugh."

"Yes because ripping off a piece of a person's soul is so hilarious," Issai replied sarcastically.

Hahri patted him on the shoulder and sat back. He grabbed his own blanket and quickly wrapped it around himself. "Let's just focus on what we can do for now. No use worrying about something until there's something *to* worry about."

A quarter-hour later, they both faced each other in soul form. Using Hahri's soul core as a focal point, Issai reached out to it with some trepidation just as he would have with his flesh and blood hand were he in his corporal body. He *had* to make this work.

Nothing happened. There wasn't even a discernable change in movement to the blue particles shimmering between them. Issai would have sighed in frustration were he still actually capable of breathing even though he knew damn well nothing was ever that easy.

Okay, that was obviously the wrong way to approach the problem. Everything, his sight, his speech, his movement was purely accomplished mentally while in soul form. He wondered if willing himself to look a certain way would work. Issai held an image of his body in his mind and concentrated on a desire to hold that shape.

A burst of excitement flooded his entire being, and he wondered what Hahri was seeing. Once again, he tried to reach out as if he possessed an arm and a hand, and was actually shocked when an arm and a hand composed entirely out of a slightly denser form of the blue light particles manifested before him. Fascinated, Issai focused on it for a long moment, experimentally flexing the "fingers" and making a fist as if he were holding a knife. The phantom hand mimicked all his movements as well as a real hand.

Next, he tried to look down and was extremely pleased when his field of vision moved as if he had moved his neck to look down. Like his arm, Issai could see the same ghostly blue outline of a torso, legs, and booted feet, but more importantly, he could finally see his own soul core. He immediately spotted the asymmetrical "bulge" on the core's right side just as Hahri had described. He wondered what would happen if he touched it with his newly created fingers.

Just as Issai reached a "finger" towards his soul core, he abruptly sensed that Hahri really wanted to know how he had done it, that he didn't want to be just an observer this time. He paused. Yes, it was probably better for them to examine it together.

Issai sent his reasoning on the matter as a rush of thoughts through the Bond, hoping Hahri grasped his meaning. He really didn't want them to have to return to their bodies to explain the process with words. Then he lowered his "arm" to his side and watched Hahri's core intently.

It seemed to take no time at all for the shimmering blue particles surrounding the other boy's brilliant core to become agitated, flickering at a much higher rate, before they began to clump together randomly until the outline of a body slowly started to take shape around the core with much the same density as the arm he had created out of those same light particles. Only when the new concentration of blue particles before him resembled a three-dimensional, ghostly outline of a bald human did they seem to settle down into their previous state.

Though featureless and hardly recognizable as his bond partner, that portion of Hahri's soul still resembled a human body enough to be functional. There they stood, two bodies composed entirely out of shimmering particles of light within a singular cloud of the same, though less densely packed, blue light particles. Issai wondered if any of this transformation would be visible to his flesh and blood eyes, wishing he could have seen the process that way. He would have to remember to ask Hahri to show him later.

Issai sent Hahri confirmation of his success and stepped closer as the other raised ghostly arms as if to stare at his hands. He reached out his hand to see if he could "touch" this simulacrum of Hahri's hand. The result was like nothing he had ever felt before. Instead of an actual sensation of texture, of temperature, or moistness, he "felt" a barrier against his hand of particles in the same way he interpreted colors with his soul-vision. His mind knew that his phantom hand should be obstructed, so it stopped accordingly without any conscious decision on his part.

A burst of startlement filtered down the Bond from Hahri, making Issai wonder if the other had interpreted the experience the same. Issai held up his hand between them and mentally urged the other boy to touch him as well. As he complied, a surge of panic rose in both of them when instead of stopping, Hahri's hand began to seemingly merge into Issai's. A rush of energy also began to enter his "arm" that felt exactly like the times when Hahri's soul had entered his body and the other had relinquished complete control to him.

Hahri jerked his ghostly appendage away and took a couple of hasty steps back that did not look altogether natural, a sort of half glide, half stumble, almost as if he had forgotten how to walk. The particles that composed his hand resembled a swarm of frantic ants for a moment before they finally settled down into their original, calmer state.

If someone ever wondered what a question would feel like physically, then Issai could readily say it felt like thousands of fingers poking at him relentlessly because that's exactly what Hahri's rush of questions felt like at the moment. He answered with the mental equivalent of a strong whack to the back of the head and an intense desire for calm. They really needed to find a better way to communicate, although Issai had to admit that the feel of the equivalent of a curse word while in soul form was an interesting experience, like the sharp, jagged edges of broken glass.

Once Hahri stopped slicing him with his soul-speech, Issai sent him his speculations about the phenomenon with Hahri's soul hand possibly being the same thing that occurred when their souls shared a body, just that they had not been able to see the exact process with their physical eyes. His bond partner's indignation instantly transformed into excitement, and Issai immediately got the sense that the other wanted to try doing it again. He marveled that Hahri's earlier fear was no where to be found.

Nodding his ethereal head, Issai raised both hands, palms out, towards the other boy in invitation. Hahri slowly mirrored the action, hesitated for a few beats, then pressed his ghostly hands forward. As before, they plunged into Issai's hands, and the flashing particles be-came part of them almost immediately, followed by that familiar rush of energy, until the two resembled some sort of bizarre conjoined twins that shared a pair of hands.

However, the melding didn't stop there. The densely-packed particles composing Hahri's arms were being pulled towards Issai's arms, breaking off bit by bit like iron shavings towards a magnet. Although Hahri had noticed it as well, he didn't pull away like last time even though Issai could feel his rising anxiety. Despite that, Hahri stepped forward, and their forearms, too, melded together.

Issai sent his unease to the other, wondering if he was experiencing any pain, but he received a negative, though the feeling was tinged with a "not more than the usual anyway" that did nothing to ease Issai's worries. Then without warning, Hahri surged forward again, and Issai found his soul-vision obscured by the other's soul-body as if Hahri was now attempting to hug him.

Issai knew the exact moment their soul cores touched. The distance pain vanished completely, replaced by a surge of energy so powerful that it teetered on the threshold between excruciating pain and the ultimate pleasure. In the same eternal instant, his soul-vision was filled with a white light so brilliant that it would have seared his physical eyes into permanent blindness.

He didn't know how long he stood there drowning in that ocean of unfathomable power and light, but it was the jarring realization that the white light had been re-placed with a more familiar sea of shimmering blue particles, a scene missing one very crucial thing, that brought him back to his senses. Hahri's newly con-structed soul-body, but more importantly his soul core, were not there.

Panicking, Issai swiveled around in a complete circle, frantically searched the entire cloud of particles that enclosed them both, but not only was Hahri's soul no where to be found, but the once wide surrounding cloud of blue light particles had shrunken down to near the size of the blue glow he had witnessed around the individual patrons of the temple.

Hahri! his mind screamed in fear, his entire being feeling the cry like the stabs of a billion knives. What had they *done?*

Then he felt it, a faint emotion almost lost within the turbulent flows of his fear and panic, a brief flash of confusion and anxiety that was not his own. A sudden realization allowed Issai to reign in his emotions before they could rage beyond the point of control.

Hahri? he sent anxiously, praying that he was not wrong.

"Issai what—what in the three hells just happened?*"* Issai heard clearly in his mind as if the words were his own thoughts, in his own mental voice. *"I can feel your emotions, but I can't see your soul core anymore! Wait—I can't move either! Not even my field of vision!"* Panic began to flood into Issai's being.

He was suddenly engulfed in a relief so profound that he would have probably collapsed under its shear weight had he been standing on physical legs. Hahri was still here; he had *not* disappeared.

Issai looked down at his soul core and would have gasped had he been able when he saw the size of the blue-white mass. It now completely filled his constructed body's torso from end to end, and even though he shouldn't have been glad to see it, the side where that piece of Hahri's soul was attached to his own still showed a clear anomaly. Like two different hues of clay mashed together, there was just something that was not quite uniform about the area.

Issai lifted his arms. They were the same as before with one very big exception. The particles from which they had been constructed appeared more numerous, more tightly compacted so that the ethereal appendages looked more cohesive, less like a child's sandcastle that could easily fall apart. He studied the glow of particles surrounding his form. Yes, even they appeared twice as dense.

"We're sharing the same space. I can even hear you talking in my mind," Issai thought, attempting to "speak" directly to the other boy. What he had to say to his partner was not something that could be conveyed with intent and emotion alone.

"Huh? Wha—so can I!" he heard Hahri practically shout across his mind.

"I think it's the same," Issai sent. *"What just happened is the same thing that happens when we share the same body and give complete control to the other. You reckless idiot! For a beat there, I thought I had absorbed your soul completely! You were damn lucky!"*

"It worked!" Hahri exclaimed, making Issai wonder if he had even heard the chastisement. *"It's so awesome that we can share the soul-bodies we created, too!"*

"I wonder why we can hear each other's thoughts now when before, while sharing a body, we couldn't"

"Probably because it never occurred to us to try," Hahri replied. *"Hold on for a beat…"* For a long while there was nothing from his bond partner, then, *"Did you hear that?"*

"No. What were you doing?"

"Just thinking about things like I normally do when we share the same body. I never once tried to talk to you while you were in control because I just assumed, apparently wrongly, that it was something I couldn't do."

"Something else we'll have to try out just to be sure. It could

turn out to be an ability we have only when we're in soul form," Issai warned.

"Speaking of abilities, should we try switching control?"

"Would that even work?" Issai sent dubiously, "I mean, this isn't even a real body."

"It's all a matter of intent in this realm of souls," Hahri reminded him. "I would think that the soul-bodies we create can be as real as we wish them to be. Let's both focus on that and see what happens."

"'See what happens…' Those are quickly becoming the most ominous words I have ever heard," Issai groused. The ripples of laughter that were currently occupying his mind also did nothing to set him at ease. This was one Old Soul that treated things much too flippantly.

However, he still did as the other suggested and quickly found himself twirling around in circles with his arms held out wide as if being uncoiled from a rope.

"Stop that!" Issai demanded.

"Just testing the waters," Hahri sent affably, Issai feeling the other's grin as if it were something physical.

Hahri held up the left hand of the soul-body and touched the center with the fingers of his right. Issai immediately felt that same sense of there being a barrier present as he had when he had touched his hand to Hahri's earlier.

"So that's what it feels like when you do it," Hahri mused. "I wonder why the same doesn't happen for me? It can't be a matter of intention because I certainly didn't want my hand to be absorbed that first time! And before you say it, it's not because you wanted to steal the rest of my soul either!"

Issai was caught short; it was indeed exactly what he had been thinking. He couldn't understand why Hahri was so confident that Issai had nothing to do with any of it. And the other boy was confident. He could feel it like an admonishment.

"Let me have control again," Issai sent instead of offering up an opinion. *"In case you haven't noticed yet, our soul cores appear to have become intermingled much like our soul-bodies. However, the anomaly caused by that fractured piece of your soul appears to still be present, so I want to get a closer look at it while we're still merged. Maybe I'll even be able to fix it with my healing ability* because *our souls have become so closely entwined."*

Issai found himself suddenly looking at the enlarged soul core.

"Wow, it's huge!" Hahri exclaimed. *"But I can see what you mean. The right side does look a bit—off. It's probably why I can still feel a bit of a—tug I suppose—even though we're essentially in the same 'body.' Do whatever you think is best."*

Once Issai could move his soul-body, he spent a long while just studying the anomaly. The mysterious matter that was their soul cores behaved in a manner that was not altogether the same as the different-colored light particles he had thus far witnessed. Since he was not actually "seeing" it as one would with mortal eyes, the best he could describe it was that the way it moved was unlike anything he had ever sensed before. There simply was no comparison, like asking a normal human being to describe what the gods saw when they looked at the earth when they, themselves, had never seen with the eyes of a god.

Nevertheless, Issai could at least see the boundaries of where the material differed from the whole, even if they were not as clear-cut as a seam in a shirt. Perhaps if he traced out the "edges" of those boundaries exactly as he felt and traced out a wound to be healed, then his mental command would also work the same for a soul-wound.

Easier said than done he soon found out when the wound he was trying to trace out was in constant motion and seemed to change position and shape with every beat. Realizing the endeavor was futile, Issai decided to simply focus on the wound as a whole and released his command to heal. Blue particles from his created torso instantly began to flow towards the soul core only to be swallowed into the shining, blue-white mass without seemingly doing anything afterwards.

With a start, as he watched the particles rush towards the core, Issai realized that the density of his soul-body was slowly starting to diminish, and that the flow of particles wasn't slowing down in the least.

Stop! Stop! he thought frantically towards his torso, unsure if that would even work. He had never tried to deliberately stop a healing.

To his relief, the flow of particles ceased, returning to their regular behavior as if he had done nothing at all.

"Well, that was certainly interesting," Hahri noted with what Issai couldn't believe was amusement. There hadn't been anything even *remotely* funny about any of that.

"Yeah, we'll see who's laughing when you suddenly find yourself in swaddling cloths again," Issai retorted. *"Unlike you, the prospect of our soul cores sucking in all the blue particles fills me with dread. Have you forgotten what we saw after killing that piece of scum last night?"*

"I wasn't worried," Hahri said rather matter-of-factly.

"You should've been," was all Issai could think to say. And Hahri once accused *him* of being an optimist.

"I wasn't just talking about what happened with the blue particles, you know," Hahri added. *"This was the first time I got to experience you trying to heal while inside your head. I always imagined that healing someone would be rather complicated, but as far as I could tell, the only thing you did to trigger it was to say 'heal' within your thoughts. Is that really all there is to it?"*

"I have to trace out the wound first, but yes. That's probably

why it failed. My mind simply couldn't latch onto that kind of wound. The soul is something we'll never fully understand, I think."

"*So—any other ideas?*"

"*Maybe—but after what just happened, I'm not sure I want to try it.*"

"*It's fine if you don't,*" Hahri reminded him, the thought flavored with absolute sincerity. It made something within Issai's being want to cringe and hide.

That more than anything decided him. "*I know, but it's something that needs to be done, no matter my misgivings.*"

"*If you're sure. Need me to do anything?*"

Issai started to say no, then paused, reconsidering. *I suppose it wouldn't hurt.*

"*Concentrate,*" he sent. "*Concentrate on the part of you that feels the little tug you mentioned earlier. Think about resisting it, or better yet, think of pulling it back, and at the same time, I'm going to try to use the hands I've created along with my healing ability to detach your soul fragment from my own.*"

"*Will that even work with our cores so intermingled?*" Hahri asked, sounding intrigued.

"*Hopefully, because I don't want to chance doing it without your soul really close. I don't want to succeed in detaching it only to have it attach itself to some other spot on my soul core. Having to touch it this one time makes me nervous enough. It's not something I want to do more than once.*"

Issai imagined the tip of his index finger like the sharp point of a knife, watching in fascination despite himself as the particles along the rounded tip slowly began to rearrange themselves until they were so densely packed that he had to focus rather intensely on them to sense them individually. He then slowly touched it to the place where the fragment of Hahri's soul had started to either meld or become absorbed by his own soul core, but the ghostly digit immediately began to dissipate as the blue particles began to move towards the core just as they had during his healing attempt earlier. He hastily drew his hand back and spent a little time concentrating on reforming the finger to its sharp point again.

This was it; he had only one method left to try, one Issai wasn't very confident would even work. He imagined the warmth that always followed his mental command traveling down his arm to the tip of the finger he was trying to wield as a blade. He was extremely relieved when a stream of blue particles suddenly traveled through his arm and began to collect within that lone digit until the tip seemed to glow a brilliant blue-white.

Willing the particles to continue to flow steadily towards his index finger, Issai cautiously touched one of the more obvious places where the soul material differed and was encouraged when his finger maintained its shape despite the majority of the healing particles feeding into, and likely absorbed by, the massive soul core. The closest he could come to describing what it felt like to "touch" another's soul in such an unusual way was unexpectedly sticking a hand into a pot of boiling water. Though he didn't feel anything like a burn, what he did feel was a sensory shock comparable to the feeling of that initial scalding.

Issai tried to ignore the chaos the direct contact was causing to his perceptions and concentrated on tracing along all the moving, differing edges that he hoped were part of Hahri's soul fragment alone. He sensed a disturbance within that portion of the core as he did so, but he was unable to really tell if he was accomplishing anything good or just damaging their souls. He certainly wasn't feeling anything like pain on his end and didn't want to risk breaking Hahri's concentration on the task he had given to his partner to ask if the other felt any new pain.

He didn't know how long he spent chasing after the edges of Hahri's soul fragment with his knife-like finger, but one moment Issai was carefully swiping it along a particularly small section, and the next, he jerked the finger completely away when a burst of startlement suddenly washed through him.

"What?" Issai demanded fearfully.

"Whatever you just did, it caused that light tugging sensation I've been feeling to suddenly disappear." Issai could practically taste the other's excitement. *"I think you did it!"*

Issai looked down at their soul cores again. Although the area of the anomaly still did not look as uniform as the other side, it was at least obvious his efforts had made a positive difference. The differing matters along the soul-wound no longer behaved quite as at odds with each other. Issai had thought that he would feel *something* when the soul detached. Had he been so focused on the task at hand that he had missed noticing something so significant?

"Before you do anything, let's watch the core for a little while longer," Issai insisted. *"Despite what you think, it still doesn't look quite right to me."*

"I take it you didn't feel anything," Hahri deduced.

"Nothing," Issai confirmed. *"That's what worries me. I wasn't expecting an explosion of pain or anything, but I thought I would at least sense its absence, even if only vaguely."*

"Maybe it's because we're currently merged within a single soul-body—our cores may be too intermingled at the moment for you to feel its loss yet or something."

"I certainly hope you're right because the alternative is a tragedy I don't even want to think about."

Even though their exchange had been brief, Issai could now barely see any sign that there was anything wrong in that portion of their soul cores. However, he still said nothing, observing it closely until he finally admitted to himself that he could no longer see anything wrong at all.

The moment of truth had arrived, and he was both hopeful and terrified.

"Let's separate and find out once and for all if I didn't just commit the mother of all screw-ups."

CHAPTER TWENTY

Watching and feeling Hahri separate from his soul-body was certainly an interesting experience. Issai had been secretly worried about whether his bond partner would be able to do it not only after melding with the soul-body he had created so completely, but also because their soul cores had intermingled. In order to not hinder the process, even if just subconsciously, Issai had decided to keep his fears to himself.

The heady feel of all that excess energy merging soul-bodies had brought had left him as abruptly as the figure composed entirely out of the blue light particles had appeared less than a finger-span in front of his face much like a manifestation of a spirit from the old tales. The separation of their soul cores, however, had not been so cut-and-dry. As Hahri's soul-body had taken a couple of steps forward, both the cloud of blue particles surrounding them and the core itself had started to expand between them.

Issai stayed rooted to his spot, afraid to even move as

a pain similar to their distance pain began to reverberate throughout his entire being. Hahri immediately paused and turned to face him, the two still-amalgamated soul cores warping in an unsettling way where they were stretched between them to accommodate Hahri's position change. Issai felt an overwhelming sense of dread. Now instead of being tethered by a stolen soul fragment, it seemed they had managed to bind themselves to each other even more completely.

"This is a fine mess we've managed to get ourselves into," Issai sent acerbically, refusing to give in to panic just yet. *"I'm open to suggestions."*

A rush of emotions from Hahri washed over him that were both apologetic and irritated as Hahri pointed a ghostly hand towards where his mouth should have been and shook his head. Issai mentally cursed. That's right; they couldn't speak with words when separated. He then got the sense that Hahri was wondering about Issai's healing ability, if he could detach them that way.

Issai immediately shook his head at the other without needing to consider it. A fragment of a soul stuck—just *stuck*—onto his soul core was one thing. Although he could easily see the differences between the material of his soul and Hahri's, *this* would be like asking him to separate all the sugar from a pitcher of water after it had completely dissolved. He sent the gist of his thoughts through the Bond, beyond frustrated about not being able to communicate properly at a time like this.

Hahri shrugged and then he was still for a long moment, giving the impression of staring intently down at their soul cores. At first, Issai only realized something was happening because his newest pain had begun to notice-ably decrease. He focused more closely on the stretched, blue-white mass, and after a short while, figured out what had changed. There was currently less of Hahri's core material mixed with his on his end of the core. He hastily sent a jumble of questions to Hahri, wondering if the other boy was the cause.

Hahri nodded without raising his head, and Issai received a strong impression of slowly "pulling."

Issai couldn't believe it was that simple, which was probably why it was working. He always did have a bad habit of overcomplicating things. Taking his cue from the other, Issai concentrated on willing his soul core back towards his body as if gently tugging on a rope. The pain instantly began to lessen more quickly.

Encouraged, Issai continued to "pull," watching as the part of the core that was stretched became thinner and thinner. Then with a final heave, the two cores separated completely in the middle like bread dough stretched too thin, the last vestiges of pain disappearing at the same moment.

Issai immediately looked down at his own core, watching in a kind of fascination as the misshapen, shining mass slowly reverted back to its original egg-shape. The bulge that had been Hahri's soul fragment was gone with no sign that it had ever been attached there at all. The burst of excitement and gratitude from Hahri soon after was all he needed to know that he had indeed been successful with detaching the soul fragment, and it had returned to its proper place.

That burst of emotion also told him one other important thing. If he was still feeling Hahri's emotions as strongly as before when they were no longer connected through Hahri's soul fragment, then the Bond, itself, had absolutely nothing to do with that accidental connection.

Saiya's going to be pissed, Issai thought, feeling a little sorry for Korin for the hell the monk was likely to receive after he told them.

He focused his attention back on Hahri, who still appeared to be examining his soul core. Although it was also back into its proper egg-shape, unlike his own, Issai could still see where the core had been fractured. The soul material was not quite moving as harmonious with its surroundings in that area as the rest of the core.

Then Hahri unexpectedly poked a couple of fingers at that portion of his core only to jerk them back as if they had been burned when the particles composing the tips immediately began to be absorbed into it. He turned to Issai, projecting a bit of sheepishness.

Perhaps it was time to return to their physical bodies. They had more than enough things to discuss to last them a tenday. Issai sent his desire to go back through the Bond, then headed for the golden collection of particles that was his body.

The cold this time was the worst he had ever felt, painful to the point that he was afraid he would shatter into a million pieces if he so much as moved a pinky. A groan to his left signaled Hahri's return.

"W-w-what I w-wouldn't give f-for a b-blazing f-fire right n-now!" Hahri stuttered miserably.

"Welcome back."

Issai's eyes flew open in surprise. He had not sensed anyone in the room at all, but both Korin and Saiya were seated on the cot across the room, the latter staring at them with an expression he had never seen her wear before, one he couldn't readily label.

"I-I'm surprised t-to s-see you t-two here s-so s-soon," Hahri said.

Korin frowned. "Soon? It's already the middle of the night. Neither one of you have moved since I came in here right before dinnertime to ask about Keison."

"W-what!" Issai said incredulously. If it was sometime during the night, then that would mean they had been in soul form for well over fifteen hours!

Hahri shot Issai a startled look. "E-even c-considering how b-being in s-soul f-form screws w-with our p-perception of t-time, I f-figured it h-had o-only been around th-three h-hours or so…"

Issai slowly reached his hands towards the bucket of hot coals in order to rub them along the warm exterior. He did not think he could hold the waiting mug of cider just yet. "I th-thought s-so, t-too." Just how long had he actually stood there working to detach Hahri's soul fragment?

"Perhaps remaining in your soul forms for such a long period of time explains what I saw when I entered the room the first time," Korin said. "Although I only saw one soul in the beginning, and it was just as transparent as before, it actually had the shape of a man this time. I could even make out some of your features like fingers, eyes, a nose, but they still were not clear enough to discern who I was actually seeing.

"For a long while, I could only see that soul, and I thought at first that one of you had left the room in soul form. However, about an hour ago, one of you suddenly shimmered into existence almost nose-to-nose with the other and then proceeded to step away. I admit it was a bit unsettling to see that soul move. It may have had the shape of a man, but it just did not move like a normal man.

"Then you both just stood there facing each other, heads bowed as if in prayer for the remaining duration. I cannot even begin to guess what you were doing."

"L-let us th-thaw out a b-bit f-first," Hahri said, carefully reaching for one of the mugs inside the bucket. "Th-

then w-we'll explain. I-It'll p-probably t-take a while."

A half-hour and several mugs of heated cider later, Issai still felt half-frozen, but at least his teeth were no longer chattering. Stuttering over his words was more annoying than the cold. He glanced over at the other pair and scowled darkly. Scratch that—having Saiya stare holes into his head the whole time was infinitely worse than either of those things.

And the prickly girl would just have to wait a bit longer for her answers because Issai had something more pressing to discuss with Hahri first. Sometime after the painful cold had started to ease, he had begun to notice that his proximity pain had changed. It had no longer felt as though his soul was being pulled apart so much as just a *disturbance*. It was the same kind of disturbance he had experienced while in soul form when he had done something to cause the blue light particles surrounding his soul core to become excited. Only now, unlike all the times before, the feeling did not seem to be settling back to a calmer state.

The feeling was also subtle and not quite so in-your-face as his previous proximity pain. It was faint enough that he could easily ignore it without the danger of it driving him mad.

"So how's your proximity pain?" Issai asked abruptly into the silence, watching closely for his partner's reaction.

Hahri had been fiddling with his empty mug, looking to be deep in thought, but at Issai's words, his whole body instantly stilled. "So you feel it, too, huh," he replied evenly, something happy and relieved flashing briefly in his eyes before his expression settled back into that of the ancient Hahri.

In that one, raw moment, Issai realized just how much

the whole issue with Hahri's fractured soul had truly bothered the auburn-haired boy, never mind how much he had assured a skeptical Issai that it didn't. To have this final confirmation of Issai's success, to have that heavy weight he had chosen to endure in silence finally lifted had been such a relief that Hahri had been unable to hide it completely from his expression.

Issai would never take the truth of Hahri's smiles for granted ever again.

"Yes. The pain has changed," Issai confirmed, the sides of his lips curving up slightly, "to something not so annoying now."

Hahri nodded, the seriousness of his eyes reverting back to something lighter. "Like my soul is humming," he said, looking at Korin and Saiya pointedly.

"Yeah…" Issai agreed, a bit startled when he realized what the other boy was hinting at. A "vibration," a "buzzing" were the words Korin and Saiya had once used to describe their own proximity pain.

Korin gasped loudly. "You did it; you were able to give Kye back that piece of his soul!" he guessed.

Issai turned to the monk. "Yes."

"But you didn't break the Bond, did you?" Saiya added flatly.

Issai turned his gaze to her reluctantly. "No, but that wasn't something I intended to do in the first place. My goal was to heal Kye's fractured soul core. At least now we know why the discomfort we suffered because of the distance between us was so different from you two, that the Old Soul Bond had nothing to do with that fragment of Kye's soul becoming stuck to mine."

"That's all well and good for *you*," Saiya spat, "but none of that is of any use to me. The only thing I'm interested in is what caused the Bond to happen; I could care less about what *didn't*."

Issai narrowed his eyes sharply. "I've told you once before that I believed the Bond is something that shouldn't be tampered with, more so now after everything we've discovered today. However, no matter my misgivings, I still intend to honor our agreement. I'll continue trying to discover what it is that binds us; it's something I think *all* of us are interested in.

"In the meantime, I think you would do good to think long and hard about whether or not you really do want to do something so drastic. I want you to think about the consequences you're willing to accept because I have no idea what will happen when an Old Soul Bond is broken. That goes doubly for you, monk."

Then he shrugged. "But that's all moot if you can't even move your souls from your bodies in the first place." He looked questionably at Korin.

The blond winced at the scathing look Saiya directed at him. "The only thing we seem to be accomplishing is invading each other's memories," the blond monk admitted with a sigh.

"That's something at least," Hahri said encouragingly. "It proves that your connection is getting stronger."

"That's not—!" Saiya started to snarl angrily.

"I know, I know," Hahri interrupted hastily. "That's the last thing that you want, but after everything I've experienced while in soul form, I think it's necessary in order for you to understand what something moving independently from you, but at the same time you are able to sense, feels like. Once you understand that feeling, then it should be much easier to recreate that sensation of separation and movement within yourself."

If anything, Hahri's words just seemed to confuse the pair even more if the rather befuddled look on the monk's face and the murder practically radiating from red eyes were any indication. Looks like Issai wouldn't have to worry about breaking any sacred bonds anytime soon, a respite he was infinitely grateful for. He couldn't help but feel that it was something he would be cursed for worse than he already was, even if all he did was tell them how it could be done.

"Speaking of separation, there's something else that just occurred to me," Issai said, flicking a knife into his right hand. Understanding flashed into Hahri's eyes as Issai touched the point to his left index finger.

"I hadn't thought of that," Hahri said, holding up his own left index finger eagerly.

Issai jabbed his finger only hard enough to draw a little blood and then looked at Hahri's corresponding finger. Sure enough, Hahri's finger remained uninjured.

"So it was because of my soul fragment all along," Hahri mused. "The soul really is a mysterious thing."

Issai smirked. "Yes, and now I don't have to worry about a bloody nose every time I want to punch you in the face."

Hahri matched him smirk for smirk. "Likewise."

"If I may ask a question," Korin cut in. "Referring to what I mentioned earlier about seeing only one of you in the room, was there a reason for that, or did one of you in fact leave the room?"

"Oh—you probably just came in here when Senn and I had merged our soul-bodies," Hahri answered.

"*Soul-bodies?*"

"That's right; we haven't told you about that yet. It's the reason why our souls looked more like a normal body this time. It was Senn's idea. He figured that since both movement and communication were all about will and intent while in soul form, why not try to will our shapeless forms into something more useful?

"They were composed completely out of the cloud of blue light particles that surrounds our soul cores, and although far from perfect, they at least held the basic shape of a human and moved more or less like one. That's why Senn was finally able to detach the piece of my soul from his core; he had a facsimile of hands and fingers to use along with his healing ability."

"That's..." Words seemed to fail Korin as he stared incredulously at the younger teens.

"...awesome, I know," Hahri finished with a wide grin. "Once we had the 'bodies,' I tried to touch Senn's 'hand' only to have it immediately start to absorb the particles. Senn inferred that it felt something like when I had given him full control while sharing his physical body, so I thought 'what the hell' and allowed his soul-body to absorb mine completely."

Korin gave Hahri such a horrified look that Issai couldn't help but chuckle. "Yeah, that's what I thought when he did it. Talk about dumb luck."

Hahri laughed. "The results were well worth the risks. Not only were you able to give me my soul fragment back, but we also might have never learned that we could talk to each other using our thoughts while in that state otherwise."

"What do you mean when you say 'merge,' exactly?" Korin asked, still looking a little staggered by all their revelations.

"Maybe 'merge' is too strong a word," Hahri reflected. "Even though the soul-bodies we created out of the blue particles completely meshed together, our soul cores were another matter. I suppose you could say they blended together, like mixing two buckets of sand to form a single sand pile. I admit that I was kinda worried when I tried to separate from him and our cores still seemed stuck together, but in the end, it was just a matter of us pulling ourselves away from each other. That's probably what you saw when you said a soul suddenly appeared, and later when we seemed to be staring at each another."

Saiya abruptly stood up, causing everyone to stiffen in alarm, but her glare was focused on Korin alone. "I think we've heard enough for tonight. We've wasted enough time waiting for them as it is. Let's go."

Hahri frowned. "Weren't you two up all last night?"

"*And?*" Saiya snarled.

"And you need sleep," Hahri continued, unfazed. "If you're so concerned about wasting time, then you need sleep because there's no way either one of you will accomplish anything if you're one blink away from collapsing out of sheer exhaustion."

Saiya opened her mouth as if to retort, then stormed towards the door instead without another word, slamming it so hard behind her that Issai feared it might splinter.

"I guess that means you'll be sleeping in here with us again," Hahri chuckled.

Korin sighed. "I am beginning to fear that her anger will never be tempered."

The monk looked so dejected that Issai wondered if something significant had happened between the other pair. Korin had always seemed to have an overabundance of energy and optimism up until this point.

"Still hoping to change her mind about the Bond, huh," Hahri said sympathetically.

"Honestly, I don't think it'll matter either way," Issai said. When both Hahri and Korin gave him a questioning look, he elaborated, "After everything I've seen today, I still believe that the Bond has to do with the cloud of blue light particles that surrounds us all. We learned that it can be manipulated, sure, but it fundamentally acts and reacts to its own set of rules.

"Unlike when our soul cores intermingled, that portion of our souls is completely melded together. I suppose you can think of it as two yolks within a single egg. I believe that's why you feel that buzzing within when Saiya and you are apart. You're stretching the part of your soul that's joined, exciting the particles like a colony of ants moving frantically, if you will. Even if I lived a million more lifetimes, I don't think I could ever understand what those rules are enough to separate us out again."

Korin seemed to collapse into himself. "I do not think Saiya will ever accept that it cannot be done," he said quietly.

"She may have to whether she likes it or not," Hahri said seriously. "After all, we've all come together like this because we wanted answers. That sole desire has set in motion forces that can no longer be stopped. Just look how much we've managed to learn in a day. Small things in the whole scheme of things, I know, but it's more than I've ever accomplished alone in over five thousand years."

"All the more reason for me to learn to move my soul from my body," Korin said. "Even if there is nothing to be done about the Bond, I still very much wish to see and experience all you have described. There must be a reason why we are able to do this."

"Maybe Soujin knows the reason already, and that's why he's trying to collect Old Souls," Issai ventured.

"Hopefully we'll get the chance to 'ask' the bastard real soon," Hahri agreed. "Speaking of, I wonder what became of Keison today? We wouldn't have heard him knock, but I would expect him to have tried the other room once we didn't answer."

"He looked pretty bad last night," Issai pointed out. "Maybe he *couldn't* come."

"If he doesn't show up tomorrow, we should definitely go check on him," Hahri said. He grinned suddenly. "After all, we might have just discovered a knife sharp enough to cut through invisible chains."

CHAPTER TWENTY-ONE

"You would think that in five thousand years she would've learned some gods-be-damned *manners!*" Hahri growled, glaring at the still-open door where they had just watched an ill-tempered little girl drag a barely awake man twice her size through as if he weighed no more than a feather pillow. The auburn-haired boy then turned his glare to the knives Issai still clutched in his hands. "Next time we share a cot, your knives are definitely *not* invited! I haven't been that close to being gutted since that damned slaver cave!"

Issai rose out of his defensive crouch beside the cot and shrugged. He did feel slightly guilty about accidentally slicing Hahri's shirt when the crash of their door against the wall had him springing out of bed with both knives already slicing upwards, but it was hardly *his* fault that Saiya thought doors should only be kicked open.

"The sun probably hasn't even risen yet," Hahri continued to rant.

"I'm too keyed up to go back to sleep now," Issai

268

said, ignoring the other boy's whining. "So what do you say we grab some breakfast and go explore the city with new eyes before Keison's potential visit?"

Hahri stopped mid-rant and looked at him sharply. "You mean in our soul-bodies?"

Issai nodded. "Merged if you're up to it. I want to be able to speak to you with words."

His bond partner's eyes lit up with excitement. "Anything in particular you're interested in seeing?"

"Hopefully, the Old Soul Keison seems to think is somewhere in this city."

A half-hour later, a merged Issai and Hahri were navigating their way out of the temple. At least, Issai hoped they were. Through their soul-vision, the world around them was one big featureless landscape of colorful rivers and clouds of particles and nothing that even resembled a manmade structure.

"Are you sure we're even going anywhere at all?" Hahri said within his mind.

"We did pass a few people just now," Issai reminded him. *"I don't think we've made it past the temple grounds yet, and it's probably still too early for anyone to be heading for the temple."*

"I hope we don't get lost." Hahri's mind-voice sounded faint, so Issai wasn't altogether sure if the other had intended him to hear it.

Once he had realized that there would be no landmarks for him to follow, Issai had immediately worried about the same thing, but then remembered that before they had created their soul-bodies, it had only been a matter of willing himself to wherever he had wished to go. He didn't see why distance would make much of a difference.

"If you're that worried about it, then we can try willing ourselves back to our bodies right now while we're still fairly close

to them."

He felt a burst of startlement from his partner, then a tinge of embarrassment. *"I completely forgot we could do that,"* he admitted. *"No, just keep going."*

"That said, maybe I should try to will us to somewhere more populated like the Merchant District or the marketplace," Issai mused. *"If an Old Soul other than Keison does live here, then those are the two most likely places he or she'll turn up at."*

"Lazy," Hahri teased, his good humor restored.

Visualizing some of the shops they had visited with the monks a few days ago, Issai willed himself to appear before them—and suddenly he was inundated on all sides by a crowd of shining, golden bodies surrounded by the now-familiar blue glow of particles. He would have yelped had he been capable as that moving mass of humanity proceeded to walk straight through his soul-body as if it wasn't even there.

The sensation was what he imagined an ocean would feel when something swam through its depths had it been a living entity. His soul-body was barely maintaining its shape as the particles of its makeup were disrupted over and over. Issai hastily made his way to the edge of that golden river, walking through a good many bodies himself, most of which paused briefly as if they, too, could sense him. Thankfully, no one's soul core seemed to have touched theirs; a desecration avoided.

"That was the most unsettling experience I have ever had," Hahri said. He probably would have shuttered had he been able.

"I think 'disgusting' is a better word," Issai said dryly. *"I think some of their particles stayed behind. I feel contaminated, dammit!"*

"That's just wrong! *Pick them out!"*

"Like I can even do that. You make it sound like they're fleas

or something."

"Fleas would be better, I think. Maybe if we think about wanting them gone, our own particles will boot them out for us."

"They'd better," Issai growled. What made it worse was he could feel every single one of the foreign particles, almost like feeling bugs crawling beneath his skin.

After thinking *really* hard about ridding himself of them, Issai turned his focus on the crowd moving past. He was glad that he had brought them here instead of the likely-more-crowded marketplace where it would have taken longer to move out of the crowds. That was one experience he didn't care to have twice.

With a start, he realized he could clearly see each person's soul core shining through the golden particles of their bodies as if through a window. Issai wondered if this new layer to his soul-vision was because of the way Hahri and he were connected at the moment. The most immediate thing that stood out was the fact that everyone's cores were at least a third of the size of his or Hahri's.

"That's interesting..." he heard Hahri say thoughtfully.

"What is?"

"The size of their soul cores," he replied, echoing Issai's earlier observation.

"When we get back, we definitely should take a look at Korin and Saiya's," Issai said.

"Yeah," Hahri replied slowly. Issai suddenly felt a strange emotion emanating from his partner that he had never felt before. *"You know,"* he continued, *"with all these differences between Old Souls and regular people—big differences in the case of our souls—I'm starting to really wonder if we're actually human."*

That stopped all of Issai's thoughts as effectively as a blow to the head. *"If not human, then what?"* Issai asked finally after a long, awkward pause.

"Who knows?" Hahri replied, his mental voice sounding much too flippant to match the complicated maelstrom of emotions that accompanied it. *"It was just a thought, so don't take it too seriously."*

"Then don't go blurting out unnerving stuff like that as if it were," Issai grumbled.

He turned his attention back to the crowd, determined not to think too deeply about why he couldn't just dismiss the other boy's speculations as absurd. For a long moment, they both watched the crowds without speaking.

Then Hahri suddenly said, *"Look at that one a little over to the right, the person that looks like they're crouching on the ground. Something looks a little off near their soul core."*

Issai complied, his gaze easily finding the person in question, who now had a small crowd of golden figures circling them. He focused hard on the little he could see of the downed figure now that the others were blocking his view, but nothing really stood out.

"I don't see anything."

"Just watch—look, the others are helping the person up. It's pretty obvious, so you should be able to see once the rest move out of the way."

Issai continued to watch as a couple of people stood on either side of the person, each taking an arm as if to help the person walk while the rest drifted away. That's when he saw it.

"That person has a really dense cloud of blue light particles within their body!" he exclaimed.

"Look at the shape of their body. I think it's a pregnant woman," Hahri added, his words flavored with both excitement and curiosity. *"The way she's walking—I think she might be in labor. Let's follow them. Imagine seeing a birth with a soul's eyes!"*

Issai had to admit that the thought of witnessing a birth while in soul form was intriguing, enough that he was willing to abandon the search for Old Souls for the moment. *"Fine."*

He kept to the edges of the crowd as he trailed the awkwardly moving trio for the next half-hour or so, not really sure which direction they were moving in, just that the crowds had thinned significantly.

"Birthing Houses are usually near the temple in large cities like this," Hahri said. *"We might have a ways to go, yet."*

"If it is, then I never saw it. They could just be taking her home after all. Maybe she just fell."

"Let's just keep following her anyway. If she's not in labor, then you can just will us back to the marketplace or wherever. We won't have lost too much time."

They walked on for another quarter-hour or so before their quarry headed towards a place where a large group of people had congregated. As they neared, Issai could see a spattering of prone bodies towards the back of the group with a flurry of people milling around them. He cautiously entered the fray, not wanting to risk another person walking through his soul-body now that he no longer felt any foreign particles contaminating his soul. Either they had been expunged all on their own or Hahri's suggestion had worked.

Rather than follow the woman they had tailed, Issai opted to approach one of the prone figures that was alone. The golden figure did indeed have the shape of a pregnant woman, and upon closer inspection, she too had that same dense cloud of blue particles below her core. Also, though it was a bit hard to differentiate from the mother's body, he could actually make out the golden outline of an infant's body within that extra dense cloud of particles.

"Hey—if that extra cloud of particles is part of the baby's soul, then where's the core?" Hahri abruptly asked.

Issai focused harder on the small figure. *"I can't see it either,"* he said after a long pause.

"I don't know about you, but I've never woken up in a new body while it's still in the womb. I always assumed that everyone else was born with their souls, but now…"

"Or maybe it is there, and we just can't see it until the baby's born," Issai reasoned. *"Look at how many things we were unable to see until we merged our souls to our current state. An unborn child's soul may just be one of many more unknowns."*

"Now I'm even more eager to see a birth," Hahri said. *"We should probably find someone closer to giving birth than this woman or the one we followed since we obviously can't wait around all day. I really don't want to miss talking with Keison today if he shows up. I want to grill him some more about Ina's supposed invisible barrier around the city."*

Issai scanned all around him for several moments before deciding on one towards the back of the group that was surrounded by four people and was writhing like someone possessed. As he stood watching at her feet, for the first time, Issai was glad that he had no physical ears to hear because judging by her frantic movements and the way she kept throwing her head back, she was no doubt screeching loud enough to wake the dead.

Even still, it was probably another hour before the baby finally made its appearance, and what happened a half-beat before it showed its first sign of life was something Issai could never in a million years have guessed. Something within the heart of that tiny golden body, deep within the dense cloud of blue particles that had indeed remained with the baby, seemed to collapse in on itself, warping the area like a crumbled up piece of parchment. It was immediately followed by an explosion of brilliant white light that lasted for perhaps another beat.

And then there it was, a blue-white, egg-shaped mass about the size of the infant's midsection, appearing as if it had been birthed by the very fabric of reality. The blue cloud surrounding the core was as frenzied as he'd ever seen it, already looking noticeable half as dense. Issai observed in a kind of numb fascination as the blue cloud gradually settled down along the outer limits while the particles closest to the new core began flowing towards the brilliant oval, behaving just as he'd seen with Hahri's and his own.

"That was..." Although words seemed to fail his bond partner, the awe infused in just those two words spoke volumes.

"Maybe we aren't moving through the realm of souls after all," was all Issai could think to say as he stared at that tiny new life. Perhaps there was something to that "Valley of the Gods" stuff the Sons of the Temple were always going on and on about...

"Korin would probably lose his shit if he saw this," Hahri added, apparently thinking along the same lines.

"Then we should tell him about it right away. At the rate he's going, he needs all the incentives as he can get if he plans on successfully moving his soul from his body anytime this century."

"We need to get back to the temple anyway. I still don't like the idea of Keison walking into our room alone with our bodies. We can always look for Old Souls afterwards."

"Agreed."

Issai made his way out of the Birthing House, not wanting to move his soul-body back to the temple while surrounded by so many people. He had no idea if it would cause a discernable disruption in the air, and given how superstitious new mothers were when it came to the events surrounding their child's birth, he didn't want to leave them with anything they could interpret as a bad omen.

Once past the last group of people, a wide stream of golden bodies off to the right immediately caught his attention. *"Is that the main road?"* he asked.

"Probably," Hahri replied. *"We can always walk back to the temple if you still want to scan the crowds. Maybe we'll even get to see someone die again."* Said so matter-of-factly, Issai couldn't tell if he was joking or not, so opted not to comment at all.

Like before, Issai slowly walked along the fringes of that human river, heading towards what he hoped was north as he scrutinized all those that passed him from both directions as well as those who entered the flow from side-streets, looking for the telltale larger soul core or denser blue glow of an Old Soul.

"I think that might be the temple," Hahri said after a while, directing Issai's attention to a point a little farther ahead where a good many people on the left were breaking off from the main flow of bodies.

"Then we might as well move straight to our roo—" Issai lost the thread of his words when his attention inadvertently landed on a figure whose cloud of blue light particles was perceptibly denser than all those around it.

Hardly daring to believe their luck, Issai focused all his attention on that person, seeking out their soul core. He would have hissed in annoyance had he been able when it seemed the people surrounding his mark would never move away, but then for a couple of beats, he finally got a brief, unobstructed view of the person's full body. Although much smaller in comparison to his own, the person's core was still a bit larger than all those around it.

"Issai, what—"

"I found one," Issai interrupted, certain that he was right.

He had a sense of absolute stillness within for the space of a breath and then, *"You're kidding me!"*

CHAPTER TWENTY-TWO

They followed the probable Old Soul as closely as they dared, becoming increasingly alarmed when the figure branched off to the left from the main group towards what Issai believed was the temple. Adding to his suspicion was the way the person was moving more slowly than everyone else, stopping for a beat or two at odd intervals as if something up ahead had briefly caught their attention. Issai hung back during those times, afraid that it was *them* that their quarry was sensing.

"Should we let them enter the temple?" Hahri asked.

"And how do you expect us to stop them?" Issai demanded. *"It's not like we can just stroll on up and pull out their soul or something."*

"Now there's an interesting idea," Hahri said, his mind-voice flavored with amusement. *"You at least can touch a soul without it disrupting your soul-body, so it might really be possible. Maybe we should try it out on the monk."*

If Issai would've had physical eyes, he would've rolled them. *"Touching one soul was enough, thank you very much.*

Let's just follow the Old Soul a bit more, see what they do. For all we know, they might just be going to the temple for something as innocent as the midday sermon."

Issai could already perceive a large crowd ahead, confirming for him that they were indeed moving towards the temple. The figure also showed no signs of stopping, following the line of blue-enveloped golden bodies for a bit before abruptly heading off to the left while the rest continued on a more diagonal path to the right.

If they were currently in the temple's main atrium, then the person was headed towards the monks' personal quarters. A cluster of what were likely monks stopped the probable Old Soul for a brief moment before waving the person on their way as if...they...knew...

Issai suddenly felt very stupid. *"It's Keison,"* he said, wincing mentally at the sheepishness in his mind-voice. Why hadn't he realized it before? They had worked themselves up for *nothing*.

A feeling like laughter filled his entire being. *"Gods— have we really become that paranoid? It's so obvious. Although— that we followed him here instead of moving instantly to the room might turn out not to be such a waste of time."*

"Oh?"

"Maybe he'll go into our room even if we don't answer his knock. Let's see what he does when he thinks we're sleeping."

Issai hurried past that same group of monks, feeling a burst of amusement from his partner when a couple of them jumped back as if in reaction to his passing. Perhaps they had even been able to see his soul-body. He would have to get Korin to ask them about it later. After what he had just seen in the Birthing House, he was curious about how much of the soul actually resided in their normal plane of existence.

When Keison stopped, Issai paused in what was probably the empty room next to Korin and Saiya's. He could clearly see a tall figure sitting on one of the cots while the much smaller one was sitting on what was likely the desk, both encased within the same thick cloud of blue particles.

Beyond that were two golden bodies sitting side by side as if suspended by air, the usual cloud of blue particles conspicuously absent. The room's walls would hide them from all three Old Souls while giving them an unobstructed view of the teen outside their door.

Keison raised a hand to knock, looking like a mime pounding on an invisible door. He paused for a few beats, then knocked again, this time a little harder. He paused for a few more, then hesitantly opened the door and slowly entered their room.

Wishing he could tell if the other was speaking, Issai left the empty room and cautiously followed after the boy into their own.

The blond teen abruptly stopped in the middle of the room as if startled, then quickly approached their cot. For a long moment, he appeared to just stare down at them. Then he reached a hesitant hand towards Hahri's cheek and instantly jerked it back the moment it contacted as if he had been burned.

"Probably feels like he touched a block of ice," Hahri commented with amusement.

Issai took the opportunity to study what he could perceive of the other's soul core through the multitudes of gold and blue light particles that encased it. Yes, there was definitely something—off—about various portions of it, much in the same way Hahri's newly healed soul core still didn't feel quite right to his soul's perception. However, as much as Keison went on and on about "invisible chains," Issai didn't see anything like that. He would just have to wait until he could see the boy in his pure soul form before judging either way.

Keison stood watching their bodies for a moment longer before abruptly turning around, catching Issai completely off guard. He had meant to leave the room before the other could see him, to maybe reveal themselves to Korin and have the monk follow them back to the room to explain while they re-entered their bodies.

The teen froze for half a beat, then instantly scrambled backwards before awkwardly falling over onto his side to rest seemingly in midair next to the golden figure that was Hahri's body.

"So much for sneaking around," Issai said dryly, watching the teen's frantic, unsuccessful attempts to right himself. *"Let's get back into our bodies before the poor kid wets himself."*

By the time Issai and Hahri had separated their intertwined soul cores and returned to their flesh and blood bodies, Keison had managed to roll off the cot. The boy currently had his back plastered against the wall beside the door, watching them with calmer, albeit slightly widened eyes. Issai couldn't help but notice the way the blond was cradling his chest protectively with an arm. Was he still hurting from what Soujin had done to him the other night?

"S-Sorry," Hahri said as soon as he was able, looking sideways at their visitor. "W-We didn't m-mean t-to scare y-you."

Keison swallowed thickly. "I thought—I thought you were Noll for a moment there," he admitted in a small voice, "that he had followed me here. The whole way, I kept feeling eyes on the back of my head, but I thought I was just being paranoid."

"And y-you w-weren't wrong," Hahri said. *"We* f-

281

followed y-you h-here."

"Why are you stuttering like that?" the blond asked, his brow furrowing.

Issai scowled while his partner just chuckled. "I-It's b-because I'm f-freezing of c-course! W-Why else d-did you th-think my s-skin w-would feel s-so c-cold?"

Keison flushed. "To be honest, you both looked dead propped up like that, like something only a psycho would do to his victims. Plus, it didn't look like you were breathing either, so I touched you just to be sure."

"Y-You s-said that y-you've t-touched Noll b-before," Hahri pointed out. "Did w-we really l-look s-so dif-ferent?"

Keison nodded. "Maybe it's 'cause I only saw Ina and Noll in really dim light."

"You don't h-have to keep s-standing there," Issai said, handing a full mug of steaming cider to Hahri. He had taken advantage of the others' conversation to down a couple of mugs of the hot liquid and was already feeling considerably better. "You look l-like you're about to fall o-over."

"Yeah," the blond teen said, suddenly looking uncomfortable as he slowly made his way over to the chair in front of the desk.

"Soujin again?" Issai prompted when it became apparent that the boy wasn't going to elaborate.

Keison stiffened at the mention of his tormentor's name, but then he clenched his fists and his mouth hardened into a thin line of determination. "That's why I didn't come yesterday," he admitted. "The night before, Soujin pulled on the chains the entire night. I really don't know how I managed to stay sane. I couldn't even go to work until today, I hurt so badly."

"Is he d-doing it now?" Issai asked, nodding at the

way the other boy was currently pressing a tightly-clenched fist into the center of his chest.

The teen looked down at his hand in surprise as if unaware of his own actions. He slowly opened his hand and brought it down to rest in his lap. He lowered his eyes in what looked that shame.

"I think it's just an echo," he said quietly.

Issai shared a significant look with Hahri, trying to convey his question with emotion alone through the Bond. He couldn't help feeling a little frustrated. Being able to speak mind-to-mind while merged in the same body had really spoiled him. Hahri tilted his head inquisitively at the sudden influx of emotions, then nodded a few beats later with a slight quirk to his lips.

"We m-might have found a way t-to help you," Issai said.

Keison jerked his head up so fast that Issai was surprised he didn't hear his neck crack. "What!"

"A soul's 'eyes' can s-see a lot more than th-these," he said vaguely, tapping the side of his right eye. "We can discuss it more once you l-learn how to move your soul from your body. It'll be p-pointless otherwise."

"I wouldn't even know where to begin," Keison said dejectedly.

"We'll teach you, so don't worry about it so much right now," Hahri said. "But before that, there's a bigger problem we need to address. Ina's invisible barrier."

Issai resented that Hahri didn't stutter once. He poured another mug of hot cider and downed it in one gulp, determined to stop his shivering.

"I haven't been taken outside the city since she showed it to me if that's what you're asking," Keison told him.

"I was thinking more along the lines of having you

take us to the exact spot where she demonstrated it for you," Hahri clarified. "I don't altogether believe her claim that it encircles the entire city, you see. After all, your obvious fear of Soujin effectively prevents you from ever daring to test her word, so deceiving you would be fairly simple."

Keison jumped to his feet. "But—what if it really does? She'll *know* if you touch it!" he insisted, voice going shrill with alarm.

"I don't plan on touching it," Hahri assured the now agitated boy. "At least not yet. I just want to *see* it is all."

"But it's invisible—"

"To mortal eyes perhaps," Issai cut in, trading a smirk with Hahri.

Keison stared at him in confusion. "What do you mean?"

"Remember what I said about a soul's eyes?"

"I think this is the place," Keison said, stopping about a couple hundred strides to the left of the southern road out of Kairash. "We probably shouldn't go forward any farther since I can't really remember how far away the barrier is from the city wall."

Issai nodded. "You can merge completely with me now," he said aloud to Hahri.

They had found that they could not talk mind-to-mind while Hahri was sharing his body. However, Issai was still hopeful that when Hahri gave up complete control to him that it was indeed exactly the same thing as merging soul-bodies.

In the next beat, power surged through his entire being, and the world exploded with colorful currents. Issai immediately turned towards the south—and froze.

"Saat! That looks really ominous," Hahri said within his mind.

The sight before him wiped out any elation Issai might have felt upon hearing Hahri's mind-voice. A dense wall of blood-red, sluggishly moving particles stood before them like some sort of barrier between the human world and the first hell, rising towards the sky to about double the height of the city wall. It was transparent enough that he could still make out the fields of white flowers and the travelers moving along the road tinted completely in red.

He watched as a couple of horse-drawn wagons moved through the wall as if it were merely an illusion even though it looked plenty real to his soul-vision. His gaze followed the wall from left to right to the limits of his line-of-sight. The uncanny wall seemed to follow the curve of the city wall exactly, giving credence to Ina's claim that it encircled the entire city.

Issai must have had quite the expression because Keison suddenly grabbed his arm and demanded in a fearful voice, "What's there? What do you see?"

"A wall of blood," Issai replied grimly, pulling his arm from the blond's grip without taking his eyes off the barrier.

"Way to scare the kid more," Hahri said sardonically. *"Remember, if he faints, you're the one that has to carry him back to the temple."*

Issai ignored him, turning towards the now horrified teen. "It's a wall of condensed red light particles that appears to encircle the city wall just as Ina claimed. As I've never seen anything like it, I can't even begin to guess how it was constructed."

"There's no way we can not touch it," Hahri said. *"I know Keison said that he could feel it, but those wagons got through just*

fine. I'm still not quite convinced that it works just as she told him. It would be quite a feat to create something that can affect people that selectively. He could've still been duped."

"Whether real or not, now that I've seen this monstrosity, I really don't want to stay in this city another day. I think we've left Soujin alone long enough. We need to find out why he wishes to keep us imprisoned here."

"What should we do about Keison? Take him with us?"

"Definitely. There may be more about the other Old Souls he hasn't told us, but despite that, just leaving him behind to be tortured by that bastard would be cruel."

"Keison will freak out, but I think you should try to walk through it right now. Even if everything Ina told him is true and some kind of beacon is set off, unless she's already in the city, it'll likely take her at least a day to actually get here to investigate. Of course, if we can't just walk through it, we'll only have a short time to figure out how to break through."

"At this point, it will be a risk no matter what we choose to do," Issai reasoned. *"Might as well go for the prize."*

"Um…"

Issai blinked and re-focused on Keison. "Sorry, I was speaking with Kye. Stay here. I want to get a closer look, and I don't want you accidentally going too far because you can't see it." He felt bad about deceiving the teen, but he really didn't want to have to deal with a hysterical kid sooner than was absolutely necessary.

Issai walked towards the red barrier until only a hand-span remained between them. This close and the wall appeared less condensed and stable, as though it had been constructed out of some bizarre form of luminous, semi-transparent crimson sand.

Before Keison could realize what he was doing, Issai stepped forward. The sensation was like running into a large windowpane without shattering the glass.

"No!" Keison shouted in horror. Issai completely expected the boy to come running, but when he glanced behind him, the blond was rooted to the spot as if too scared to move. "You said you wouldn't touch it!" he accused.

"Don't worry; we don't plan on being here when Ina shows up," Issai told him calmly. "Just stay back for a moment."

He pressed a hand firmly against the barrier. Like air made solid, Keison had told them. At the time, Issai couldn't imagine what the blond teen meant, but now that he was touching it, he decided that the strange texture could be described no other way. It wasn't slick like glass or porous and rough like a dried sponge, nor was it particularly hot, cold, cool, or warm. It was just *there*, a purely mental acknowledgment of its existence.

That last thought gave him an idea.

"Hahri, can you step out of my body for a moment? I want to try to walk through it when I can't see it."

"Keison couldn't see it," Hahri reminded him.

"I know. What I should have said was 'can't perceive *it.' I'm going to shut my eyes as well."*

"It's worth a shot."

Within moments, Hahri's soul-body stood beside him, translucent and nearly featureless, but still identifiable as a human body. Issai noted that the transitions between states took less and less time to complete each time they did them, a fact that would come in handy in the future, he was sure.

"What are you doing?" Keison called worriedly.

"Testing its capabilities," Issai replied.

"We really should be getting out of here!" Keison insisted.

"Just a bit longer," Issai said as he shut his eyes and

proceeded towards the barrier again, this time with a bit more momentum.

Bam!

"Dammit!" Issai muttered, stepping back and rubbing his forehead.

A rush of amusement came through the Bond, and Issai turned to glare half-heartily at his partner. Not that the other would be able to actually *see* his expression in his current state. Then before Issai could beckon him back into his body, Hahri's soul-body walked into the barrier.

The result, in Issai's opinion, probably looked a lot more hilarious than his own face-plant. The moment he had collided with the barrier, Hahri's entire form seemed to fly apart like a raindrop striking a cobblestone, leaving behind a much smaller, shimmering blob that was probably the manifestation of his soul core in the material plane.

Issai received a barrage of Hahri's wordless curses through the Bond before the other's soul reentered his body without even trying to re-form a soul-body.

"That has got to be one of the weirdest things I have ever felt!" Hahri said the moment their souls were melded again.

"Did it hurt?" Issai asked curiously.

"No, not exactly. It just really muddled my sense of reality for a moment. I had a hard time perceiving you until the chaos settled. I felt like I was lost for hours!"

Issai frowned. *"It was only a few moments between you hitting the barrier and then hitting me with your curses."*

A sudden cry of alarm behind him had Issai instantly whipping around, his knives sliding into his hands. A young, brown-haired girl about a finger-span shorter stood behind Keison, one hand clutching his right shoulder tightly and the other wrapped tightly around his

288

middle. By the look of absolute terror on the boy's face, she could be only one person.

"Shit!" Issai spat, and launched himself at them.

Then between one step and the next, he felt Hahri push his consciousness to the forefront with more aggression than he had ever used before, and suddenly they were only one stride away from the pair when a haze of red flooded his vision in the same instant something solid brutally slammed into his face. Issai bounced back sharply and landed hard onto his back, feeling Hahri's presence retreat as a shock of pain reverberated throughout his back and face.

What in the three hells had *happened?*

A warm liquid began flowing down into his eyes and mouth. Issai spat it out the moment he tasted salt on his tongue, wiping furiously at his eyes with the back of his hand that still, thankfully, clutched a knife. Issai rolled over and forced himself to his knees, the inside of his head throbbing as if it might burst. When he finally managed to raise his head, his eyes immediately fixed on the distorted image of two people moving erratically towards the barrier.

"Get up! They're almost to the barrier!" he heard Hahri urge faintly within his mind.

Keison was frantically trying to jerk out of her grasp while also dragging his feet, but the slight girl continued to pull him along by the wrist with an abnormal show of strength.

Issai's body refused to cooperate, the world jolting upside down and causing him to fall back to one knee the moment he tried to stand.

"Can't," Issai gasped, pressing his fists against either side of his head as it continued to throb painfully.

A faint curse floated through his mind beneath the

pain, then suddenly Hahri was pushing for control again and Issai let him have it. Hahri immediately dropped both knives, raised both hands straight above his head, and then swung both arms down as hard as he could as if throwing something at the retreating figures.

Issai saw it for only half a beat, a ripple in the air as though the very fabric of reality had been torn and the top part of the world had slipped down a bit, before Keison and Ina went down hard as if they had been trampled from behind by a herd of rampaging bulls. Neither one was moving.

Hahri slowly staggered to his feet, failing down twice more before Issai's legs finally held. He hastily wiped the blood that continued to stream into his eyes and then pressed the same hand against the wound on Issai's forehead, wincing at the sting. He tried wiping at the blood pouring out of Issai's nose, but soon gave it up as a lost cause and pressed his lips tightly together to keep the disgusting liquid from getting in his mouth.

He reached up to pinch Issai's nostrils closed to stem the flow, but one agonizing touch revealed that it wasn't just broken, but *crushed*. Issai cringed to think of what his face probably looked like right now.

"I can't believe that actually worked," Hahri said, looking in the direction of the still bodies lying within the white blossoms about a hundred strides away.

"What the hell did you do?" Issai demanded as Hahri carefully bent down to retrieve the two knives he had dropped earlier.

"The same thing I accidentally did to Korin a couple of days ago," Hahri replied, slipping both blades into the arm-sheaths hidden beneath Issai's sleeves before he started to walk, or more accurately, limp towards the downed pair. *"Remember when I threw him against the wall with only a*

gesture?"

"We never did look into that, did we..." Issai couldn't believe he had forgotten about such an important thing. *"There for a moment, it looked like you had warped reality."*

"Who knows? I was trying to aim for Ina alone, and she did take the brunt of it, but..." He sighed. *"We were just out of options. I just hope Keison isn't hurt too badly."*

"He would probably forgive us anything as long as we keep him safe from Soujin." Issai paused for a few beats then asked, *"What happened back there? One beat we were running and the next my face felt like someone had bashed it in with a tree trunk!"*

"I'm not sure. If I didn't know better, I'd say we face-planted into one of the bitch's barriers."

"It did seem like I saw a flash of red before I ended up flat on my back," Issai agreed. *"We're all damn lucky that neither one of us blacked out."*

"Should we take Ina back to the temple for a little chat?"

"No," Issai said at once. *"First we need to get her to open the barrier, and then get her to tell us everything she knows about Soujin—neither of which will happen without resorting to the kind of methods the monk will definitely not approve of."*

"Right. Where should we—oh look, I think Keison is waking up."

Issai turned his attention back to the scene before him just as they reached the pair. Keison was moaning softly and looked to be trying to turn over. Hahri stiffly went down on his knees beside the blond and helped him roll over. Other than a minor bloody nose, Keison did not show any outward injuries.

"S-Senn?" Keison croaked, frowning confusedly up at them. "What's going on? What happened to your *face?*"

Hahri wiped the blood from his mouth and pointed to the unmoving body beside the teen. "Ina happened, that's what."

Keison's eyes went comically wide as his gaze followed Issai's finger. He yelped, and violently jerked away from her body.

"Is she dead?" he asked, a tinge of hopefulness coloring his words.

"Probably not. I was only trying to stop her, not kill her. Sorry about the 'kick' to your backside, by the way. We were a little desperate."

Keison gasped. "I remember now! Ina grabbed me from behind and I shouted. Then one moment you were by the barrier and the next you appeared right in front of us as if out of thin air! Next thing I know you just flew back like someone had thrown you!"

"We think we hit one of Ina's barriers. I don't know how she managed to create one so fast, but we definitely didn't see that one coming. Senn's nose must be pulverized."

"Huh?" For a few beats, Keison looked puzzled before understanding flashed in his eyes. "Oh, I'm talking to Kye, aren't I? Gods, this is so weird!"

"You'll get use to it," Hahri assured him. "If you can stand, we need to tie Ina up before she wakes. Senn always carries some rope looped to his belt, enough to at least—"

Without warning, Ina's hand shot out and grasped one of Keison's ankles, and a thick, red film began to spread up his leg so quickly that it had already completely covered the teen's body up to his chest before he could even gasp with shock.

"Move and he dies," Ina warned, her voice breathy and strained as she laboriously pulled herself to her knees without letting go of Keison's ankle. The red film had now completely covered the completely terrified teen's head. "I've placed a barrier around him. He probably only has enough air for a quarter-hour. Attack me again and I'll press the barrier against his nose and mouth completely."

CHAPTER TWENTY-THREE

Rage boiled up within Issai, made all the more potent when joined by Hahri's own rage.

"Do that and you'll be dead before you can even blink," Hahri said quietly. By the brief flash of fear in Ina's eyes that she couldn't completely suppress, Issai figured that the ancient Hahri had surfaced. "I'm guessing that Soujin would be pissed if that happened."

Ina flinched as if Hahri had slapped her, then turned a glare hot enough to melt steel towards Keison. "Traitor! I thought you were just trying to escape the city, but how dare you give *him* information about us and our lord!"

Hahri snorted. "He didn't. We found out the bastard was up to something all on our own."

"Right now, I think Noll is with her," Issai informed him. *"Be careful. Keison never did mention whether or not he had any special abilities."*

While Hahri verbally sparred with the Old Soul, Issai had taken the opportunity to study her with a soul's eye. Although he couldn't see past the golden particles of her body to glimpse her soul core in his current state, he could clearly perceive that a large quantity of those golden particles were not the same in the same way he had been able to spot the foreign particles that had contaminated his soul-body when all those people had walked through him back in the Merchant District. With Hahri in control of his body, Issai couldn't look down at himself for comparison, but he was fairly certain that he was right.

"We?" Ina's eyes suddenly narrowed in suspicion. "The other one's with you, isn't he?" When Hahri said nothing, she laughed, the tone more sinister than amused. "I can't believe you two have the balls to merge again after what Soujin did to you," she sneered.

Both Issai and Hahri stilled completely. "What the hell are you going on about?" Hahri demanded, his voice low and deadly.

She giggled. "Still can't remember? I suppose I can give you a hint. If you think this is the first life you've met then think again. Does the name 'Vorn' ring a bell?"

Hearing that name come from the mouth of an enemy violently shook both of them to the core, so much so that Hahri actually physically flinched.

"What do you know of that?" Hahri hissed.

Her smile was condescending as she shook her head. "I think we've talked enough."

She squeezed Keison's ankle tightly, causing the boy to wince, then carefully slid her hand up his leg, tracing a path across his torso, up to his shoulder until finally coming to rest on his right bicep. She dug her fingers into the flesh as if the red barrier wasn't even there, making him wince again.

"Get up," she ordered the blond harshly as she climbed unsteadily to her feet.

When Keison just sat there, she yanked his arm up

until it seemed she would pull it from its socket. Only then did the boy reluctantly comply, swaying a bit as if dizzy.

Hahri jumped to his feet as well and made as if to lunge at her, but a hiss of warning from her stayed his hand.

"Do you really think we'd let you take him?" Hahri growled.

"You have no choice," she replied smugly.

"I would rather die!" Keison cried, his voice sounding muffled as if shouted from behind a pillow that had been pressed over his face.

His dark eyes darted to Issai's forearm then back up to Issai's eyes, pleading. Issai felt his heart clench painfully at what the boy was asking.

"Give me control," Issai said firmly. If it had to be done, then *he* would be the one to carry the stain.

A variety of emotions from his partner washed through him—startlement, violent refusal, stubbornness, exasperation, as well as something else that was so complicated that he had no hope to decipher it. However, Issai would not be swayed. Not this time.

"Give it to me," he repeated softly. No argument, no anger, just something that would be.

That strange emotion flooded his being again, then Hahri simply retreated without a word.

"You think that because he is an Old Soul that he has no reason to fear death," Ina said, "but he has every reason, as do the rest of you, because even if he's reborn, you'll never find him again. But *we* will."

Issai narrowed his eyes. "We'll see."

Both knives slid into his hands and he lunged at Keison. In that moment, Ina's eyes widened in panic before she suddenly shoved Keison hard directly at Issai, turned, and ran towards the barrier. One of Issai's knives struck Keison at chest level as the blond fell into him, the blade sliding off the red film without penetrating as if it were as strong as a granite wall.

"Issai!" Hahri screamed urgently in his mind as he staggered back with the other boy's unexpected weight.

He cursed as he caught sight of the fleeing woman's back. She was only a few strides away from the barrier.

Issai thrust Keison to the side and threw a knife at her with everything he had in him without a moment's thought, unsure if he could even reach that distance. It embedded itself in her left shoulder, the shock of the impact causing her to tumble forward only a couple of strides away from her goal.

Without even conferring with each other, Hahri instantly took back control of Issai's body and shot off after Ina with all the speed of an arrow. The flash of red was all the warning they received, and Hahri barely managed to get an arm up to chest level before they crashed headlong at top speed into one of Ina's barriers for the second time that day. Issai felt the agony of his arm shattering as they were flung back in reaction, but Hahri was already struggling to rise from the moment they had hit the ground.

Ina was crawling towards the barrier one-armed, his knife no longer sticking out of her heavily bleeding shoulder. The barrier they had crashed into was still there, small and only about the width of four grown men standing shoulder-to-shoulder.

Through sheer stubbornness, Hahri made it back onto his feet and stumbled after the crawling figure, wasting a few precious beats having to go around the small barrier. Only Ina's legs were still on their side of the barrier, and Hahri made one last desperate leap, reaching out with his good arm in an effort to snag her boot. His fingers grazed Ina's heel just as she pulled it completely into the red mass of particles.

For the second time, agony shot through Issai's left arm as they landed directly on the ruined limb, the pain so excruciating that he was certain he would have blacked out had Hahri not been within his body to share the pain. Issai didn't know how, but Hahri still managed to immediately climb to his knees and try to follow Ina through the barrier, but the moment his hand touched that red wall, Issai knew they had lost.

"*Saat!*" Hahri screamed aloud, banging Issai's uninjured fist hard against the once more functioning barrier in thwarted fury. He sat back onto his haunches and cradled Issai's injured arm against his chest as they both helplessly watched such a potential treasure trove of information stumble farther and farther from their grasp.

Then Issai became aware of movement behind them, and he immediately pushed for control. He turned his head and saw Keison staggering over to them about a hundred paces away, his body still covered from head to toe with that red film. His hands were frantically clawing at his throat as if a noose were tightening around his neck, which, Issai realized with horror, wasn't too far off the mark.

Ina had claimed that Keison only had enough air for a quarter-hour. He was pretty sure at least that amount of time had already passed if not more. Issai hurried over to the teen as quickly as his injuries allowed.

"It's—hard—to breath," Keison wheezed as soon as the violet-eyed boy was within earshot. He looked utterly terrified.

"Don't speak," Issai warned. Already, the blue cloud of particles surrounding Keison's body appeared significantly less substantial. "The air within has probably almost gone completely bad. Sit down and try to hold your breath as much as you can. You need to buy us as much time as you can if we're to have any hope of saving you."

"I don't think the bitch was lying when she said they would find him before we could if he died today, and I think the kid knows it. That's why he looks so terrified right now."

"She thought I was going for her with my knives. I saw the panic in her eyes. That's the only reason why she pushed Keison into me—to shield herself. After being so unwilling to give him up before, likely fearing punishment from Soujin, the only reason I can think for her to do it at that moment was she believed remaining in her current body was more important to Soujin, and that she was confident they would be able to retrieve Keison again in the future."

"We absolutely cannot allow any of that to happen." Hahri said determinately.

"I only have one idea to try," Issai cautioned, staring grimly at Keison's red-coated body. *"Ina's barriers are all composed of light particles. They're different from the blue particles, of course, but I'm hoping that they all fundamentally follow the same rules, that I can separate them in the same way that I separated the fragment of your soul from my core. If it doesn't work, then we're probably all screwed."*

Issai scowled. *"I really don't want to do this here, but Keison would be dead long before we could get him back to the temple."* He glanced over to the southern road that was still filled with quite a few travelers despite it already being past midday. He could only pray that no one decided to wonder over, or worse, that the Guard decided that they looked suspicious enough to investigate. *"We need to separate. Form a soul-body and wait for me."*

He focused once again on Keison. "Stay as still as possible. We're both going to leave my body, so don't be alarmed when our souls appear."

Once Hahri was gone, Issai moved out of his body as quickly as he could manage and wasted no time in forming his soul-body and joining with Hahri's. He then kneeled down beside Keison and touched a ghostly hand against the barrier. The feeling of texture to his soul sense was something smooth and solid and completely alarming.

The blue cloud surrounding the boy's body was a frenzy of movement, mirroring the growing agitation that Issai felt perfectly as he realized just how much of those particles Keison had lost. An image of the man he had killed a couple of night ago entered his mind, how the blue cloud around him had disappeared completely just before he died, and his heart sank.

"This barrier is different than the one around the city," he told Hahri, his mind-voice bleak. *"The red particles are almost static; I can barely feel any movement at all. They're only one step away from merging completely into a single structure. I don't know if they can be separated any longer!"*

Suddenly Keison's body toppled over to the side, followed at once by a mass disappearance of more of those blue particles.

"Whatever you're planning on doing, you had better do it quick!" Hahri exclaimed.

Issai focused a large concentration of their blue particles into his hand and thrust it at the red film covering Keison's face, trying to dig his fingers into the barrier. They merely slid off without making so much as a crack. With Hahri's soul fragment, he had only had to push at the different core materials with the intent of healing as if he were cutting a seam and the two souls had separated, albeit slowly and with some resistance. But the two soul cores had been alive with movement as opposed to this infuriating barrier that was all but inert. It wasn't going to work, and it was all he had.

Issai clenched his hand and hit the barrier with it in a fit of anger. The extra particles he had collected into his hand were released in a flash of brilliant blue light, and he felt something in the smooth material beneath change. He jerked back his hand in surprise and saw a small patch of sluggishly moving red particles over the area of Keison's nose.

"That's it! Whatever you just did, do it again!" Hahri urged excitedly.

Issai hastily flooded his hand with more of the blue particles and then slammed his fist as hard as he could into the same spot over Keison's face. This time he felt the surface of the barrier give, and when he removed his hand, golden particles were completely visible through a hole in the red film the size of a coin. Issai resupplied his hand a third time and smashed the area just under that hole.

Rather than behave like shards of a broken pane of glass, the red particles became like the sparks of red light he had seen flowing in the multitudes of shimmering currents of colored particles that flowed all around them. He watched as they slowly drifted from beneath his fist towards a nearby particle stream of sparkling purple and disappeared within as if absorbed.

Issai quickly pulled back his hand when he noticed that some of Keison's blue particles were starting to stick to his hand. The hole in the barrier was now large enough to have completely uncovered Keison's mouth and nose.

"That's enough for now, I think," Issai said, moving back to his feet. *"As long as he can breathe, the rest can wait until later. I don't want to leave my body so vulnerable for another beat longer if I don't have to."*

"Then let's try to enter it while we're merged like this," Hahri suggested. *"It'll be faster."*

To Issai's surprise, entering his body in their current form felt no different than when he did it alone. Even the bone-chilling cold felt the same. However, the blinding pain in his arm and face completely caught him off-guard. Damn—he had totally forgotten about the mess Hahri had made of his arm and nose. The way his forehead throbbed and his vision blurred, he suspected that, along with a likely concussion, he might have also fractured his skull.

He definitely needed to heal his wounds before they went back to the temple, but first, he needed to make sure Keison was in fact still breathing. Issai carefully and stiffly moved onto his knees in order to hover over Keison's prone body, trying not to wince and aggravate the pain in his face as his shattered arm was painfully jostled.

Keison's body still looked as though it had been dipped in a pool of blood, but at least the teen's chest was moving up and down in a more or less normal rhythm even if he was still unconscious. The red film was completely gone from a central area just below his eyes to a bit above his chin, the edges around the hole curved and smooth rather than sharp and jagged.

"He's one lucky bastard," Hahri commented as Issai slowly fell back onto his haunches. *"If this had happened a couple of days ago, you wouldn't have had the right knowledge to help you figure out how to break that barrier."*

"And as always, luck wanted nothing to do with us *since Ina managed to get away,"* Issai replied sardonically. He glanced back at the southern road and along the perimeter of the city wall, but his eyesight was just too hazy to be reliable. *"My vision is pretty much shot right now, but I'll try to keep my*

eyes open while I heal myself. Keep a look out for trouble as best you can."

He felt a burst of sympathy from his partner. *"I'm glad I don't have to worry about your wounds manifesting on my body any longer. It would have sucked if you had to heal the same injuries twice."* A feeling of wry laughter, then, *"Hell, just feeling these kinds of injuries twice would have sucked."*

Issai fixed his eyes to a point in the distance between the road and wall in order to give Hahri the best angle, then turned his focus inward to begin tracing out his injuries, starting with his head. Once the feeling of knives stabbing into his head disappeared, the rest of his injuries were much easier to take care of, though his arm took twice as long to heal than his nose.

Issai sighed wearily and stretched his newly healed arm out, pleased that not so much as an ache remained. His vision had also cleared enough for him to see movement along the right edge of the city wall that quickly materialized into five figures slowly heading west towards the southern road.

"That's probably the Guard," Issai said aloud as he turned towards the still prone teen beside him. "It's a damned miracle that we haven't been spotted yet, but I don't want to push it."

"You'll have to carry Keison," Hahri pointed out unnecessarily.

Issai growled. "If the kid knows what's good for him he'll wake up. *Right. Now!*"

Issai smacked Keison's cheeks hard between his two hands, taking into account the thin barrier still coating most of the kid's face.

Keison sat up so quickly that he and Issai almost bumped foreheads.

"Good," Issai said with satisfaction, climbing to his

feet as the blond stared up at him with a look of wide-eyed confusion. "Now, get up. An even worst task awaits us."

"Which is?" Hahri asked as Keison went from staring to frantically touching his face and neck.

Issai's expression turned sour. *"Convincing Saiya to leave with us."*

CHAPTER TWENTY-FOUR

"No," Saiya said flatly, looking from Issai to Korin as the monk sat across the room wringing his hands anxiously.

"Ina may be hurt, but they still have a perfectly sound body to use in Noll," Issai reasoned. "We can't count on them staying away for long. We would especially be screwed if Soujin decided to come clean up their mess for them. Meeting him on his terms when we're still almost completely in the dark is the worst thing that could possibly happen at this stage."

"*No.*"

"Saiya…" Korin trailed off, looking at his bond partner pleadingly.

"Look," Hahri spoke up, pulling himself away from the door he had been leaning against, "there's no way we can stay here. Don't you understand—she *knew* about Senn and me, things about our ancient past that should've been impossible for her to know. She erected that barrier to keep *all of us* here. Not just Keison. That's more than

305

enough reason for a jail break."

Without warning, Saiya drew her sword, causing everyone to flinch back simultaneously. She pointed it at Korin. "I gave you your time," she hissed. "If you insist on leaving now without fulfilling your promise to me, then I'll just break that gods-be-cursed bond *my* way right now!"

Hahri was suddenly in front of her, yanking the sword out of her hands and smacking her hard with an open palm on the side of her head.

"Dammit kid!" he barked angrily as she lunged for the sword with murder in her eyes.

He shoved her back roughly with his free hand, and Issai caught the back of her shirt and yanked her even farther away from Hahri. "If you would just take that humungous stick you've got shoved up your ass out for one moment, you would clearly be able to see that we've been doing nothing *but* help you! You kill Korin now, and the only thing that will accomplish is helping that Soujin bastard by making us wait for the monk to grow up again while the separation from him slowly drives the *both* of you mad."

Saiya jerked out of Issai's grip, alternating her glare equally between Hahri and Issai as she silently backed away from them until her back hit the desk, looking like an animal cornered. Both Korin and Keison watched the scene from their perch on the same cot, frozen and silent as if worried the slightest movement might set Saiya off again.

Hahri relaxed his defensive stance when it became apparent that she wasn't going to try for the sword again, and his angry expression melted into something less severe. "Right now Senn knows more about the forces governing our souls than any of us could understand even after an eternity of trying. He is the best hope you have to ever deciphering the mysteries of the Bond. So what's it gonna be? Are you gonna run off now like a brat throwing a tantrum, or are you gonna come with us and just maybe have your wish fulfilled?"

As Saiya and Hahri silently stared each other down, Keison suddenly screamed and toppled to the floor, shattering the suffocating tension as effectively as a bolt of lightning striking the middle of the room.

"Soujin—he's—" the boy managed to moan before shrieking fit to wake the dead and curling up into a fetal position.

"*Saat!*" Hahri cursed, rushing over to the writhing teen and tossing Saiya's sword to the shocked monk as he knelt down. This was the first time Korin had witnessed the boy being tortured. "Ina must have reached Soujin already! We have to go *now!*"

"Merge soul-bodies with me!" Issai demanded, falling to his knees beside his partner. "If Soujin did indeed attach some sort of invisible chains to Keison's soul, then he'll probably be able to follow them straight to us! Now that he's pulling on them, I might be able to perceive them this time!"

Hahri nodded. "You two stand back!" he directed at Saiya and Korin as Issai and he scooted back to sit against the wall.

A few moments later, Issai was gazing down once again at Keison's red-filmed body. He focused on where the tormented boy was currently fisting his hands against his stomach. Ina's barrier was making it extremely difficult for him to perceive all the varying particles beneath, as if trying to look through an extremely dirty window.

"I can't 'see' past that blasted barrier, dammit! We don't have time for this!" Issai growled in his mind.

He filled both hands with a multitude of blue particles until they were shining more white than blue and drove both fists down onto Keison's stomach and the arms protecting it as if they were a sledgehammer. Red particles went flying in every direction like sparks from a disturbed campfire, and Keison's body seemed to spasm violently in response to the impact.

The blond teen might have also screamed, but Issai wasn't sure if it was in response to the barrier shattering over his torso or to the three faint lines coming from the heart of his now visible soul core, quivering like ropes being pulled taunt. They were so insubstantial that had he not been looking specifically for something abnormal and the material had not been sufficiently "excited," Issai would have easily missed them.

The effect was exactly the same as he had observed when he had been inadvertently pulling at Hahri's core when he had still carried a fragment of his partner's soul. The lines continued on outside Keison's body to a distance far beyond what Issai could perceive.

It was no wonder that Keison was screaming so horribly. The kid must feel as if his soul was being literally torn in half.

"Do you see?" Issai asked.

"The bastard pulled out pieces of his soul!" The disgust in Hahri's voice was palpable. *"Can you do something about it?"*

"Yes," Issai replied hesitantly. Without Soujin being in the room, there was only one course of action he could see. *"I can 'cut' them."*

The resulting jolt of emotion from Hahri was what he imagined shock would feel like if it were something as material as a rock slamming into his face.

"To lose a piece of his soul, no matter how small, forever—do we really want to do that to him?"

"I don't, but the alternative—leaving him behind for Soujin to find him—would probably be a worse fate. If Soujin had taken a large piece then I would never consider it, but... This is all we can do for him."

"Then do it," Hahri said firmly, *"and let the burden of this deed be shared equally between us."*

Issai did not at all like the way Hahri's final words had reverberated throughout his soul, as though Hahri had made some sort of cosmic pact with the gods that had branded the other boy's soul in a dangerous way. But now was not the time to confront him about, especially when whatever his bond partner had just done had the feel of something permanent.

He willed a bunch of blue particles to the tips of a couple of fingers and then walked over to a point about a hundred paces from Keison's body, wanting to spare as much of Keison's soul as he could. This time the process was a bit trickier as there was no "seam" to work with on the three stretched pieces of the teen's soul. Like with Ina's barrier, attacking the problem as if it were a wound to heal did not so much as cause a scratch in the soul material when Issai dug his finger across a strand.

Issai directed more of his blue particles to the tips of his thumb and index finger and then grasped all of the soul strands between them firmly while gripping a point along the strands about a finger-span to the left with his other hand. Hoping that what he was about to do wouldn't be as painful to Keison as he feared, Issai violently wrenched the strands held firmly between his fingers to the right while willing the blue particles to dig into the soul material at the same time.

All the strands instantly snapped as easily as if they were strands of hair, releasing a backlash of energy that completely disrupted Issai and Hahri's combined soul-body. His senses in disarray, it was a long while before Issai could focus his mind enough to turn his attention back to Keison. The boy's body was no longer curled in on itself but thrashing around as if he were having a fit. Another body, Korin judging by the size, was now kneeling beside him trying to hold the writhing body down.

His heart sank.

"Hahri can you hear me?" Issai sent urgently.

"Things were a bit weird there for a moment, but yeah."

"Help me form our soul-body again. It looks like Keison's in agony! I have to try to heal the damage!"

Even though it was probably only a few beats, it seemed to take an eternity before they managed to form another soul-body. In an instant, Issai was kneeling beside Korin and scrutinizing Keison's soul core. The damage was immediately apparent; the unique bits of material that formed the core in that area moved erratically compared to the rest of the core.

"You've never been able to heal anyone except yourself and me," Hahri said worriedly. *"Can you?"*

"After healing the injury to your soul and breaking the barrier around Keison today, I think I finally understand the 'how' about my ability more thoroughly if not the 'why'—why I, alone, seem to be able to do it."

Using a surge of blue particles at his fingertips, Issai carefully ran them over the damaged area, concentrating on an intent to match the "torn" places to the un-damaged, surrounding material. Right away, he could feel that it was working, that the material was beginning to move more naturally. He continued to work until Keison's body fell still and he could no longer sense that he was causing any change. Removing his hand, Issai scrutinized the area and was relieved to see the soul's equivalent of healed scars.

"So—does this mean you'll be able to heal everybody now?" Hahri asked, his entire being buzzing with excitement.

"Not their physical bodies. My power lies within my soul, is fueled by it, so because our souls are bound and if it's a body we inhabit, then I can heal it. Given that only a soul can touch a soul, I wouldn't even know where to begin using my flesh and blood hand."

"Speaking of, we need to get back into our bodies. Keison's condition notwithstanding, we left the rage monster with an important question to answer. Not to mention Soujin who, if he wasn't already on his way here, he probably is now *since we've broken his leash on Keison."*

This time, they didn't have the luxury of warming up slowly. As soon as Issai was firmly within his body again, he spared only a few moments to rub his hands vigorously over his arms to get his circulation going before crawling over to Korin and Keison. He was only vaguely aware that Saiya had not moved from her place against the front of the desk. As long as she wasn't a threat, he would concern himself with her later.

"How is he?" Issai asked the monk as he sat back onto his haunches beside him.

Keison's face looked ashen and was covered by a sheen of sweat and multiple trails of tears, but his expression was calm as he opened his eyes and regarded Issai with a weak smile. Issai was surprised that the boy was actually conscious.

He felt Hahri come up behind them as Keison answered hoarsely, "I still feel a bit of a strong ache, but the worst is gone. Are they gone for good now?"

Issai made a face. There was no easy way to say it so might as well be blunt. "It wasn't anything like invisible chains I cut; it was pieces of your soul, pieces that Soujin probably stretched out of you the first time you met and

311

kept as kind of a tether to him since they were still attached to your soul core. The pain he tormented you with was solely within your soul even if it may have felt otherwise, and the pain you felt now towards the end was me cutting that tether. I'm sorry, but it was the only way to free you from him."

Keison shook his head. "There's nothing for you to be sorry about. If the only price I have to pay to be free of that demon is feeling this minor ache in my chest for the rest of my life, then I got off really cheap."

"We need to leave Kairash soon," Hahri said. "Do you think you'll be able to travel?"

Keison struggled to sit up, and Korin reached over to help him the rest of the way up. "Even if my legs were broken, I'd find some way, believe me. I'd like to be long gone by the time Soujin gets here."

Issai looked over at Saiya, who was watching them all intently with a strange look in her eyes. "And you?" was all he said.

He thought the monk would add something, but Korin just looked back at her expectantly.

Saiya stared at them for a long moment before finally turning her head away and nodding curtly. Korin's shoulders sagged in relief. He went over to the cot where Issai belatedly noticed that Saiya's sword rested on and picked it up. Saiya's gaze was once again on her bond partner, her face expressionless. The ancient monk smiled softly and took a couple of steps towards her, holding out the sword hilt first.

The first thought Issai had was that the monk was crazy. The second was to shrug the whole thing off, remembering that Korin had no sense of self-preservation when it came to his bond partner.

Saiya slowly took the hilt from Korin's hand and re-sheathed it in one smooth movement.

"Now that that's settled, we need to decide where we're going," Hahri said.

"Aideya," Korin said at once.

Hahri blinked in surprise. "Why there?"

"Prior Tourn told me when I first set out in search of Saiya that he had heard many rumors about the movement of foreign troops throughout the kingdom. Plus a street child told me that something unusual was going on involving the Mahze." Both Issai and Hahri stiffened at that name. "Given what you have told me about being pursued by what looked like entire armies as well as what that Mahze slaver lord told you about Soujin, well, I thought perhaps it would be a good place to start gathering information."

"Have to admit, that does sound promising," Hahri said. He glanced at Issai, and the violet-eyed boy nodded. "All right, now we just need to get some supplies. We'll leave that to you, monk. Keison, I'm sorry, but we really don't have time for you to go back to your boarding house. We've already lost too much time as it is, and Senn still has to break through Ina's barrier."

The blond shook his head. "I already have the only thing I wish to take with me," was all he said.

"Then let's head out."

As Issai followed Hahri out the door, his partner stopped so suddenly that he nearly walked into his back. Issai glance over the other's shoulder and was greeted by the sight of over a dozen anxious-looking monks crowding the corridor in front of their room.

"Korin, I think you had better handle this," Hahri said with a tinge of amusement.

Korin immediately stepped around Issai. "What is going—oh I see. Brothers, we are all fine. Everything is fine," Korin assured them with the fakest smile Issai had ever seen him wear.

"We heard the most horrible screaming!" the foremost monk exclaimed, trying to look past them into the room with an expression that said he fully expected to see the walls painted with blood. "Just like the other day…"

"It was…" Korin trailed off with a frown, clearly at a loss of how to explain something his Brothers would probably never understand.

Hahri reached back and grabbed a startled Keison's arm, pulling him to the forefront. "Nothing to worry about. We just freed this boy from the torment of a demon, is all," Hahri said with a grin that normally would have made Issai want to kick his teeth in had he not felt his own lips curve up into a smirk at the look on the monks' faces.

"This barrier shouldn't be as hard to 'crack' as the one over Keison's body," Issai told Hahri after studying the red monstrosity for a long moment. *"It will be more like pounding through wood than rock."*

They were currently standing merged within a single soul-body at the edge of the barrier along the eastern side. They hoped to confuse the trail by making a hole there as if they planned to head out-kingdom when in fact they intended to circle back towards Aideya along the northern borders of Kairash. However, they really couldn't be certain that they had even managed to leave the city unseen, so it was probably just wishful thinking anyway.

Their bodies were being watched over by Korin and Keison, a fact that had Issai eager to be done with the whole thing. As they had made their way to the barrier, his skin had begun to crawl faintly, reminding him of the

314

time Hahri and he had had to flee Subu. They were almost out of time.

Issai flooded both his hands with blue particles as he had done to break through the barrier over Keison's chest and slammed them both into the red wall with everything he had in him. Red sparks flew everywhere in an explosion of white and blue light, and they hadn't even fully disappeared from his perception before he was hitting the barrier again. That second hit sent him sprawling completely through the newly created hole, barely managing to keep his feet as he tripped over a small portion of the barrier near the ground that was till intact.

Hahri immediately separated from him without comment, and they both hurried back to their physical bodies. The crawling of his skin was almost doubly pronounced once Issai was back in his body. Luckily they hadn't been gone from their bodies long enough for the chill to set in. It was starting to look as though they would need every once of energy they had and then some.

"Come on. We've got to go *now*!" Issai said, already walking through the hole he had created that was now invisible to his normal eyes. The moment he passed the barrier, he let out a string of rather nasty expletives.

"I hope you can run really fast," Issai said to Keison as the blond teen came up behind him.

"Huh?"

Issai pointed to the black line that had just appeared across the eastern horizon. "Fast enough to outrun an army of cavalry."

ABOUT THE AUTHOR

C.G. Garcia lives in a small West Texas town whose claim to fame is having the world's largest Rattlesnake Round-Up. She has a degree in computer science, but due to life's twisted sense of humor, ended up working in a pharmacy. A lifelong lover of all things fantasy and science fiction, she is also the author of *The Supreme Moment*, the first of her *Fractured Multiverse* novels. Visit her blog at http://CGGarciaAuthor.blogspot.com for updates on upcoming titles or just to chat.

Book 3 of the *Old Souls* trilogy
coming Fall 2014